Praise for JUDY BAER

"I can totally see why author Judy Baer's books are award winners and bestsellers! *Million Dollar Dilemma* is a fabulously rockin' inspirational romance. Fans of inspirational, chick-lit and contemporary romance will enjoy this book."
—*CataRomance Reviews*

"*Million Dollar Dilemma* is a million-dollar treasure you must read!"
—*Armchair Interviews*

"*Million Dollar Dilemma* is sophisticated in structure and story, but sweet and accessible."
—*NBC10.com*

"Whitney Blake...becomes not just a fictional character, but a 'girlfriend'—so much so that readers might have to remember they can't meet her for a cup of coffee. This is...real life, good and bad... subtle nuggets of wisdom.... Experiencing life with Whitney does offer a sense of camaraderie...fun twists and witty lines... Baer's writing is fresh and imaginative as she seamlessly weaves diary entries into a story many will relate to and enjoy."
—*Christian Retailing* on *The Whitney Chronicles*

"Just like Bridget [Jones]...chick-lit readers will appreciate all the components of a girl-friendly fantasy read. Quirky characters...flashes of genuine humor keep even the poignant segments...from becoming too heavy. ...the results are genuinely enjoyable."
—*Publishers Weekly* on *The Whitney Chronicles*

"*Bridget Jones's Diary* for evangelicals.... This is romance... and it's often amusing. Baer [brings] poignancy to the plight of the good girl who is growing older."
—*Booklist* on *The Whitney Chronicles*

A CENTURY
OF STORIES
NEW HANOVER COUNTY PUBLIC LIBRARY
1906-2006

JUDY BAER

NORAH'S ARK

Steeple
Hill
Café

Published by Steeple Hill Books™

STEEPLE HILL BOOKS

ISBN-13: 978-0-373-78566-7
ISBN-10:   0-373-78566-6

NORAH'S ARK

www.SteepleHill.com

Printed in U.S.A.

For Sandy Dehn—our walk and talks are precious to me
and your faith and wisdom are a shining beacon.
Thank you for being my friend.

Chapter One

❧

WELCOME TO NORAH'S ARK
HAVE YOU HUGGED YOUR IGUANA TODAY?
Norah Kent, owner-operator of Norah's Ark Pet Store
and Doggie B and B—Bed and Biscuit

I stood back and studied the sign I'd placed in the window. Creative marketing for a pet store has its own unique challenges. It's hard to know, really, if an iguana will lend itself the same "isn't that cute" factor as my Cuddle A Puppy Tonight! campaign had. It would help if I had an extra dime to spend on professional advice, but I usually have at least a hundred and fifty extra mouths to feed and that adds up. Granted, the fish and birds don't take much, but the mastiff puppies I'm currently housing make up for it.

"New Monday-morning promotion, Norah? What will it be next, Grin At Your Guppy or Tickle Your Toad?"

I didn't have to turn around to know it was Joe Collier from the Java Jockey, the coffee shop and hangout across the street from my pet store.

"What do you think?"

"Makes me think I'd rather hug *you*."

"Get a grip, Joe, this is important business." I didn't turn around to look at him because I knew he was serious and didn't want to encourage him. Joe's been pursuing me ever since the day my menagerie and I moved into the storefront near him two years ago.

I left a perfectly nice, secure, decent-paying job managing a veterinary clinic and being a veterinarian's assistant to pursue a dream of owning my own business, and not even hunky, persistent Joe is going to derail me now.

"When are you going ease up, Norah? Norah's Ark has as much walk-in traffic as my coffee shop. You do as much business as anyone on the street."

I turned around to look at him. Joe is six feet two inches tall, has curly black hair, pale blue eyes and the best muscles a lifetime membership at the sweatiest gym in town money can buy. He always wears a white, long-sleeved shirt with the cuffs rolled up his forearms, jeans and loafers without socks. That's no easy feat in Minnesota during the winter, but Joe's a guy for all seasons.

"There's no time for a small business owner to 'ease up.' You know that." I waved my arm, gesturing at the rows of businesses housed in quaint, former Victorian homes flanking both sides of Pond Street. Pond Street was named, tongue in cheek, because it runs directly into Lake Zachary, one of the largest, most populated and popular boating lakes in the city. In fact, every street in Shoreside runs directly toward the lake, like spokes on a bicycle. The avenues, which would normally run in the opposite direction, are more in an every-man-for-himself pattern. The slightly rolling terrain and difficulty of finding one's way around town only made it more appealing to people. Over the years, Shoreside has become an exclusive and trendy—if confusing—place to live.

"None of us would be here if we 'eased up.'" The summer traffic here is great but winters can be slow. We have to work when the sun shines—literally.

"So just slip out for a couple hours this Saturday night and I'll introduce you to this great Italian restaurant I know. Think of it as an opportunity to pay tribute to my maternal ancestors. What do you say?"

Joe has a smile so beguiling that it can melt ice cubes. If I don't give myself some space to think, I succumb to it every time.

"I'll let you know later."

"Not much later, I hope," he teased. "I have a whole list of other beautiful women to ask out if you turn me down." His dimples dimped—or whatever it is dimples do—but I still resisted. "I'll tell you after I close the store tonight, okay?"

"You're a hard sell, Norah. Maybe that's why I like you." He chucked me under the chin as he does my dog Bentley, a mixed breed Staffordshire terrier, beagle and who-knows-what-else, and sauntered back to the coffee shop.

If he thinks my hard-to-get persona is attractive, that means that saying "no" is only going to fuel his fire. I'll have to think of a new tactic to keep him at bay.

It's not that I don't like Joe. I do. Almost too much. The problem is that I'm just not *ready* for Joe. He wants a serious girlfriend, someone with marriage potential who is ready to settle down, and I'm not that girl—yet. Sometimes I worry that he might not be willing to wait.

Still, I love owning my own business and being independent and I want to have that experience for a while longer. I'm a throw-myself-into-something-with-total-abandon kind of girl. When I marry, I'll be the most enthusiastic wife and homemaker ever, but right now I am focused on the shop. Besides, although I've never admitted it to another living soul, I'm waiting for bells to chime, to feel the poke of Cupid's arrow as it lands in my backside or sense a shimmery-all-over feeling that I imagine I'll have when I fall in love. It's my personal secret. Everyone thinks I'm a sensible realist. Hah! Nothing could be further from the truth.

I decided to leave the iguana sign up for a day or two to test the response and was about to reenter the store when Auntie Lou came out the front door of her store to sweep the sidewalk. Surreptitiously, I watched as she tidied up the front of Auntie Lou's Antiques. Her name is actually Louella Brown and her age is—well, somewhere over a hundred and fifty, I think. Auntie Lou is the oldest antique in her shop, cute as a bug and wrinkled as a raisin. She also dyes her hair a fire-engine red-orange that makes Lucille Ball's and Carrot Top's tresses look anemic. This morning her distinctive hair was tucked under a cloche hat and she wasn't wearing her upper plate so she looked especially raisinlike. Still, I found her smile appealing when she waved me over for a visit.

"How's my pretty today?" Auntie Lou asked. She always says that. When she does, I immediately flash back to Dorothy and the Wicked Witch of the West in *The Wizard of Oz*. If I had a dog named Toto, I'd grab him and run.

"Great, how are you?"

"Arthur kept pestering me all night and Ruma-tiz, too. Those boys are pure trouble."

Translation: her arthritis and rheumatism are acting up again.

"Sorry to hear that."

"Oh, to be young and pretty like you!" Auntie Lou reached out and touched a strand of my long, dark hair, which is currently in one of its wilder stages.

I inherited my naturally curly hair from my mother who, no matter how hard she tries, can't get those kinks and waves to settle down. Mom's blond and beautiful and has settled for an upswept do that tames it fairly well. I, on the other hand, have let my dark hair grow as long as it will and usually harness it in to a whale spout sort of ponytail that erupts from the top of my head and hangs to somewhere between my shoulder blades. People—especially kids—always want to touch my hair to see if it's real.

My mom also has remarkable gray-green eyes which, happily, I also inherited. As a child, I would look into her eyes and feel as if I could actually see her tender heart enshrouded in that smoky gray-green haze. My dad says I have the same eyes, "only more so." He insists I actually wear my heart on my sleeve and it's my entire soul that is on display in my eyes. It's an interesting concept but I try not to think about it. I'm not sure there's a good mascara sold to enhance one's soul.

I *am* a big softy. This much is true. I'm a total pushover for children, the elderly and anyone who is an underdog or down on his luck. I am also a complete and total sucker for anything with four feet, fur, gills, wings, claws, tails or webbed feet. I volunteer as a willing midwife to anything that gives birth in litters, broods or batches. I love tame and wild, pedigreed and mutt alike. I've been this way since the first time I grabbed our golden retriever Oscar by the tail as a tiny child and he licked my face instead of giving me the reprimanding nip I deserved.

My parents still remind me of the Christmases I'd cry when I saw a doll under the tree instead of stuffed animals and the bucket of oats and toddler swimming pool I kept filled with fresh water in the backyard "just in case a pony came by." I rode the back of our velvet floral print couch like it was a bucking bronco until my plastic toy spurs shredded the pillows and I was banished to pretending to ride a horse around the backyard. I must have looked deranged, now that I think of it, whooping and slapping myself on the butt to make myself go faster. Good thing I didn't own a riding crop or whip.

My dad is a veterinarian and my mom a nurse, so there was usually something with wings or paws bandaged up and living at our house while it mended. In fact, I assumed that everyone had a pet snake until I took mine to my friend's house to show her mother how pretty he looked now that he'd shed his old skin. That, I was quick to discover, was a very bad assumption. She did forgive me, however, as soon as the paramedic revived her.

Anyway, I'm a softy for all the unique characters on Pond Street, too.

"You got a good mouser over there?" Auntie Lou inquired. "I'm in need of a shop cat, a working feline. How much will it cost me?"

"Not much. I'll drive you to the animal shelter tonight and we'll find something perfect for you. I think a calico kitten would be a great accessory for your antiques. He'd sleep on that soft cushion on the platform rocker in the window...."

"How do you make a living, Norah? I want to *buy* a cat from you."

"Let's adopt a kitten and I'll sell you a kitten bed, food, toys, catnip and a scratching post instead."

Auntie Lou shook her head helplessly.

"And I'll make you sign a paper saying you'll buy him a lifetime supply of food from my store, if that will make you happy."

"Done, you silly child." Auntie Lou patted me on the cheek and turned to reenter her shop.

I like to consider myself an adoption agency, not a pet store. I *place* animals in homes. I spend time with prospective pet owners helping them decide what type of pet is best for them and then help them find the perfect one. I've even considered adding "pet consultant" behind my name. Dad says I'm nuts, but I actually make a great living selling all the pet accessories people need for their perfect pet. I have a very loyal following—all people as nutty about animals as I am. I also run the Doggie B and B—Bed and Biscuit—out of the back of the shop for loyal customers who want to travel and have their pets in a safe and familiar place. The business keeps growing, especially now that I include all pets, not just dogs, and have begun serving homemade birthday cakes to those who celebrate their special day away from family. Once a customer caught me and his beagle wearing paper birthday hats and howling out an eardrum-splitting rendition of "Happy Birthday To You." Needless to say, I got a huge tip and a lifetime fan. Only animal people understand these things.

Of course, I do have the usual pet store animals in my store—at least two of everything just like Genesis 7:8. *"Of clean animals and of animals that are not clean, and of birds, and of everything that creeps on the ground, two and two, male and female, went into the ark with Noah, as God had commanded Noah."* Except the rabbits, of course. I always start with just two, but, well, they *are* rabbits after all. Anyway, if it was good enough for God and Noah, it's good enough for me.

I've been a Christian since I was ten years old. As a child, I was drawn to all the verses of the Bible that refer to God's four-legged creatures. Even the most lowly, a donkey, for instance, held significance for Christ. When He rode into the city of Jerusalem, he didn't do so on a chariot. Instead, he came humbly, a serene, peace-desiring king on a donkey's unbroken colt. *"Go into the village ahead of you…you will find tied there a colt that has never been ridden: untie it and bring it. If anyone says to you 'Why are you doing this?' just say this, 'The Lord needs it….'"* The commonplace becomes exceptional when God is involved.

Everyone, it seemed, was having a difficult time staying indoors on a beautiful day like this. Next out of her store was Lilly Culpepper, our local fashion maven. Lilly and I moved onto Pond Street and opened our little shops within a few weeks of each other and have ridden the up-and-down rollercoaster ride of small business ownership together ever since.

She runs a funky clothing store called The Fashion Diva next to Norah's Ark and is a walking advertisement for the things she sells in her shop. Today she wore a long, red Santa Fe–style crinkle-pleated skirt, a short boxy sweatshirt the color of old mushrooms, high-heeled black boots and a gray felt fedora. And it looked good. I wonder how many hopeful shoppers leave her store with similar outfits hoping that they'll look like Lilly when they get home and put their new clothes on. And I wonder how many of those shoppers realized that at home, those same clothes look like the pile of wrinkled, mismatched laundry they already have lying on their closet floors.

What Lilly doesn't—and can't—sell is her style. She looks good even in a gunny sack and a pair of galoshes. I know this for sure because one year we went to a costume party as a sack of potatoes and potato fork. She looked great and I looked like I'd been wrapped in brown crepe paper and had a set of pronged antlers strapped to my head. Next time *I* get to be the vegetable.

"Joe asking you out again?" she greeted me with no preamble. Though she came nearer, she didn't walk toward me. Lilly doesn't walk, Lilly *sweeps.*

Anyway, as she swept toward me, I said, "Good morning to you, too."

"If you'd say the word, he'd get down on bended knee and ask for your hand in marriage."

"My hand isn't much good to him without the rest of me."

"You could do worse," she advised me. She fingered the chunk of jewelry at her neck. It was a hodgepodge of beads, colored cubes, macramé lumps and various ribbons. That, too, looked fabulous on her. On me—or 99.9 percent of the world's population—it would have looked like a terrible blunder from the craft factory. No doubt she'd sell at least two or three today to people who admired it on her.

"Don't wait too long," she warned. "That little waitress at Tea on Tap has been eyeing him lately."

"What's the tea lady doing in the coffee shop? Scoping out the competitor?"

Lilly gave me one of those pitying looks she saves for when she thinks I'm being particularly obtuse. Usually I get them when we're talking fashion.

"What else is happening on Pond Street? I seem to be out of touch."

"It's all those animals you surround yourself with. It doesn't give you enough time for people." She studied me with a surgical glare. "You need a date that doesn't have four legs and a tail."

"Shh. Don't say that too loud. Bentley might hear. You know how sensitive he is."

I was only half kidding. I rescued Bentley from a shelter. He'd been abused in his former home and, in my professional opinion—such as it is—Bentley has serious self-esteem and confidence issues. These may also stem from the fact that, due to his indiscriminate parents' genetics, he's not the most intimidating presence on the block. Or in the pet store. Or anywhere. He may be stocky but his heart is pure powder puff. I'm sure I saved Bentley from extinction. Nobody else would have been crazy enough to adopt a dog like him. He knows that and has committed the rest of his life to loving me—what a great swap.

Happily, Lilly ignored me and began to fill me in on the latest from the rumor mill on Pond Street.

"Belles & Beaus is adding another masseuse."

Belles & Beaus is a day spa located in a huge restored Victorian up the street. It started out as a hair salon with two stations and a lot of out-of-date magazines, but has rapidly become a very chic and stylish spot. Then again, everything along Pond Street is becoming that way. The Bookworm now has author signings and poetry readings, the Drugstore's old soda fountain *is* the place for kids to hang out and you can—much to Joe's dismay—buy a latte at Barney's Gas Station right along with your unleaded premium.

Someday I'm hoping that Barney will realize that his sign, *Barney's Gas*, isn't quite specific enough. I've had more than one person come into my shop laughing and ask what kind of gas Barney has anyway. I usually leave that question alone. It's an explosive issue.

"The store beyond Belles & Beaus has been sold to someone who's planning to open a toy shop."

"Cool." A toy store—my kind of people.

"And guess who said hello to me when I was at the Corner Market today!"

"Sorry, I left my mind-reading kit at home today."

"Connor Trevain, *Commander* Connor Trevain." She said it in the tone of an awestruck groupie.

"Back for a visit, huh?" *Commander* Connor owns the fleet of cruise boats that sail Lake Zachary, although he's never spent much time in Shoreside. He actually was a commander in the Navy, a graduate of the Naval Academy and served as a ship's captain. It was well-known that he "came from money" as Auntie Lou would say. The fleet has some fabulous boats, the largest, the *Zachary Zephyr* is regularly rented for weddings, anniversaries and class reunions. The food and service are amazing and the surroundings romantic. It's a *très chic* place to be married. The smaller boats take tourists sightseeing around Lake Zachary, sometimes stopping at Ziga's, a supper club the Trevain family owns on the far side of the lake.

"No. That's the best part!"

"I thought you said you saw him."

"Not that. The best part is that he's not here for a visit. He's here to stay!"

That made about as much sense as wearing Bermuda shorts to shovel snow. Last I'd heard he was suffering away his time with some boating venture in Hawaii. "Why?"

"He's decided to be 'hands on' with the business. Isn't that exciting? He plans to captain the *Zachary Zephyr.*"

"Well, shiver me timbers, think of that." I put my hands on my hips and stared at my friend. "So what?"

"*So,* he is *rich* and *handsome* and *single,* that's what!"

The sun came out and the fog in my brain cleared. "And you have your eye on him?"

"Both eyes. He's going to make the scenery around the lake more spectacular than ever."

"Are you interested in dating him?" I asked, never quite sure what direction Lilly is going in with her rambling conversations. She's a smart girl but fixated on clothes and, occasionally, men.

"Are you kidding? Of course, but he won't look at the likes of me." She grabbed my hands. "Wouldn't it be wonderful if he asked me out?"

Her eyes got wide as two saucers. "I have to check to see what's on order for the store. I'll need new clothes. Who knows when I might run into him!" She eyed me up and down like a disapproving school marm. "It wouldn't hurt you to get something new, either." With a swirl of red, she shot back into her shop, where, I knew, she'd spend the rest of the day poring over fashion magazines and doodling with her own clothing designs.

I love Lilly. She's funny, beautiful and my polar opposite. For every fashionista outfit she has, I have a pair of denim jeans and a sweatshirt. Of course, she doesn't haul fifty-pound bags of dog food, change litter boxes or deal with untrained puppies in her business, either.

"And…"

I spun around to see Lilly poking her head out the door again.

"…the new cop is on duty. We can all sleep well tonight." Then she disappeared again around the doorjamb and didn't return.

Whew. Feeling as though I'd just been through a windstorm of trivia, I shook myself off and went back to tending to the only business I should be minding anyway.

Chapter Two

✤

"Do you, Samantha Renée, promise to love and to care for this new member of your family? Do you promise to change his litter box, give him fresh water every day, be kind to him and protect him from harm? If so, answer, 'I do.'"

"I do," came a breathy little whisper.

I tried to stifle a smile as I looked at the pair across from me—a little girl with blond curls, pink overalls, a ruffled blouse and a white Persian kitten. Samantha held the kitten's paw in the air with her hand and they both seemed to nod solemnly. I make sure everyone takes the Solemn Oath of Adoption seriously. Samantha's parents stood behind her grinning widely.

"I now pronounce this adoption proceeding complete."

I whipped an embellished computer-generated adoption certificate off the counter and handed it to the little girl. Her blue eyes grew as wide as saucers at the official-looking paper to which I'd attached a gold seal, a few stars and a photo of the kitten. I always feel like the Wizard of Oz when I do my adoption spiel, like I'm handing out bravery, a heart, a brain or, in this case, a friend for life.

Then I began taking pictures with the Polaroid camera I have for just such auspicious occasions and doled them out to all the proud participants.

Samantha and the kitten, which she'd already named Squish because of the shape of his face, followed her father to the car to stow the litter box, litter, food, scratching post, toys and various and sundry necessities mandatory for a fourteen-ounce ball of fur to take over an entire household. Samantha's mother hung behind.

"I can't thank you enough." She grabbed my hand and pumped it. "I've never seen our Sammie so excited…or so eager. I believe she is really committed to caring for that kitten. I may have to remind her of her responsibilities sometimes, but now she knows that kitten is *hers*. That 'adoption' ceremony makes it so real for her. What a brilliant concept!"

"That's the idea," I said modestly, although I, too, believed I'd thought of it in one of my more inspired moments. I did everything in my power to make sure the pets I sold were well cared for. The little adoption proceeding has been a clever and effective tool. Now parents drive across town to buy a pet from "the lady who makes my kid take it seriously."

I can't help it—taking animals seriously, I mean. It's a direct command from the Big Book itself—right up front. *"And God said, 'Let us make humankind in our image, according to our likeness and let them have dominion over the fish of the sea, and over the birds of the air, and over all the wild animals of the earth and over every creeping thing that creeps upon the earth.'"* We are all His creations, and as those created in His image, we as humans have responsibility for His other creatures and handiwork. It's way cool, of course, but also a big task and sometimes I don't think we're doing a very good job of it. If we were, every creature would be fat and happy and we wouldn't have a need for rescue shelters. Until that happens, I'm just going to hang out here at Norah's Ark and do what I can.

That thought reminded me that I'd promised Auntie Lou to help her find a kitten. She doesn't care about pedigrees— "Pedigree, smedigree" she'd said once. "You love a pet 'cause it's yours, not because you've got a list of its ancestors." That means she needs to adopt the cat and buy only the trimmings from me rather than the other way around.

Auntie Lou is a bit of an anomaly on Pond Street. She lives above her store in a cozy little apartment. She doesn't drive a car and I doubt she ever has. She's been here as long as anyone can remember. Joe speculates that when she began selling things in her store, they weren't actually antiques yet. Pond Street is home to Auntie Lou and we shopkeepers are her family. She never talks about having any other relatives and it's assumed she has no one else. She's a real throwback in this material world and that's why I'm so fascinated by her.

The bell at the door stopped my musings as a tall blond

man with rigid military bearing strode into the shop and glanced around with something akin to disapproval, as if the colorful parrot, a black-capped lory named Winky, who was loose in the shop, might do something dastardly to his lovely yellow polo shirt. Winky is a handsome fellow. He is primarily red but accessorized with bands of blue, green wings and a dash of yellow.

Not that my new customer didn't have reason to be alarmed, of course. Winky is no gentleman. But instead of making mayhem, Winky decided to greet him. "Hello, Big Boy…awk…" Then Winky let out a wolf whistle that would put a construction worker to shame and the bird winked at the startled man.

That's how he got his name, from a lady who had grown rescued him from some bad owners. She had grown too ill to care for him and had made me promise I'd find Winky another good home. I've been trying, but Winky has a smart mouth and ribald sense of humor, so he's been a challenge to place. The trouble with parrots is that their life span may be longer than that of their human. I've suggested to more than one customer that when they write their will that they include custody instructions for their birds. That's a great way to separate the serious customer from the casual looker.

"May I help you?" I asked, realizing someone other than Winky should be working the store.

"I…ah…no…well…yes, I suppose you can." He didn't really look comfortable in the pet store in those sure-to-pick-up-fur navy trousers of his. "I just wanted to greet the owner of this establishment. Is he in?"

Ohhhh. No points for that one.

"*I'm* Norah Kent, owner of *Norah's* Ark. May I help you?"

He had the grace to look embarrassed. "Excuse me. I thought it was *Noah's*…I assumed…"

Assume nothing, I thought to myself. Especially not on Pond Street.

He shook himself free of that and extended a hand. "I'm Connor Trevain. I own the *Zachary Zephyr* and the other cruise boats on the lake. My current administrator is retiring and I've decided to be 'hands on' for a while. I wanted to meet the merchants up and down Pond Street and introduce myself." He flushed a little. "I already blew it with you, didn't I?"

I do not have the crusty shell of M&M's. I melt everywhere. "Of course not. Welcome to Shoreside."

He relaxed and smiled. It changed his entire demeanor. At once it made him less intimidating and more approachable. It also made him more handsome than the stern, businesslike expression he'd worn earlier. Oh, boy, was Lilly going to be excited about this.

"Have you been to all the other shops?"

"I met Joe at the coffee shop. And Barney at the station."

"Isn't he a gas?" I asked, testing his sense of humor.

That seemed to fly right over his head.

"I've also been to the Corner Market to meet Chuck and Betty."

I didn't have the heart to tell him that Chuck's name is really Olaf and that he'd been dubbed Chuck because of all the ways he could tell you to cook a pot roast. If the Barney joke went by him, he'd never get that one.

"And I've been at Auntie Lou's Antiques." A frown flitted

across his features. "It's very…crowded…in there. And she's very…quaint."

I could tell he was trying to be polite. Auntie Lou's is sensory overload for the uninitiated.

"So you do have a few places left to visit." I wondered if I could get to the phone and call Lilly before he got there so she could put on fresh lipstick.

"Yes." He sounded so put-upon that I stared at him.

"You don't sound very happy about it."

"It's not that. This is just quite a change from my former life. It will take some getting used to."

"We're worth the effort," I assured him. "Pond Street and its merchants will grow on you."

"Yes, some of them already have. It was nice meeting you, Norah," he said in parting.

So that was Connor Trevain. Lilly was right about one thing. He was definitely going to improve the scenery down at the dock.

"Are you sure this is the right one for me?" Auntie Lou asked as she held a fat calico cat with a purr like a 747 rumbling in her ear.

"Are *you* sure? That's the question."

"He's pretty cute."

"A perfect calico."

"And he seems to like me."

"No kidding." The cat blissfully kneaded Auntie Lou's shoulder with his declawed paws. "He adores you." I crossed my arms and looked intently at her. "Then what's the problem?"

She flushed under the bright patches of blusher—or rouge, as she called it—on her cheeks. "I haven't lived with anyone or anything for thirty years. I don't want to make another mistake."

I blinked. "A mistake?"

"That's what my husband was," Auntie Lou admitted cheerfully. "A rascal, that fellow. It's a wonder that he didn't put me in the grave with him."

This was all news to me.

"He couldn't keep a job or didn't care to. Lazy as the day is long." Her expression softened. "But so charming. He treated me like a queen, you know. Made me forget that I had to support us most of the time. Then he got sick and I nearly lost my mind tending to him and trying to keep food on the table…." Her voice drifted with her memories, into the past. "I didn't regret a moment I spent caring for him but after he was gone, I realized that sometimes it can be just too hard to love someone who hasn't the same ability to love back." She eyeballed the cat. "Do you think this guy is up to it?"

My heart ached for Auntie Lou. She'd loved and lost and, even with a pet cat, was afraid to love again.

"I'm sure of it. And *he'll* earn his keep. The lady at the desk said his former owner told her he was 'an affectionate animal and a great mouser.'"

"Then why did they give him up?" Auntie Lou asked suspiciously.

I checked the card from the front of the cage that held the cat's history. "Looks like she went into a hospice program, Auntie Lou."

The old woman's expression softened. "So you got left behind, too, did you?" she whispered into the cat's soft fur. The roaring purr intensified. "I suppose we belong together then, two old rejects."

Deal closed.

Then she looked up, her eyes twinkling. "Now don't you go lecturing me about calling myself a reject. I couldn't be one or you wouldn't spend time with me, you sweet girl. Now go get me some papers to sign or swear us in or whatever it is you do in your shop. I want to get this guy home before I change my mind."

Leaving the pair looking lovingly into each other's eyes, I went to the shelter's desk to tell them a pet had found its home.

"Did you see him yesterday?" Lilly accosted me in front of the Java Jockey on Tuesday morning looking wild-eyed and beautiful in a lavender chiffon top and shocking purple leggings. Her hair was piled in high curls on her head and she wore shoes that looked like instruments of torture, toes so pointy that she could have had them declared dangerous weapons. She had mini chandeliers hanging from her luscious lobes and silver chains draped around her neck. Improbable, impossible and outlandish, on Lilly it was a look to-die-for.

She plopped into one of the outside chairs and put her double espresso latte with sugar-free vanilla flavoring and a chocolate-dipped coffee bean onto a table. I joined her with my decaf with soy milk.

"Whatever happened to preppy clothing? You know, wool skirts, penny loafers…."

"Another day, Norah. Wait until you see what I've ordered for fall." Then she realized that I'd distracted her from her original thought. "Well, *did* you?"

"Connor Trevain, I presume."

"Isn't he gorgeous? I can just see him at the helm, driving the boat or whatever sea captains do, squinting into the mist, not knowing what dangers may face him out on the open water…." Lilly threw her head back and gazed dreamily toward Lake Zachary.

"He'll be on tour boats, Lilly. Unless Gilligan's Island is somewhere in the middle of Lake Zachary, I don't think he'll have a problem."

"Oh, you're no fun!" She stamped her foot and I remembered that she could probably disembowel me with that shoe.

"I'm plenty of fun. I'm just not fantasizing over Connor Trevain."

"Don't you like him?"

"Lilly, I don't even *know* him."

"He's rich and good-looking."

"But is he a Christian?"

"He can always become that. It's harder to become rich and good-looking."

My shoulders sagged. "Lilly, don't you know me at all?"

She looked contrite. "Sorry, Norah. I know how important that is to you, but does it hurt for him to be cute, too?"

"Of course not. But he'll be much cuter to me if he's a Christian."

Lilly and I discuss this often. She's right on the edge of accepting Christ but pulls back every time she thinks of something she might have to give up if she accepts Him fully. So far she's asked me if she'd have to give up wearing pretty clothes and lipstick, dancing, playing cards, drinking wine and having fun. I keep telling her that that is between her and God. Once she accepts Him and invites the Holy Spirit into action in her life, she'll know what pleases Him and what doesn't. Plus, it will be so much fun to please Him that if she sees something she does need to give up, she won't mind. She can't get her mind around that concept yet. I understand. It's hard to comprehend how God can fill you up so that you never feel like you're missing a thing.

"What kinds of men *do* you like, Norah? I blabber about this one and that and you just take it all in, never saying a thing."

"I'm not shopping right now, Lilly. It's hard to conjure up a list for you."

"You like Joe. He's charming, great-looking, nice and tall. Those things could go on your list."

"I'm not making a list!"

"Well, you should."

"Why?"

"What if someone comes along and he's perfect and you aren't prepared? He might get away!"

Lilly's logic defies reason. Or if it defies reason, can it be logic? Lilly's way of thinking always dumbfounds me. It's also part of why we're friends. I'm never bored around Lilly.

As we sat there talking, I noticed Lilly's antennae go up. I can see it in her eyes when there's either an interesting fashion statement or a cute guy nearby. Her posture straightens, her eyes light up and her nose twitches just the tiniest bit. She says it doesn't, but I know. I'm an eyewitness.

Unfortunately the object of her interest was behind me

and although I could hear the clink and jangle of metal on metal, I didn't see him until he stopped at our table.

"Good morning, ladies" he said to us. I turned around and came eye to buckle with a uniform-clad police officer. He stood with legs straddled and hands linked behind his back, just like on television. He did have the impenetrable black sunglasses but was missing the crisp blue hat which would conceal all expression on his face. And...could I believe my eyes? Was that a *horse* standing behind him?

Chapter Three

❧

"Well, hello. What a hunk you are!"

"Norah…" Lilly's shocked voice warned.

I paid no attention as my gaze made its way across the most incredible horse I've ever seen—a gleaming chestnut with muscled flanks, high, strong withers and dark, intelligent eyes. He was drop-dead gorgeous.

"*Norah!*"

I looked up and blinked. Lilly's shaken and bewildered expression slammed me down to earth in a hurry. Leave it to Lilly to think I was talking to the man, not the horse.

Without a pause, I pushed away from the table, stood and locked eyes with the massive gelding decked out in a highly buffed, supple black leather saddle and murmured appreciatively, "I wish I had one of you in my shop."

Then, with great intention, I turned to the stony policeman. "What an awesome horse. I didn't realize we were getting a *team* of police protection."

Lilly sagged with relief once she realized that I wasn't addressing the man's attractiveness—which was certainly obvious. I made a mental note to talk to her later and convince her that not every woman views the world the way she does—by noticing the men first and only later seeing the scenery.

The cop, a hunk in his own right, with square shoulders, a broad, solid body that tapered to narrow hips and an unreadable, impassive face, nodded slightly.

"Nick Haley. I'm Shoreside's new police officer." He didn't offer his hand or make any effort to smile. His face—the part I could see below the low hat and mirrored sunglasses—was worth studying anyway. Very nice, if you like strong jawlines, golden tans and lips that were probably very good at everything they did, from smiling to kissing....

"That is so awesome!" Lilly blurted, trying out her ingenue persona on him.

It didn't work. Not even a twitch of a smile.

"Mounted police, what a great idea," I said, delighted at the thought of having another animal—a huge and beautiful one—in the neighborhood. I had to drag my attention away from the gleaming sorrel shifting in the sun, his neck and flanks shiny and new as a freshly minted copper penny. His ear twitched as an audacious fly tried to land on its tip.

"Mounted only part-time," he corrected me. "I work with

several local police departments at community events. Because Shoreside hosts so many outdoor parades and events Sarge will be rotating in and out. Your mayor and city council decided that they wanted a police presence able to move in the crowds around the lake and one that wasn't quite so…"

"…intimidating as a police car?" I finished for him.

"Yes." He cleared his throat and began to scratch the magnificent animal on the neck. "This is my first day on the job. I want to stop by with the horse and meet each of the business owners. This is Sergeant Thunder."

"He's a real sergeant in the police force?" Lilly gasped. "I didn't know they did that. Do horses have to go to the police academy or something?"

The officer's finely drawn lips twitched. "Sergeant Thunder is the name given to him before he was recruited by us. Purely a coincidence. I call him Sarge for short."

"Oh." Lilly sat back to digest that. Lilly isn't big on animals. She doesn't hate them, but she doesn't pay much attention to them, either—except Winky, who gives her a lecherous wolf whistle every time she enters Norah's Ark.

"My name is Norah Kent. I own Norah's Ark. This is Lilly Culpepper of The Fashion Diva. Welcome to Shoreside." His handshake was warm, firm and rough with calluses. They were a working man's hands like those of my grandfather, a farmer. I had the sense of being protected even as Nick and I shook hands. Perfect vibe for a policeman to emanate. Still, a smile would have been nice, too.

Lilly dropped Valley Girl and went straight for Queen Elizabeth. "Charmed, I'm sure," she murmured huskily as he took her hand. Lilly is always adopting personae other than her own. They're like clothing for her. She tries something different for whatever mood she's in. She slides in and out of movie star guises like other people change T-shirts. Personally I like her best when she's being Barbara Walters or Kelly Ripa. If Lilly is wearing a tailored suit and a hat, it's Margaret Thatcher every time.

I reached out and touched Sarge's flank. It twitched and rippled as if my finger were an unwelcome fly but he made no other movement. Neither horse nor rider was going to let you see them sweat.

"It was a pleasure to meet both of you. Now if you'll excuse me…" The officer made a clicking sound with his tongue and Sarge obediently backed off. They were a team, all right.

After they moved away, Lilly squirmed excitedly in her chair. "What a dream!"

"The horse is great," I agreed.

"Not the horse, silly. The man!"

"Did you even notice the horse, Lilly? The one that was twelve hundred pounds heavier than the guy leading him?"

"What if you met a guy someday who was perfect for you but didn't like animals?" Lilly said exasperatedly. "Then what would you do?"

"A guy who didn't like animals couldn't be 'perfect' for me. It's like that policeman and his horse, or Bentley and me, we're a pair, a team, and that's all there is to it. I'm in no danger of falling for a man who won't have anything to do with God's furry creatures."

"You and your animals. One of these days you're going to have to start looking at men, Norah, or you'll end up one of those crazy cat ladies whose house smells like a litter box and has kittens born in your bed."

My first notion was to gross her out and tell her that it didn't sound like such a bad life to me, but I know what she means. I don't want to live forever with a parrot with a ribald mouth and a dog with more emotional issues than he has fleas as my only companions.

We didn't have time to debrief the advent of the new police officer any further because at that moment Joe walked out of the Java Jockey and headed for the lake. He turned briefly to wave at us.

Lilly pointed to Joe's broad, muscular retreating back as he sauntered down the sidewalk. "Maybe you should marry Joe. He's handsome, successful and crazy about you."

"There's only one small problem, Lilly. I don't want to get married right now." I slapped the heel of my hand against my forehead. "Oh, yes, silly me. There are *two* problems. I'm also not in love with him—not that way, at least not yet."

"But you like him, don't you?"

"Of course, but…"

"Has he asked you out lately?"

"We're going out for Italian food on Saturday."

Lilly clapped her hands and leaped to her feet. "I've got just the dress for you."

"Dress? Lilly, when was the last time you saw my legs?" Granted, I do wear a skirt to church on Sundays—but it isn't my usual uniform. That's anything with a Norah's Ark logo on it.

"Exactly my point." She grabbed my hand and tugged

until I reluctantly followed her across the street into The Fashion Diva.

The Fashion Diva has every bit as much élan as Lilly does. My friend is an artist at putting items of clothing together in unexpected ways. Today she had a beach-party theme on her wall, a collage of summer clothing—shorts, halter tops, flowing skirts—that appeared to be worn by invisible bodies playing volleyball. She'd tacked a scrap of webbing and two sticks to the wall to indicate the net, deflated a volleyball and arranged it as if it were sailing midair.

"Cool wall," I managed before she shoved me into a dressing room and began flinging clothes in behind me.

"Lilly, I can't just walk out of my store and leave it untended."

"You try these on. I'll watch for customers. If anyone comes to buy one of those gargantuan puppies you have, I'll call you."

"They are mastiffs. They're supposed to be gigantic."

"They grow up to be Volkswagen vans. Why don't you sell miniature poodles, the kind people can carry in their purse? Such a trendy look right now."

"Animals are not accessories, Lilly."

A big sigh came from outside the door. "Okay, okay. How does the skirt fit?"

"Like a collapsed canvas mainsail."

There was a long silence outside the dressing room door, then another sigh. "Let me see."

I trudged into the painful light of day. The skirt she'd given me was actually canvas-colored, with rivets, stitched pockets and a slit on the side which was probably supposed to show off my long, shapely leg. Instead, it made me look like one of the concrete foundation footings they were pouring for the new bank being built down the street.

"Oh, dear. Maybe we can't do this quickly after all."

"Exactly. To entertain yourself, put together a couple outfits that will make me look human rather than like squat, ugly buildings. I'll try them on later just to satisfy you. No promises I'll buy, though."

"You are my newest crusade, Norah, even if I have to order clothes made of denim, flannel and sweatshirt fabric, I will make you a representative of Fashion Diva style."

Terrific. Being Lilly's pet project is always a pain because she's relentless in whatever she sets out to do. The only one she's ever had to admit defeat on is Auntie Lou whose style can be best described as a Civil War combined with consignment store chic.

Why, I wondered as I hurried back to feed the animals, didn't she just advertise on the side of a bus rather than make me, a cute but admitted sow's ear—fashionwise, that is—into a silk purse?

At noon, I jogged up to Belles & Beaus to make an emergency bird feed delivery. They've installed a large cage in the foyer and I filled it with peach-faced lovebirds to greet their customers. I love a lovebird—makes sense, doesn't it?—because they are playful and energetic and yes, can be taught to give kisses. Though it's a completely up-to-date spa, the main floor has been kept to look like the Victorian house that it is. Lush pinks, lace, teacups, ornate furniture and all the things the Victorians loved are accounted for in this place. It would make me wacky to have to work in such sensory excess, but it's popular with its clientele. I admit I can stand it quite nicely, however, for as long as it takes to have a facial or a pedicure.

On the way back to the Ark, I stuck my head into the open door of the building that was to be the new toy shop. The man and woman stripping wallpaper in the back of the room jumped as if I'd fired a rifle when I knocked on the door.

"Not open until next week," he yelled.

"I don't want anything except to welcome you to the neighborhood." I took a step inside the door. "I'm Norah Kent, from Norah's Ark pet shop."

Reluctantly, as if they were walking in cold molasses, the couple moved toward me. They were in their midfifties, dressed in jeans, T-shirts and tennis shoes.

Something had gone awry in these people's lives. I could see it in the deeply etched frown lines bracketing his lips and the deeply cut wrinkles making her forehead nearly as furrowed as the Shar-pei puppies I sometimes sell.

These people, with their grim expressions, didn't look like they belonged on happy-go-lucky Pond Street. Neither did they look like owners of a toy store. Or maybe I'd confused them with the cultural image of Santa Claus. Toy store owners didn't *have* to have round bellies, pink cheeks and perpetually be saying, "Ho-ho-ho."

"I'm Franklin Morris and this is my wife, Julie." He reluctantly stuck out his hand for a shake.

Franklin and Julie. Simple, commonplace names for ordinary people. What kinds of monikers had I expected? Big Bad Wolf and Cruella De Vil?

"Looks like you still have some work to do before opening day." The fellows who built the pyramids didn't have to work any harder than these guys would to get this place done in a week.

"Yes," Franklin said tersely.

"Are you hiring any help?" My voice was beginning to sound falsely chipper—annoying even to my own ears.

"No."

"Doing it yourself, then?"

"Yes."

Well, don't talk my ear off!

"We're in a little over our head. The building is in poorer shape than we realized."

Overwhelmed. Now *that* I can understand.

"If you need help, holler. We treat each other like family here on Pond Street."

Franklin and Julie exchanged glances, their expressions indicating that they weren't sure if this was good news or not. Then Julie rallied. "Thanks so much for stopping by. I'll visit your pet store after we get settled."

I had to be content with that. First Connor, then the policeman and now the new toy store owners. Suddenly there were a lot of strangers on Pond Street.

I hadn't noticed Auntie Lou sitting in the shade in a big balloonlike hanging wicker basket chair left over from the late seventies until she accosted me with her broomstick. She was so short that her feet didn't touch the ground and the chair all but gobbled her up. She was still wearing her cloche hat but did have her teeth in now which smoothed out a few wrinkles. Occasionally Lou's choppers clatter when she talks so it's fifty-fifty which is actually better—teeth in or teeth out. Sometimes it sounds like she's playing the castanets when she talks.

"How's the cat doing?" I looked around but didn't see him in her window.

"Big slug is sound asleep on my bed. Eat, purr, sleep. Eat, purr, sleep. That's all he does."

"Isn't that what he's supposed to do?"

"What about mousing? A batch of field mice could set up shop right next to him and he'd never blink," she said with a smile.

"Give him time, Lou. He's just getting settled in."

"Settled-schmettled. He's just as lazy as my former husband."

And, I realized, that the backhanded statement had somehow been a compliment for both the cat and the man.

"Can you sit awhile?" Auntie Lou asked hopefully.

"Not now, but I'll come over later and pin up that dress you need hemmed."

"You're a good girl, Norah. What would I do without you?" Auntie Lou patted my hand with such gentle affection I felt tears coming to my eyes.

Chapter Four

❧

My place is a townhouse situated on Lake Zachary that I purchased from my father, who'd once owned it as investment property. I'd renovated it and made it my ideal retreat. After work I hurried there for Bentley, who had opted for a morning at home over a day at the shop with me. Bentley enjoys his peace and quiet but he's not immune to getting lonesome. Especially for *moi*.

How do I know my dog likes it quiet? At Norah's Ark, every time Winky starts whooping it up or a batch of puppies start squealing, he flops on the floor and manages to get his front legs and paws up over his ears as if to say, "Turn down the volume." When my television is too loud, Bentley stands in front of it growling at the screen until I adjust the sound. Bentley definitely needs his quiet time.

Actually, what Bentley *really* needs is therapy. I rescued him from a shelter nearly two years ago. One day I saw the Humane Society sign and turned in to the lot as though someone else was driving the car and I was simply along for the ride. The car parked itself, expelled me from the driver's seat and my legs, under no direction from my mind, walked inside.

I've never been able to go into a Humane Society without coming out with a pet or two—or three, if you count that ferret—that's why I regularly mail my donations rather than deliver them in person. Someone other than me should have a chance to save the entire animal kingdom. But that day, maybe because I'd just moved into my home and tripled my living space, I'd felt a giddy sense of freedom.

That same lack of restraint kicked into high gear as I heard myself say to the receptionist, "I'd like to see the dog here that needs rescuing the most."

Without a blink, she led me to a cage at the back of the dog room holding a pathetic black-and-white creature. Mangy and flea-bitten, with mud up to his belly, his head was drooped so low that his nose nearly touched the floor. But as we neared, the pup's head came up, his deep brown eyes connected with mine and *zing,* Cupid's arrow—Lilly says it was actually *Stupid's* arrow—hit me right between the eyes.

That "love at first sight" thing? I'm not sure it happens with humans, but it does with dogs. Bentley and I started a love affair right then and there.

"A bath might help," the woman said. "Maybe I

shouldn't have shown him to you until he was cleaned up, but you *asked*...."

"Any story on him?" His eyes never left mine.

"Not that I know of. He'd been showing up at some garbage cans behind a restaurant, waiting for someone to drop something he could eat. Apparently the staff started 'dropping' more food than the manager liked, so he called us. Our vet thinks he's part beagle, part Staffordshire terrier and maybe a dribble of pit bull, although you'd never know it by his disposition. We've nicknamed him Romeo because he's so eager for love.

"It wouldn't surprise me if he'd been abused because he's nervous," she continued. "But he's also a survivor, no doubt about that."

I stared at the little mixed package. His head, ears and soft eyes recalled a beagle, but his solid, stocky body and thick, shiny hair were reminiscent of a Staffordshire. His physical look reminded me of Sylvester Stallone of *Rambo* fame. His personality? Pure Rodney Dangerfield.

Of course, as Paul Harvey says, it's easy to guess "the rest of the story."

Bentley has come out of it beautifully—physically, that is. He's black-and-white, with a black eye patch, one black ear and one mottled gray one. He has the stocky body of a strong dog thanks to that dash of pit bull in the soup, most likely. His nose is one great big black licorice dot and his expression is sweet. He's all bark and no bite, although he can growl fiercely from the pit of his stomach if he's frightened. He frightens himself quite regularly by looking in my full-length mirror.

But while Bentley has physical bearing, he's a neurotic canine. He's allergic to loud noises, most men and cheap dog food. At first, even my dad couldn't get close to him without Bentley planting his feet firmly and rumbling from somewhere deep in his belly. A street dog has to learn to fight even if its true nature is more Romeo than Rambo.

When Dad finally got sick of all the dog's posturing and took two steps toward him, Bentley dropped to the floor and rolled on his back, belly exposed for scratching, panting happily. Bentley has a highly ineffective force field of protection. Talk about being all bark and no bite.

Anyway, Bentley was at the door to greet me with the giddy, I'm-so-happy-to-see-you-because-I-thought-you-had-abandoned-me act he does—a series of flips and circles, frantic running to and fro across the living room floor making excited woo-wooing sounds and finally, a dramatic collapse into a heap at my feet.

If I could ever affect a *man* that mightily—sans the running across the floor, of course—even I would get married.

Then, as I stepped from the foyer into the large living-dining area, my ears were assaulted by a nerve-jangling screech, a "Well, hello, baby!" and the excited flapping of wings. Again, if a man were to greet me with as much enthusiasm as Asia, my mynah bird—Asia, as in Asia Mynah—my heart would go pitter-patter.

As it is, the only pitter-patter I ever hear is the one making its way across my hardwood floor—my Flemish giant rabbit, Hoppy, coming to see what the fuss is about. He sat up and twitched his nose at me and gave me a look that said, "Lettuce, I must have lettuce"—I always imagine he's speaking in Arnold Schwarzenegger's voice—before bounding, as much as a fourteen pound rabbit can bound, to the kitchen to sit in front of the refrigerator and wait for me to do his bidding.

Fortunately rabbits get along quite well with dogs if introduced properly. Besides, Bentley believes that Hoppy is the Alpha dog in the family and the epitome of the canine species. Hoppy is also litter-box trained, a patience-trying process that involves ever-ready alertness and nimbleness—on my part. See Hoppy raise her tail, see Hoppy relax her ears, see Norah run for the litter box, see Hoppy train Norah…and so it goes.

Bribery is actually a very good way to train rabbits—children, too, I've heard, but that could be an urban legend. That's why Hoppy's box is always sporting a toy and a slice of apple or a sprig of parsley to make it the pièce de résistance. It's also why I pet and praise her there for jobs well-done. It's no wonder that she sits in the dumb thing just for fun even now that she's got complete house-rabbit ranking.

I scratched Bentley, moseyed to the kitchen, gave Hoppy a piece of lettuce and was about to start supper for myself when the telephone rang.

It was my father. "Your mom and I are taking a few days off. We're going up to the North Shore. She's found a bed and breakfast she wants to try. If you need me, I've got my cell phone."

They've been on a perpetual honeymoon for as long as I can remember. They hold hands, steal kisses, hug, and especially when I was a teenager, kicked up my gag reflex on a regular basis. Still, that's what I want my marriage to be like, too. If…when…

After I'd gotten the details of the trip and had started to grill myself a cheese sandwich I realized that the theme of my entire day had been "I'd get married if…" Now what's *that* about?

I took my sandwich and a cup of tea to the deck and ate it while staring out at Lake Zachary. Maybe Lilly was finally getting to me, making me worry that true love—the kind with bells—would never happen to me. Dating is one thing but finding a soul mate is quite another. Maybe that's it, my soul is lonely—lonely for someone I can share my faith with as well as my life. Joe's a churchgoer, there's no doubt about that, so maybe…

A gull dive-bombed me, startling me out of my reverie. It had to be Lilly's influence or Joe's insistence that our relationship be allowed to grow more serious that caused this particular train of thought and brand of misery in me today. "When *You* want it," I said, tilting my head back and imagining the God of the Universe caring about trivial little me. Comforted, I returned to the kitchen to dig into the refrigerator to see if I had any other food which hadn't met and surpassed the expiration date on its packaging.

"Vavavoom!" Joe commented as I opened the front door. "Great look."

I suppose it's great if you're going for the Electrocuted Idiot theme, but I didn't say that. Instead I waved him into the house. "It was all Lilly's idea. She thinks I should wear my hair loose and my slacks tight instead of the other way around. I feel like I stuck my finger in a light socket."

I referred, of course, to my unfettered hair which, unrestrained, floats like black seaweed around my face. The slacks, also Lilly's idea, were black, slender and cropped just above the ankle. She'd insisted I wear a red silk blouse with a mandarin collar, ornate black frogs and a delicate design stitched in gold thread. The best thing about the getup was the fact that she'd "allowed" me to wear black thongs on my feet so that, although I felt like a poster child for an Asian import company, my feet didn't hurt.

Joe, looking incredible as always, sockless and in a white shirt and dark trousers, cupped my face in his hands and pressed a kiss on my forehead. "Maybe we should find a sushi bar instead of eating Italian."

"No, thanks. This is a tribute to your ancestors, remember? We'll eat pasta until we almost burst and then spoon spumoni and tiramisu into the crevices. Then we'll roll home groaning and saying we'll never eat that much again. But on the way we'll run into a Baskin-Robbins and eat some more. It's your family's way, I've seen them in action."

More than once, actually. Joe invites me to all his family's get-togethers and I often join him. Other times, on holidays, when I know Auntie Lou is alone, I cook a big meal and invite her and, as Lou puts it, other "human strays" I can find to join us. Once, by putting it out there that I would be home for Thanksgiving, I ended up entertaining not only Auntie Lou, but an out-of-town pet food salesman, Barney of Barney's Gas, Lilly, a courier who came to my door with a package from my parents, a new neighbor in my complex and three people from church who said they didn't have plans and were going to go home and open a can of soup.

"But when you give a banquet, invite the poor, the crippled, the lame, and the blind. And you will be blessed...." God invites everyone to His party. He doesn't believe in exclusivity and neither do I.

"You aren't as ill-suited for Lilly's attire as you'd like to think. Frankly, when you aren't in a sweatshirt and jeans you're…"

The way Joe was looking at me, I was afraid his next word might be "delicious," so I hurried to interrupt. "Care for some appetizers? A soda?"

"We'd better get going. I made reservations for seven."

Joe drives a Jaguar XK convertible, elegant yet sporty, just like he is. He's also charming, funny, generous, smart and a whole host of other good things. Maybe, I thought, as we careened, top down, toward his favorite little Italian restaurant, I've held too tough a line where Joe is concerned. Some women would saw off an appendage to claim he was theirs and here I am, fending off his advances and trying to be his friend when he wants more.

It must have been the top down on the convertible that scrambled my brain because I decided that, for the night, I would play with the idea of spending the rest of my life with Joe. I've spent so much time pushing him away, that it seems only fair that I give him at least a chance at proving he's the one for me.

If I were rating him on good manners, looks, charm and the ability to order great Italian food, he'd get an A+.

I was still picking at my tiramisu when Joe asked, "What is Lilly doing tonight?"

I leaned back and nearly purred, like a kitten sated on warm cream. Actually, most everything we'd eaten—shrimp pizza in white sauce, ravioli, fettuccini—has been made with pure cream, so the metaphor wasn't that far off.

"Lilly? She had a date."

"With that engineer she was seeing?"

"Oh, no, as far as I know, he's history. You aren't keeping up."

"I don't have enough time to do that and run my business," Joe joked.

It's true. No one does. Lilly plays dating "catch and release." Like the fishermen who populate Lake Zachary, she wants the thrill of the catch, not the fish itself. We tried to count one day, just how many men Lilly had dated in the past two years and even she couldn't remember. Lilly depends upon the cliché "there are always more fish in the sea" and she's always on the lookout for a new variety.

"I think Lilly has her eye on Connor Trevain," I commented as the waiter poured me another cup of coffee.

"He'd be an exotic catch if there ever was one." Joe pinioned me with his gaze. "Is that what you want, Norah? Someone exotic?"

"Me?" I squeaked. "Do you think he likes jeans, sweatshirts covered in dog hair and eau de parfum of Fish Food? I don't think so."

"But what do *you* want in a man?"

I felt an earnestness descend over Joe. The conversation was going in a direction I hadn't expected. Still, I had promised myself I'd give Joe this chance, so I didn't brush him off.

"You can almost guess, can't you? He has to be a Christian and love animals as much as I do, for starters. And he has to dote on Bentley. That's a given. Anyone who fills those qualifications has potential." I tried to keep my voice casual, but the thickly curtained, muted booth in which we sat seemed to suck up the lightness and made me sound grave.

"I know you wouldn't take a second look at someone who didn't share your faith, Norah, but an animal lover like yourself? Do other people as passionate as you exist?" He was smiling a little, half curious, half amused.

"I hope so. I believe I was put on this planet to care for God's vulnerable creatures, Joe. I can't turn my back on that."

"I'm a Christian and I like animals. Especially Bentley." He said it so softly that I barely heard his words. "Where does that put me?"

My hand moved of its own accord to his cheek. "It puts you in a very select group of my precious friends, Joe."

"Just friends?"

Oh, oh. Here we go.

"I know I've been pushing back whenever you try to approach this, Joe. The shop, the renovations in my home, the business decisions…"

"Norah…" he chided.

"Okay, so I'm scared." I crossed my arms over my chest feeling suddenly very vulnerable. "How's that for honesty? Finding a life-partner is a big deal. What if I make a mistake? What if my choice is bad? Then what?"

He looked at me so gently that I felt like crying. "Where is God in this process?"

I felt a warm rush of humiliation spurt through me. Some big talker I am! All this stuff about meeting a man who loves God and yet I really hadn't consulted Him about it other than a drive-by prayer or two.

"Hypocrite in the room, I admit. It just seems so *permanent*. I know I can't have anyone in my life that doesn't understand how I feel about—" I paused, feeling a pun coming on "—the *under*dog!"

"Are you scared of me, Norah?"

I certainly am when he looks at me like that, I thought. My defenses start crumbling like Hoover Dam being hit by a nuclear weapon.

"Okay, okay. I get your point. No more playing games with my emotions—or yours. I'll quit stuffing it when I'm attracted to someone—even you."

"*Even me?* What a romantic you are, Norah." A smile played on his beautiful lips and his eyes twinkled. "I'll take these as words of hope."

I punched him in the arm. "Just because I promise not to play games with my emotions doesn't mean anything will come of it, you know."

"I'll take that chance." He picked up my hand and gently kissed each knuckle.

When he dropped me off at my front door and drove off, I stared after Joe for a long while.

"Well," I muttered as I let myself in and prepared to have Bentley slam into my kneecaps in a frenzy of glee, "we'll see what comes of this."

It wasn't until I was snuggled into bed with Bentley under the covers with me—he has his own pillow which he uses just like humans do—that I began to think about the ramifications of my conversation with Joe.

Then Bentley began to snore beside me and I was reminded that there wasn't anything to worry about. It would have to be one very special man who'd be willing to share his bed with my dog—and that was a requirement I didn't plan to bend easily.

Chapter Five

✣

My phone rang at six on Monday morning. Fortunately I was up, showered and making myself a cappuccino to go with my bagel. The animals have no concept of "sleeping in" so they're training me to get up earlier and earlier. Someone once asked me if I'd ever consider having a rooster around the Ark. No way. If I want another alarm clock, I'll go to Target.

"Hi, Dad," I said as I picked up the receiver. He's the only one I know who keeps ridiculous hours like these.

"It's me, Norah."

And it was certainly not my father. "Auntie Lou? Is that you? You sound funny."

"Nothing funny about it." Her voice was fuzzy. Or maybe

she just didn't have her teeth in yet. "Are you coming to work soon?"

I eyed my bagel. "I'd planned to leave in fifteen or twenty minutes, after I eat breakfast and skim the paper."

"Could you stop over here first?"

Odd. Auntie Lou likes to sleep late because she often stays up late into the night watching old movies and doing crossword puzzles. The doors to her shop never swing open before ten-thirty.

"Sure, I'd be glad to."

"If you don't have that extra key to my store at home with you, my key is under the pot with the artificial geraniums in it. You might have to dig a bit as I laid some stones on top of it, too."

"You won't be up to open the door?"

"If I could get up, I wouldn't be calling you, dearie."

I felt a wash of panic run through me. "Are you sick?"

"Not so's you'd know it."

"Then what's going on?"

"Oh, Arthur pushed me out of bed this morning and Rhuma-tiz helped him," she said obliquely.

"You fell out of bed?" I translated.

"More of a bad slide, but I ended up on the floor just the same. Fortunately I grabbed my cell phone on the way down. All I need is a little help up, dearie. I hope I didn't bother you too early."

I was already wrapping my bagel in a napkin and pouring my cappuccino into a carry cup as I answered. "Auntie Lou, how long did you wait before calling me?"

"Oh, not long. I got a chance to see the sun come up through my bedroom window. Pretty."

"I'll be right there." Leave it to Auntie Lou to find the good in falling out of bed and lying on the floor half the night.

"No hurry. I'll be here when you get here."

No hurry? What am I going to do with that woman? Independent and free as a bird, stubborn as a mule and patient as a saint, she'd no doubt waited until it was convenient for *me* before calling. I wanted to hug her and shake her all at once.

Fortunately I'm walking distance from Pond Street. I was on my knees pawing in the dirt under the fake geraniums when I heard someone clear their throat behind me. I glanced sideways at a pair of polished black leather boots and four equally glossy hooves. On their way, no doubt to the art fair in the park. I found the key and rocked back on my heels to look at Officer Haley and Sarge. Sarge, even more imposing from this angle, shifted restlessly and the metal rings on his headstall and bridle jingled faintly.

"Anything wrong?" Nick Haley inquired mildly.

If I hadn't been so rattled, I might have taken time to appreciate the melodic timbre in his voice. Instead, I just got annoyed.

"Do you *ever* take those things off?" I asked, referring to his mirrored glasses. "And if you do, I wish you'd do it right now. I need you to come upstairs and help me."

His eyebrow arched over the frame. Then, slowly, he pulled the glasses off, revealing a strong, handsome face with unexpectedly blue eyes, long dark lashes and high cheekbones. Whoa. Eye candy.

"I got a call from Auntie Lou asking for help. She's fallen out of bed and can't get herself up, sort of like the television commercial, I'm afraid. Though she didn't admit it, I'm sure she lay there most of the night so as not to disturb anyone's sleep. She's small but solid. I could use an extra pair of hands."

He tied Sarge in a quick release knot, took the dirty key from my hand and opened the door. Together we ascended the stairs to the second floor of Auntie Lou's shop and entered the small, cozy but cluttered apartment where she'd lived for as long as I—or anyone else on Pond Street—could remember.

If the shop was fascinating, her apartment was mesmerizing—full of charming bits of Auntie Lou's history and favorite things that had come into the shop and been squirreled away in her personal stash. She loved old hats. A dozen of them were perched on hat forms around the room sporting plumes and feathers or intricate beading and competing for space with hand-painted vases, antique books and statues of dancing figures.

But this wasn't a museum and we weren't on a tour. I headed for what I knew was her bedroom and opened the door.

Auntie Lou lay on the floor in a puddle of sunlight. She'd put a hand across her eyes to keep out the sun and the big calico cat sat sentry over her. Her nightgown was pure *Little House on the Prairie* and the cane she'd taken to using lately lay on the floor out of reach.

"I hope you didn't hurry on my account, dearie," she managed. Her throat was dry and her voice cracking.

"I certainly did. How long have you been lying here? And is anything broken?"

"Only my pride, child. Only my pride."

Without speaking, as if we were reading each other's minds, Officer Haley and I braced ourselves and lifted Auntie Lou to her feet. Her knees buckled a bit and she sank gratefully onto the bed.

Officer Haley moved into the kitchen and returned with a glass of water which she sucked down with gusto.

"Should we call a doctor?" he inquired gently.

"Mercy sakes, no! There's no medicine for being old and silly. I don't know what made me think I could hop out of bed for a drink of water like I was a teenager. Arthur is a bad bedfellow, that's all I can say.'

Officer Haley looked at me over her head, puzzlement in his beautiful eyes.

"Arthur. Arthritis. Auntie Lou and Arthur have a marriage of inconvenience," I explained.

"Now you two run along and don't tell another soul about this. I feel so foolish that my face must be red as a jar of beet pickles as it is!"

"No promises, Lou," I said sternly. "We're your family here on Pond Street. We can't look after you if you never tell us what's wrong."

"Nothing subtracting forty or fifty years from my age wouldn't help." The calico was rumbling like a diesel truck and rubbing his head on Lou's arm. "Now go away, both of you. I've got Silas here to help me get dressed."

Lou chuckled at the expression on Nick's face. "Silas is my cat. Named him after my dear departed husband. Both sweet, useless layabouts."

"Are you sure…" he began.

"Sure as can be that you aren't the one to help me get dressed, mister. You, either, Norah. Go rescue a gerbil or something. I'm fine."

With that, she grabbed the cane Nick had propped by her bed and waved it at us threateningly. Our rescue mission was obviously over.

Back out in the sunlight, we found Sarge snacking contentedly on a patch of grass.

"Officer, I'd like to thank you…"

"Nick. Call me Nick."

"Oh, well, yes, thank you," I said, sounding vaguely dimwitted. I wish he'd put his sunglasses back on. Those eyes of his rattled me as though they X-rayed my soul. Instead, he stood there, tapping the bow of the glasses against his leg, making the coins in his pocket jingle.

"Tell me, has this happened before?"

"No. She sometimes complains that she's so stiff she needs a hoist to get out of her chair, but when I suggested a lift chair so she could stand more easily, she huffed and puffed and said she didn't want to be expelled from a chair like a bottle rocket and that was that. As far as I know, Auntie Lou has never had a major health issue. She's just old."

"How old?"

"She says she went to grade school with Methuselah and junior high with seven of the Apostles, but other than that, I have no idea."

Finally, he laughed. "Okay, so it isn't a recurring event. I'd just like to know in case…you know."

"I'm glad you're willing to watch out for Auntie Lou. I

am, too. And everyone on Pond Street would notice if she didn't show up at the shop for a day or two. Maybe I can convince her to go to the doctor for a checkup."

"Does she have any family?" he inquired.

"None that she's ever mentioned." I felt my chin come out defensively. "We're her family. *I'm* her family."

Although I'd never thought about it like that before, I knew it was true.

We're stewards, after all, responsible for the earth and creatures God gave us and for those who can't care for themselves. *"Care for the orphans and widows in their distress...."* What can love and gentle care hurt? Absolutely nothing.

"Then she's very fortunate to have you."

"Fortunate to have *me? I'm* fortunate to have *her.* Auntie Lou is a treasure, Nick. Just wait until you get to know her. You'll see."

I reached out and stroked Sarge's neck. "He's beautiful. Have you always ridden horses?"

"For the police? No. I was a narcotics agent for several years. Then I had a little—" his voice faltered "—accident and I needed a change, an assignment a little less...dramatic. That's when I backed off narcotics and went back on the force. When they needed someone part-time for the mounted patrol, I applied. I rode a lot as a kid and that was actually what I'd intended when I originally joined law enforcement. It seemed a natural choice. Now, as you know, I do crowd control for special events as well as normal police work. Shoreside has enough events around the lake, parades and fairs to keep me busy."

Though his tone was pleasant, it felt as though he'd

strung barbed wire around a certain topic he'd mentioned—an accident, *his* accident. *Ask me about the horse,* he hinted silently. *Don't ask me what happened to get me here.*

"Well, I think he's magnificent. There aren't many jobs I could enjoy more than the one I already have except those involving horses or dog training or…"

"Give me horses any day," he responded quickly. Sarge shifted restlessly and the creak of his saddle and the clank of stirrups reminded us how patiently he was waiting.

"Thanks for helping me with Auntie Lou," I murmured. "I know you must have more to do than…"

"Anytime. And I'll keep an eye out for her, too."

Feeling grateful and a little giddy, I went to open Norah's Ark and fed the masses.

At 10:00 a.m., two of my favorite Bed and Biscuit clients arrived. Winslow Cavanaugh galumphed into the store, tongue lolling out of his mouth. He's a lovable galoot, pampered as much by his owner as Bentley is by me. A few steps behind, Cassia and Adam Cavanaugh entered. Adam was carrying a lurching pet carrier with feral sounds and hisses emanating from the breathing holes.

Winslow and Pepto have been coming to my B and B for several months now. The Cavanaughs travel a lot—overseas, I think—and the happy-go-lucky dog has made himself right at home in the back of the store. Pepto, a cat with the disposition of a viper and personality of an evil dictator of some small, suffering nation, has only deemed to grace us with his presence because he has no other option. I've made it my goal to win over the big, ornery cat and we're making some headway. I love a challenge. Especially a furry one.

Once I got them settled, I returned to the front of the store in time to see Lilly sweep in and gracefully receive her admiring squawk from Winky. Today she was wearing something chiffon and mustard-yellow, a dress perhaps, although it looked as though it had been put together with safety pins. She had matching knee-high, lace-up boots, a vibrant orange ribbon woven through the blond curls she'd piled on top of her head and a necklace and earrings made out of more safety pins. On her, stunning. On me? Stunned.

"Don't you look like a ray of sunshine?" I greeted her. Or a yellow paint spill.

"You like it?" She twirled and the chiffon floated around her in a gauzy cloud. "I thought I might run into Connor Trevain again today and I wanted to look, you know, nice."

"Nice? You look like lemon sherbet. Delectable, mouthwatering even."

"That's what I was going for."

"Trevain is still in your sights, is he?"

"He hasn't been out of them since the day he arrived." A small pout formed on her lower lip. "But he's been so busy with those boats of his, he's hardly had time to stop in to say hello. Did you come to work early today?" Lilly inquired as she picked up a piece of lettuce and fed it to the iguana.

"Earlier than I'd planned." I gave her an abbreviated version of Auntie Lou's arthritis and left out the help I'd received from Officer Haley. I didn't want anyone to get the idea that Auntie Lou was incapable of caring for herself. Still, it wouldn't hurt to have others watching out for her just in case she fell in her shop.

"Maybe she's too old to be running that place all alone. When my grandmother was her age, she moved into a retirement home."

I ignored her implication. Auntie Lou is not Lilly's grandmother. She's unique and can't be compared to anyone else. I studied Lilly for a moment. "Something's different about you today, Lilly. What's up?"

She looked at me coyly, as if I'd caught her with her hand in the cookie jar. "I've made up my mind about something."

"Tell me more." Lilly prides herself on being flexible. To make up her mind—and stick with it—is definitely an occasion to be curious about.

"I'm getting married."

I felt my jaw drop and my eyes bug out with shock.

"You don't have to look so surprised. I'm almost thirty, you know. It's time."

"But, but, but…" I made a noise like a sputtering engine. "Who?"

"It's a secret."

"Why?"

"Because he doesn't know about it yet." Lilly fluttered her eyelashes and I saw her perfectly painted lids. "But he will soon enough."

"Who…why…how…"

"Connor, of course. Why? Because he's handsome,

charming, wealthy, debonair and perfect for me. How? I'll be as charming and wonderful as I can, that's how."

Lilly can be plenty charming and wonderful, but I'm not sure she's picked a viable target with this one. "What if he's not interested in being married?"

She waved a dismissive hand. "Oh, I'll worry about that later. For now I just want to go out with him."

"More than once?" I thought of her serial dating and short attention span where men are concerned.

"Of course more than once! A lot." She put a polished finger to her lips. "You're the only one I'm telling because you are my best friend."

"Shouldn't you mention it to Trevain?"

"Of course not. He has to figure it out for himself."

"Lilly, what if he doesn't want to get serious with someone right now?"

"That's what love is about, Norah—the unexpected. Affairs of the heart cannot be decided by logic alone."

I have to grant her that. And it made her intentional plotting even more ridiculous.

"I know how you are about love and marriage, Norah," Lilly added. "It needs to be blessed by God and all that, but this will be okay—really."

Blessed by God and all that?

It was more than just a toss-off matter for me. God's blessing is the key to the whole thing, as far as I'm concerned.

Lilly has been trying to play hide-and-seek with God. Sometimes she tries to avoid Him completely. Other times she asks a hundred questions about what it's like to give one's life to Him. She's got some ideas from childhood about a judgmental God and it's got her hung up. She forgets that the same God who sees our sin and judges it as wrong, is the One who has the ability to forgive the sin, wash it away and forget it ever happened. He doesn't keep a tally of wrongs like some humans do. He forgives and forgets *"Far as the east is from the West."* When Lilly's ready she'll jump in—Gucci-clad feetfirst—I just know it.

Chapter Six

❦

Now that Lilly had announced her new project—the unsuspecting Connor Trevian—it was time for me to get back to work.

"Sorry I don't have time to help you plan your wedding, but I have a tuna fish cupcake to make. It's Mr. Tibbles's birthday today and he's coming to stay a few days."

"You mean that pompous black cat, the one that acts like he's Winston Churchill?"

"That's him."

"You'd rather do that than plan my wedding?" Lilly said incredulously.

"Let's just say that I know for sure that Mr. Tibbles is coming. I'm not so sure Connor is going to go willingly down the aisle." I met Lilly's gaze with my own. "What's up with you, anyway?"

Lilly pouted a bit, threw her blond hair back from her face, stomped in her high-heeled butter-colored boots to a chair behind the counter and sat down. Her starlet persona, no doubt about it. "Do you think I'm flighty?'

Uh-oh. Trick question.

"Ah, well, it depends on your definition of the word *flighty.*"

"Airheaded, dizzy, short attention span, blonde jokes, erratic, unreliable, capricious."

"If you know the definition of *capricious* you probably aren't flighty."

"Be honest, Norah. You're the only one I can rely on to tell me the truth, the whole truth and nothing but."

"First I need to know who called you flighty."

"Oh, that accountant I've been seeing. He says we can't continue a relationship because I'm much too erratic and impulsive."

No wonder Connor is looking so good.

"In that case, you *are* flighty. Look at how you are dressed. You strive for erratic and impulsive."

"And cutting edge fashionwise," Lilly defended, already looking a bit happier. "You're right. I *like* what I am. If he doesn't, he's not the man for me." She jumped up and gave me a hug, swathing me in the fragrance of lavender and something mossy. "I'm so glad we're friends, Norah. I can trust you. You tell me the truth and never go behind my back. Thank...thank..."

"...God?" I finished for her.

"Yeah. Him." Her eyes narrowed as she studied me. "If

you're the kind of product He turns out, then I do want to get to know Him better…someday." Then she threw her head back and swept out of the store like a runway model. No wonder she'd made her accountant nervous. Lilly was a full five fingers, a definite handful.

So she was watching me, looking for God in me. My grandmother said I might be the only sermon someone like Lilly ever hears. That should keep me on my toes.

When I pad around in my pajamas and big white bunny slippers, Hoppy goes crazy. She thinks she's got company and keeps returning to my feet to sniff them. Her little nose practically vibrates with excitement. I'm thinking of getting a second rabbit so she'll have some company. It's easier to put two does together than two bucks, so I'll have to get another female. If I introduce a male, within weeks, I'll have way too much company in the house.

I leaned down to touch her soft fur. "You bunnies are just like humans, aren't you? Two women can get along fine, but put a man in the mix and—poof!—there's trouble." We eyed each other soulfully, human and rabbit, and for a moment, I was sure Hoppy knew exactly what I meant. Then she tried to bite off my slipper's nose and I snapped out of that daydream.

When my doorbell rang, my attack powder puff, Bentley, slid off the couch, rolled on the carpet, staggered to his feet and took what he thinks is an aggressive stance. It *might* be aggressive, if he'd ever learn to stop wagging his tail. Bentley, for all his former woes, is an optimist. "Sure," his posture says, "I'll protect my mistress even if she is wearing stupid slippers, but, no matter who you are on the other side of the door, I'd rather just lick your face."

Then he must have gotten a whiff of pizza, because he raced to the door wriggling like an otter on a waterslide.

Lilly was on the other side of the door with a double pepperoni and cheese pizza, bread sticks and a liter of soda. She walked in without invitation and plopped the food down on my table. "Girl's night," she announced. "I'll get the plates."

Never one to turn away a delivered pizza, I gathered glasses and napkins and settled into one of the cushioned chairs in my dining room.

"What's up?" I finally got around to asking as Lilly doled pizza onto plates.

"Oh, nothing. Want a bread stick?" She waved them under my nose.

"'Nothing'? You brought a family-size pizza for 'nothing'? Lilly, we could solve the world's problems over this thing. What's wrong?"

"I saw Connor after work."

I watched a piece of mozzarella make a tightrope between my mouth and a slice of pizza. "And?"

"And he's perfect for me, Norah. Absolutely perfect. I love the way he looks, the sound of his voice, his aftershave...."

Smitten. Deeply smitten. Besotted. Love-struck even. I reeled in the cheese with my teeth and tongue.

"...but I'm not sure how to get him."

"'Get' him?" There was a tone in Lilly's voice that I hadn't heard before, especially where men are concerned. Anxiety.

"You know. Make him realize I'm the one for him."

"Lilly, you do that all the time. You can do that unconscious! You're sweet, beautiful, funny…."

"I can be," she agreed, "but not this time. This time it feels
like I'm a schoolgirl with a crush on the captain of the foot-
ball team. I can be all those things because I haven't really
found anyone I want to spend my life with. Now, when it
counts, I'm scared stiff!"

Lilly, scared stiff, is a sight to behold. Her blond hair was
in a loose halo around her head, she wore snug designer
jeans, high-heeled boots, a frothy peasant blouse and a
thick, silver-studded belt that nipped in her slender waist.
Her earrings matched her belt which matched the chain
around her neck, which matched her thick silver brace-
let…scared stiff looks great on Lilly.

"I really care this time, Norah, and as a result, I'm like a
clumsy, unsophisticated kid who doesn't know what to do
with her knees and elbows, let alone the rest of her!"

"Sounds quite charming to me." Sometimes I wonder if
Lilly only likes guys who don't initially show much interest in her. I sprinkled red peppers on the pizza and then surreptitiously slipped Bentley a piece of crust. "Maybe Connor
likes that kind of woman."

"I don't think so."

Something in her tone made me look up sharply. "Why
do you say that?"

"Oh, he's nice to me, it's not that, but I don't feel any spark
coming from him."

"'Spark'? As in lighting a fire?"

"You've got it. The reason I recognize his lack of interest

is that I've given off that same vibe myself, to men I know are crazy about me but that I'm not terribly interested in."

Ah. The root of the matter. Lilly is one of the most competitive people I know. She is unwilling to lose anything she sees as competition. She can give the off-putting vibes but she can't take them when they're aimed her way.

"Why don't you give it a chance, Lilly? Connor doesn't know you and, frankly, you don't know him. Allow yourselves a little time."

Lilly fluttered her long French manicured nails in front of her face.

"Who knows?" I offered. "Maybe you won't like him as well as you think you will—and he'll like you even better."

I studied her and was surprised to see a glaze of tears in her eyes.

"Sometimes I get sick of being a strong, independent woman, Norah. I want to be swept off my feet and carried into the sunset. Do you understand that at all?"

Do I? Me, who's waiting for Cupid's arrow and shimmery shivers and wedding bells? "Of course I do, Lilly. Just don't panic. Desperation is not a scent you want to give off, you know."

"It's more clear-cut for you," she said accusingly, wiping her eye with a stiff paper napkin. "You think God's going to clunk you on the head with a guy some day. I don't think I want to wait for that."

It would certainly expedite matters if God just dropped my ideal husband into my lap. No wondering if or when Mr. Right comes along. No insecurity about myself because I'd know that this man is meant for me. No wearing makeup every day of the week just to make sure I don't scare Mr. Right off with pale cheeks and no mascara on my lashes. The idea had merit, although I was wise enough to keep that idea to myself.

Still, Lilly was feeling better when she left sometime later. Pizza therapy is one of my favorite medical prescriptions.

On my way to the post office on Tuesday morning, my step slowed as I neared the new toy store. The door was open yet I was reluctant to stop in, considering the odd reception I'd had last time I was there. But fools venture where angels dare not tread, so I mounted the steps and went inside.

What a transformation! What had been dingy and drab had been changed into a scene from one of my favorite books as a child, *The Secret Garden*. The walls were freshly papered in muted pink Victorian cabbage roses that gave off an aura of a musty but elegant past. There were dolls everywhere—Madame Alexander dolls, Barbie dolls, fat baby dolls and collectibles with delicate porcelain faces and bemused expressions. A huge round crib hung with thick mauve ribbon and delicate rosebuds was piled high with teddy bears. Another crib was full of jungle creatures—fat, jolly monkeys, floppy-necked giraffes, lions with wild manes. It wasn't until I was halfway to the jungle display that I realized the room had been divided in half. Behind the area filled with dolls was the "techno" room. PlayStation consoles, video games, cars on racetracks and everything that either plugged in, used batteries or made loud obnoxious noises was displayed here.

"What do you think?"

I was so engrossed that I gave a startled squeak and spun around to find Julie Morris standing behind me. Though she looked a little strained, today she had a smile on her face.

"You're a phenomenon! I had no idea this place could look so good." Meeting Julie and her husband the other day, I hadn't believed there was a playful bone in either of their bodies. Heartened, I pressed on through the fantasyland they'd created.

"Would you like to see my favorite part?" Julie asked shyly.

I wonder how a person gets so timid—especially one who intends to be a business owner dealing with the public all day long.

Julie led me to a table filled with baskets. In the baskets were tiny toys and packets of candy. Diminutive dolls, race cars so small their wheels would make M&M's look large, little coloring books and paper dolls. My particular favorite, for a dime apiece, was fake fingernails on green plastic fingertips with hair sprouting from the first knuckle.

"I had these when I was a kid! I played an ogre in a school play in third grade." I picked one up, popped it on my index finger and quoted, "'I'm sure you'll be delicious, little girl, I'll save you for dessert.'" Why *is* it, I wonder, that we allow kids to read fairy tales as violent as the evening news?

Without thinking, I picked up a Chinese finger puzzle. It was the kind I could never get my fingers out of when I was a child, poked a finger in each end and recalled the panicky feeling that I'd have to spend the rest of my life with my index fingers connected by a little straw tube.

"Uh-oh, I think I'll be buying this. Do you have scissors?"

Julie laughed, pressed my index fingers toward each other and showed me the trick to getting my fingers free. "That's why I love this table. It has things on it cheap enough for children to buy on their own, and gadgets old enough to appeal to their parents."

Covertly I studied her. Julie is a pretty woman, if one can see through the premature frown lines and deeply carved grooves around her mouth. She doesn't seem a likely candidate to own a toy store but she certainly knows how to devise a charming one.

"What made you come to Shoreside and start an old-fashioned toy store?"

I felt, rather than heard her hesitate.

"We needed a change of scenery and I wanted to do something fun."

"Well, you got that part right, I…"

The back door opened and closed again with a slam and a teenage boy bolted into the room. He wore baggy jeans with more pockets than there were in my entire closet, a black T-shirt with some bizarre figure on the front with its mouth open to reveal fanged teeth and a hairdo that spiked into needle-sharp tips embellished in orange. All he needed were the fake monster fingertips to complete his ensemble. He opened his mouth to say something to Julie, saw me and snapped it closed again. Without a word he clomped on heavy black boots to the back and up a set of stairs to the second floor. Had I not known it was a fifteen-year-old boy on those stairs, I would have thought it was a team of Clydesdales making their way up the flight of steps.

"Your son?" I ventured. The stricken look on Julie's face told me it could be none other.

"You'll have to excuse Bryce. He can be...difficult."

Bryce looked as if he were born to be "difficult." The creases and worry lines on her face began to make sense. I'd have them, too, if I had to live with an attitude like the one I'd seen in the few seconds Bryce Morris and I had been in the same room together.

I didn't speak, sensing that there was more that Julie wanted to say.

"We're hoping that this move to Shoreside will be good for our family. A fresh start."

She saw the question on my face.

"We...Bryce...needed to start over...another school district." She looked pained. "He got in with a bad crowd. We felt it would be a good idea to move someplace farther out of the city. You understand, of course, that we don't want this to be public knowledge. He's a good boy, really. A kind heart."

I squeezed Julie's hand and silently determined to put the Morrises at the top of my prayer list.

Connor was sitting at a small table in front of the Java Jockey, sipping espresso from a small china cup and staring toward Lake Zachary. When he saw me, he waved me over, jumped to his feet and gestured toward a wrought-iron chair.

I hate the cliché "Curiosity killed the cat." Violence of any kind toward animals is abhorrent to me. But I figure curiosity isn't going to get me without a fight, so I pulled up the chair and sat down.

"Funny, but even now I can't get enough of the lake—or any water for that matter," he said. "Sitting here, looking across it is still a delight to me."

"It couldn't hurt that you have six luxury cruise boats moored at the dock."

He smiled and his even white teeth flashed in the sun. Tucked as they were into a handsome face with a perfect golden tan, it was quite a sight. I understand why Lilly hears wedding bells when she looks at him.

"Have you taken one of my cruises, Norah?" He said it so casually he might have been asking if I'd ridden one of his bicycles.

"A few times, for weddings."

People around here often rent cruise boats for anniversary and wedding receptions. It's a perfectly self-contained, no worries, floating restaurant. Only one time did I see a problem with having one's wedding reception on board. We were sailing nicely around the lake celebrating the nuptials of our friends when someone realized that the bride and groom had not made it to the dock. They had become so lost in each other's eyes that they also lost track of time and, literally, missed the boat. By the time the captain had turned the ship and sailed back to pick them up, the bride, still in her white dress, and the groom, looking like that little banker, Mr. Monopoly on the board game, appeared pretty dismal. She had tears tracking down her face while her groom was obviously trying to answer that age-old question of newly married men—*What have I gone and done?* Fortunately, a standing ovation, striking up the band—okay, string quartet—and a buffet cheered them considerably.

"I'd like to have you join me sometime. As my guest. Would you consider that?"

"How generous of you! I'd love to...." My brain went into gear two beats behind my mouth. Recalling Lilly's building infatuation with this guy, I wanted to make sure she got the attention, not me.

Although he is probably asking me just to be sociable, Connor's reputation for enjoying beautiful women precedes him. And I'm no doubt worrying prematurely. Look at Lilly and then look at me. Unless he gets a thrill out of women wearing their hair in an aquatic animal imitation—my whale spout of a ponytail—I'm not in danger of holding his attention for long.

"Will there be many of us from Pond Street on board?" I asked innocently, hoping he'd get the hint.

I could read nothing in his well-bred features. His tone was pleasant. "What a fine idea. A party. Brilliant. That would be a good way for all of us to get acquainted."

A high, sharp sound coming from my shop caught our attention. Bentley stood in the doorway of Norah's Ark holding his dog dish in his mouth, making the high-pitched squealing noises and staring accusingly at me, eliciting guilt in me from every pore. Little stinker.

"Looks like your dog is hungry," Connor pointed out unnecessarily. "And who is minding the store?"

"Annie. Sometimes she works at the Java Jockey. Joe and I share her."

"You love what you do, don't you?" Smile lines crinkled pleasantly around Connor's eyes.

"I do. I grew up knowing that I wanted to live with a menagerie around me and the more the merrier. Especially dogs. Norah's Ark is perfect for me."

"I felt the same way about the water," Connor admitted. "I couldn't get enough. I was sailing things in the bathtub before I could talk. It's as though I was—" he fumbled for a word "—created to sail."

"We're all created for something," I agreed affably, "there's no doubt in my mind about that." I glanced toward the store. Bentley was now lying on his back, legs straight in the air playing dead doggie, bowl still clutched in his teeth.

"I suppose I should take the hint and go feed my dog before rigor mortis sets in."

"I'm surprised he hasn't come running over here to get you."

"Bentley? Oh, no. He'd never do that. He doesn't like to cross streets."

Connor looked at me incredulously. "A dog that refuses to cross streets?"

"It must have had something to do with his life before I got him. Bowled over by a car, maybe. A near miss of some kind. Of course, Bentley doesn't like a lot of things."

Like fireworks, staircases, heavy metal music, blenders, motorcycles, electric can openers, suitcases on rolling wheels, the doggie park or, believe it or not, fire hydrants. And those are just his more noticeable idiosyncrasies.

Living with Bentley is an adventure in paranoia. He sees himself in a mirror and goes berserk, ostensibly protecting me from himself. His phobias and suspicions are legion. Fortunately, his capacity for love is even greater.

Connor stared at me strangely. "I don't believe I've ever

met anyone who seems to like dogs, and every other animal, as much as you do."

"Love me, love my dog," I said cheerfully. Connor, who
really didn't know me very well, had no idea how serious a
statement that was.

Chapter Seven

✥

I glanced up from the paperwork I do every Wednesday—
ordering leashes, fish food and cat toys—to a jingle of the
bell I kept in the store's entry. There stood a large figure in
the doorway, backlit by bright sunlight. The body nearly
filled the entry, a silhouette of broad shoulders, narrow hips
and lean muscles. I was reminded of an action-adventure
movie where the hero enters, a larger-than-life figure come
to save the day.

And I wasn't that far off. He looked so different without
his uniform, spit-polished boots and mirrored sunglasses on
that I hardly recognized Nick. Today he was wearing dark
trousers of some soft, rich-looking fabric, a pale blue polo
with a black belt and shoes. Better yet, his eyes weren't hid-

den behind those distance-keeping glasses. He looked tanned, fit and, I searched my mind for a word Lilly might use—dazzling.

Then I realized that he also looked frozen in the doorway, so I hopped off my stool and went to greet him. I didn't come close in the clothing department in my khaki shorts and standard polo embroidered with a Norah's Ark logo.

"Welcome! Come on in." I beckoned him in. "Do you like things with wings, scales or fur?"

His jaw was set with the same resolve I sometimes have when I go to the dentist—even though the business card says *Gentle Dentistry,* I don't quite believe it. After all, my dentist's name is Dr. Payne. "No. No pets."

"Then you've come to the wrong place," I said cheerfully. "Unless it's me you want to see."

"Do you have a minute?" He looked uncomfortable, as if something might attack him. Of course, Winky was giving him the evil eye and had remained silent, which usually meant he was considering parrot mischief.

"Sure. Annie's in back cleaning the B and B so there's even someone on duty. We had a big party last night for one of my 'guests.'"

"You're still talking animals, right?" He looked unsure.

"Yes. I have a cat named Pepto staying here who has a bit of an attitude problem. He made his way to the top of the curtain rods and brought them down with him." I had to chuckle. "You should have heard the noises that came out from under those curtains. I thought the water pipes would freeze and the mirrors crack! Quite a little set of lungs that Pepto has."

He was looking at me as if I were speaking Swahili so I gestured toward the outdoor tables across the street at the Java Jockey. "Would you like caffeine? You're looking a little pale around the gills." There I go, diagnosing him with a fish disorder.

He didn't seem to notice. In fact, he brightened considerably.

"Sure, yeah. Okay. Fine."

We took a table in the corner to avoid the bright sun. Feeling frisky, I ordered a large latte with soy and hazelnut flavoring. Talk about living on the edge. Both caffeine and sugar in the same drink, a combination that always loosens my lips.

"You're looking purposeful," I commented as I studied him. "Is your visit business or pleasure?" His biceps bulged and I could see veins in his forearms that hinted at dedicated muscle building. He also had long pale scars running from beneath the left sleeve of his polo shirt to his wrist. A car accident, I guessed. The healed wounds looked like they'd been carved by jagged glass.

"Actually, I wanted to see if you'd had a conversation with Auntie Lou about her fall out of bed."

"She's fine. 'Meaner than ever,' she says." I was pleasantly surprised to realize that he was concerned for my elderly friend. Though everyone knows Auntie Lou, she doesn't have many close friends that call on her. Everyone on Pond Street assumes I am the go-to girl when something concerning Auntie Lou comes up.

She loves music and can get a little carried away with the volume on her little old portable stereo in the store. She plays her LPs as loud as she can—until someone sends me over to tell her to turn it down. Sometimes I catch her in the back of the store, eyes closed, humming, shuffling her feet and communing with Lawrence Welk and his friends. She also likes Elvis, but people seem to get less tired of his voice emanating from the back of the shop. Mostly I'm delegated to talk to her about not feeding the gulls in front of her store or leaving mannequins bare except for elaborate hats, in the store windows.

"You don't think there's a danger of something like that happening again?" His forehead creased in genuine concern.

"Oh, I didn't say that. She'll probably do it sometime. At least she keeps her cell phone beside her—even in bed."

The frown went away. "Good. I'd hate to think of her lying there, waiting for help…."

"That's very sweet of you. Is this your duty as a police officer or as a concerned neighbor?"

"A little of both. I have grandparents, too, you know." He smiled then, really smiled and I saw how truly handsome Nick is. He doesn't smile often but when he does…let's just say, it's worth the wait.

"Where did your grandparents live when you were a child?" I asked, intrigued.

"On an island in the middle of Lake Michigan. Gramps was a fisherman."

"And you saw a lot of them?"

"I stayed on the island every summer and worked for my grandfather."

"So you like the water."

Nick turned to look out at Lake Zachary, still as a mirror

rimmed with a frame of lush trees and lawns dotted with large lake homes. "I do. This is an ideal location for me."

"Then I'm glad you're here." I surprised myself with my enthusiasm over his good fortune. I guess I'm glad he's here, too.

We carried on a rambling conversation about the lake, the weather, favorite foods: His are prime rib, mashed potatoes and corn. Mine are milk chocolate, dark chocolate and white chocolate. And hobbies: Nick is rebuilding a 1969 Camaro in his garage. My hobbies are the same as my business—animals, animals and more animals.

It was a rather cozy tête-à-tête until Joe walked out the front door of the coffee shop and noticed us. As he walked our way, I could see that he looked troubled.

"Hey, Joe, everything okay?" I patted the seat of the chair next to me and invited him to sit down.

He accepted the offer by dropping heavily into the chair. "Just the usual. Somebody wants vacation time and I don't have anyone to cover it so that means I'll be working nights next week. The espresso machine is trying to express itself in ways that make me think I'll have to have it repaired. Same old, same old." His gaze darted between Nick and me but he didn't say any more.

"Nick was just asking about Auntie Lou," I offered. "About her health," I added vaguely.

"I'm not sure she has much time left at the shop," Joe said bluntly.

"Do you know something I don't?"

"Of course not, but she's old. Old people lose steam, that's all. She should be somewhere she can take it easy instead of working like she does."

"Put her out to pasture, you mean?" For some reason, the idea of Joe suggesting that Auntie Lou's "steam" was dwindling upset me.

"Hardly that. But I worry about her sometimes."

"She is a little frail," Nick added, trying to bridge the gap that had broken open between Joe and me, "but she's got lots of spirit."

"I think it's great that both of you are concerned, as I am, but Auntie Lou isn't finished yet." I pushed away from the table. "I have to get back to work or I won't get my order in on time. Nick, thanks for the coffee."

He started to rise, but I waved him back into his chair. Such a gentleman.

Joe cleared his throat. "Don't forget about my niece's violin recital on Friday."

I crossed my eyes at him. "If it's as bad as last time, I'm bringing earplugs."

"My sister says she's improved a little."

"Only 'a little'? Joe, I suffered hearing loss at her last recital. I'd rather listen to a bagful of cats fight than Mozart's Adagio in E major played by a nine year old."

He shrugged helplessly. "My sister is expecting you."

"Only for Maria, then." I grinned and turned my back on them, reminding myself to stop at a drugstore to buy myself some cotton balls to plug my ears. I left the two of them together to find something to talk about.

The recital was even worse than I imagined it could be. Joe's niece blistered out a classical piece that no doubt had its composer turning over in his grave, if not trying to claw his way out to rip the violin from the child's hands. And she was one of the better ones. Even Joe's comforting arm around my shoulders didn't help. Throughout it all, the music teacher sat with a blissful smile on her face, nodding and looking proud.

"Is that woman attached to reality at all?" I whispered to Joe after the wailings and screeches were done. "If I had to listen to those shrieking sounds all day, I'd be deaf as a post."

I moved a little closer to the buffet table where the prodigies' mothers were serving pieces from a cake shaped like a violin. Accidentally, I bumped into a tall woman who hovered over the cake plates. "Excuse me, I didn't mean…" She turned toward me. It was the guilty party. The one who'd taught all those innocent children to play like coyotes howling at the moon, like tires squealing on wet pavement, like turkeys having their tail feathers plucked…. There should be a law against what this woman does to music.

She smiled at me with that serene, unearthly smile. As she did so, I noticed a tiny earplug protruding out of one ear. She didn't answer but gestured me to move forward through the line. *No fair!* Couldn't she be penalized for using illegal equipment? Surely wearing earplugs was frowned on by a Teachers of Musical Instruments Association or something. There's got to be an organization to prevent cruelty to parents.

"I'll buy you dessert to make up for this," Joe said later. At least I think that's what he said. I'm new at lip reading, having had to start it only this evening, after the concert.

"Bribery won't work. You owe me more than a crummy

piece of pie for loss of hearing. Don't ever do that to me again, Joe. Never invite me to anything where your family plays, sings, acts or orates. Promise?"

Joe smiled and took my hand in his. A dark curl fell onto his forehead and his eyes were mysteriously shadowed by the light of the streetlamp. "'Love me, love my family.' Isn't that what you say?"

"I say 'Love me, love my dog,' Joe. And Bentley doesn't play a violin."

"My family loves you, you know."

"They are wonderful people. They can make magic in the kitchen. Your family is chock-full of fabulous cooks with generous hearts and great intelligence. They were standing behind the door, however, when musical talent was handed out."

Joe ignored my comment. We've had this conversation before and he and I are in full agreement about the no-talent part. We just disagree on what to do about it when these recitals come up.

Still, in the end, I did forgive him for only a piece of sour cream raisin pie at Tea on Tap. Weak, I am so terribly weak.

"So what do you think?" He pushed the crust from his pecan pie in my direction. I'm a crust girl, myself. One of my all-time favorite foods is pie crust rolled flat, sprinkled with cinnamon and sugar and baked in sheets to break off and eat all by itself, a taste I acquired in my grandmother's kitchen.

"Can't think," I dodged. "My brain is still jangled from the noise." By the look in his eyes, I knew that Joe was getting ready for a conversation I didn't want to have.

"Someday you might have a little girl or boy playing in a recital, you know. *We* might."

A lead ball dropped into the pit of my stomach.

"Joe…"

"You can't avoid this forever, Norah." Impatience flashed on his handsome features.

"Nor do I want to. But I want to avoid it now." I don't know what makes me so resistant to the idea of marriage just yet. "The time isn't right."

"Maybe it's the *man* that isn't right. Is that it?" He looked at me with so much hurt in his eyes that I ached for him. But not enough to change my mind.

"You said it. I didn't." I reached for his hand, but he drew it back.

"Do you think there's someone better out there for you? Is that it?"

"I have no idea, Joe. Quit being obtuse. I haven't looked. I'm not interested in looking. Don't you see? That's the problem. I'm just not ready."

I haven't heard bells yet.

I know Joe so well that I quickly realized that he was about to give me an ultimatum of some sort. Unfortunately, well as he knows me, he still forgets that giving me an ultimatum is as problematic as coaxing an unwilling donkey into a trot.

"I know, I know. You aren't 'ready.' You have feelings for me, but….if you do decide to fall in love I'm first on the list."

"Not only first on the list but second and third, as well. I just need some time."

"Time's going to run out eventually, Norah. Then what?"

Joe's eyes were soft and a little sad. He's been patient with me for nearly two years. A pang of guilt shot through me even though I know that until I am sure—and that God has confirmed it for me—I couldn't do more than I was doing now.

"I can't ask you to wait forever, Joe. I want you to follow your heart. If there's someone else you might…" My throat ached as the words came out.

"It's not that." He took a deep breath and then he smiled. "I just thought strong-arm tactics might work with you."

I was relieved and overwhelmingly grateful that he still had patience with me. "Joe, you are a prince," I began. "And you *are* first…"

"…second and third on your list. I know, Norah. I know. Maybe you want to see other people."

"Other people?" I parroted idiotically. "We hardly even see each other!"

"I've been pushing you too much, haven't I, Norah? Maybe I need to back off and give you some space." His voice was firm and determined. His eyes looked raw and painful as two holes burned into a blanket.

He's doing this for me.

"Joe, that's not…"

"I think it is. I can't seem to entice you to marry me by pushing, Norah. Maybe I can do it by backing away."

My throat clogged with an emotion I couldn't identify. I'd never felt more loved by him than at that moment.

"I see it in your eyes, Norah. You need space and time. You've told me that all along, but I didn't want to listen. Now—" he smiled weakly though there was nothing else weak about him "—I realize that's the gift I have to give you.

Time. Freedom. You are at liberty to see anyone you choose, Norah. I won't get in the way."

"It's not about that, Joe. I'm just waiting to feel…to hear…" I couldn't get the word *bells* out of my mouth.

"And I'm here when you start to 'feel' it."

"There's no one else I want to see," I blurted, suddenly, unexpectedly feeling panicky. "No one."

"Me, either. But you need space. I love you, Norah. But I want you to come to me willingly if you come at all. I've waited nearly two years. I can wait a few more months."

I was filled with an overwhelming gratitude at his words and, to my shame, another niggling thought. *Only months?* Maybe Joe was right. I was even balking at a timetable for my freedom.

"It's not going to change my feelings for you," I began.

"No? I hope it does."

Surprise must have shown on my features.

"I hope it makes you love me more. Enough to marry me."

"And if it doesn't?"

He shrugged as though there were thousand-pound weights on his shoulders. "It's a chance we'll have to take."

I think I surprised him when I shot up, threw myself across the table and hugged him. I certainly surprised myself and the waitress coming to refill our coffee cups. "Joe, you are the most awesome man on the planet."

He grinned and pushed me back to my side of the table. "Remember that. It's not every woman that has the opportunity to marry a superhero."

Later, as I watched his taillights disappear around the bend,

I felt a sense of heaviness in my heart. What's wrong with me? Am I being selfish about building my business? Is he the one for me and I'm too blind to see it? I tipped my head back and stared at the star-sprinkled sky. Lord, what's a girl to do?

Then, because I heard Bentley in the house moaning like he'd been eviscerated, I went inside to rescue my lonely doggie.

"Hi, Norah. What's new?" a gravelly voice said as I opened my front door.

"Not a thing, but thanks for asking." I put my purse down on the foyer table and sat down on the couch so Bentley could jump up beside me.

"What's shaking, baby?" came the next question.

"What's shaking with you?" I inquired politely.

"Great balls of fire!"

"That's no answer. How was your night?"

"Overworked and underpaid."

"I know the feeling." Bentley snuggled next to my leg and sighed happily.

"Gimme a kiss, will you?"

"No." Then I decided to be blunt. "You have terrible breath. You're a stinky bird."

An indignant flutter came from across the room. "I'm a mynah bird!"

"You're a stinky bird."

Finally Asia Mynah acquiesced. "I'm a stinky bird."

Asia Mynah and I have some variation of this conversation every time I come through the front door, another at bedtime and a third when I uncover his cage in the morning. His vocabulary is prodigious, a hundred and fifty words or more, because his previous owner spent hours working with him. Frankly, I have more intelligent conversations with Asia than with some humans I know.

Feeling exhausted all the way down to my bones, I put my feet on the ottoman that also serves as my coffee table and switched on the television. I tried to watch the news, but Bentley barked until I turned to the *Animal Planet*. Fortunately they were having a special on rhinoceroses and, because Bentley doesn't like things with horns or dry skin, I was able to switch back in time to see the weather.

I leaned back on the couch and closed my eyes.

Hi, Lord. Busy day, huh? My head is swimming. Everything has been going so smoothly and now there's all this change. Auntie Lou falling out of bed, the odd new people at the toy store, Connor Trevain, coming back to run the cruises, Lilly's obsession with him and Nick Haley and his horse. Oh, yes, and Joe's agreeing to give me space. What's Your take on all of this? Anything You want me to do? My favorite spot is in the center of Your will, Lord, so I ask that You keep me there, even when conditions change around me. Thank You, as always, for all the blessings You send my way. Help me to share them with others. And thanks for allowing me to be a steward of Your creatures. Without animals, this world would be a grim and forlorn place.

Oh, yes. Help Auntie Lou deal with Arthur and Ruma-tiz.

In Jesus' name. Amen

Feeling as if I'd touched all the important bases, I went to bed.

Chapter Eight

✤

"Norah, did you pick up my newspaper this morning?" Lilly breezed into my store on Monday morning with a frown on her face. "I'm on my way to the Java Jockey for coffee and biscotti and it's not here."

"Sorry. Can't help you. I haven't noticed it outside your door for two or three days."

"I'm going to call to complain that it hasn't arrived."

"What hasn't arrived?" Chuck from the market walked in the door. We on Pond Street meander in and out of each other's businesses with alarming regularity.

"My morning paper. It hasn't been coming lately."

"Yours, either?" Chuck looked surprised. "You are the fourth person I've heard complain this week and there are probably many more who don't come by the meat counter. I called the paper and they insist that the deliveries were made."

"Who'd want a bunch of old newspapers?" Lilly wrinkled her nose disdainfully. "Weird."

It *is* weird. No one ever disturbs things around here. There are too many people who know too much about each other's dealings for anyone to get away with monkey business—not that running off with daily newspapers is getting away with much.

We didn't have time to consider the disappearance of the morning news because at that moment, Connor walked into the store. He looked as though he'd combed his hair with sunlight and his white captain's uniform was so bright it was blinding. I almost expected him to hold up a bottle of laundry detergent or give a sales pitch for bleach.

"Good morning, Norah…Lilly. Beautiful day."

Lilly trilled as if he'd said something brilliant and it took everything in my power not to roll my eyes or gag.

"Good morning to you, too, Connor," she said breathily. *Uh-oh. She's doing Marilyn Monroe.*

Connor's raised eyebrow told me that he was wondering about the abrupt transformation in Lilly.

"Can I get you something?" I asked, speaking into the silence between them. "Kitty litter? Pigs' ears? Flea powder?"

Lilly turned to glare at me. She thought I was being an idiot, I know. Asking him if he has fleas is not a good come-on. That's okay. I think she's being one, too. *Marilyn Monroe before breakfast, I'm sure!*

Connor was already looking a little dazed when Winky decided to enter the conversation. "Nice buns, cutie pie," he chortled. And he wasn't talking about a bakery. Whoever trained this bird to talk should probably be incarcerated.

Of course, there *is* a lot of truth in Winky's observation.

Looking as though someone had just poured boiling water on his face, Connor stammered, "I just thought you might…stores don't open yet…I need coffee…would you like to join…"

"We'd love to!" Lilly chortled. She grabbed me by one arm and Connor by the other and pulled us toward the door so that we popped *en masse* onto the sidewalk. It didn't matter to Lilly that Connor had come into *my* shop rather than hers to invite someone out for breakfast. She has it bad. I hope she's not setting herself up for a big disappointment.

Coffee shops are hugely confusing. One would think that a coffee shop just sold coffee. And they do, sort of, but you need to know how to speak the language, otherwise it's like going into an Asian market and just asking for "vegetable." Dark roast, light roast, espresso shots, raspberry shots, foam, no foam, the decisions are endless. There's no sitting down to relax with a cup of coffee these days. You have to make an executive decision first.

Once we settled ourselves on the terrace, I sat back to observe. Lilly was being full-on Lillflirty, charming, funny and altogether lovely. Connor, I couldn't read. He's a perfect gentleman, engaged and polite. They would be good for each other. Lilly would bring lightness into his life and Connor would offer levelheadedness to hers. I smiled inwardly at the thought of Lilly finding someone truly right for her.

Snap out of it! One cup of coffee does not a romance make!

Feeling silly about my overactive imagination, I looked up and saw Joe walking across the terrace with a coffee-pot in hand.

"Don't you charge for refills?" I held out my cup for a shot of the straight, no funny stuff added, brew.

"Eleven billion pounds of coffee are drunk each year in the world. I think I can spare a couple cups. Besides, it's a special occasion. Connor's 'welcome to Shoreside' party." Joe put the coffeepot on the table and sat down. The way his eyes darted between Connor and Lilly, I knew he was thinking what I was thinking. Maybe Cupid's arrow would lodge for these two.

The scenery is spectacular, I thought, even with my back to the lake. Watching Joe and Connor is pure pleasure. Even a woman on a self-inflicted diet can still look at the me*n*u.

Triggered by a scent of soap, leather and horse and the sound of a clinking chain, a tingle raced through my body. I knew immediately that Nick was standing behind me.

"Good morning, Officer. Join us?" Joe invited.

Nick took a chair from an adjoining table, turned it backward and straddled it much as he sat astride Sarge.

"What's up on the crime scene?" Connor asked, smirking as if he'd made a hugely funny joke.

Nick didn't laugh. "Several people have been complaining of overturned garbage cans, garden plants pulled up by the roots…." I recalled the scar on Nick's arm that I'd observed yesterday. I understood it now. He'd had his funny bone surgically removed.

"Don't forget the missing newspapers. Belles & Beaus says theirs have been AWOL for a week."

"I see the headline now. Big-City Crime Hits Idyllic Small Town. Can you handle it? Or do we need to call in a SWAT team?"

The desultory conversation rambled like a meandering stream for a few more minutes and after we broke up, I followed Lilly into her shop to get the clothing catalog she'd insisted I study. As soon as we were inside, she spun to grab my hands. Dressed in a pale and frothy pink shirt, white slacks and shocking pink boots, she looked like a life-size Barbie doll, a Barbie in love.

"Norah, I think Connor likes me!"

"How could he not like you?"

"Do you really think so?"

"Lilly, you've broken more hearts than high cholesterol!"

She leaned against the display counter which held a bedazzling array of bright, chunky jewelry, costume watches and beaded bags. "He's the one for me, Norah. I just *know* it."

I've never seen Lilly like this before. Maybe she and Connor *could* sail away into the sunset together—literally, I mean. Or at least to the other side of Lake Zachary.

"Who's minding the store?" Auntie Lou asked on Tuesday afternoon as she boiled water for tea in her cozy but cluttered kitchen. Auntie Lou opens and closes her store as she feels like it. No regular hours for her. It doesn't seem to hurt business, however, because even though she puts a Closed sign on the front door, she sits on the sidewalk in a rocker greeting people as they pass. I think Auntie Lou must do more business with her store closed, than most antique shops do when they're open.

"Annie. Joe hired a high school boy to work for him for the rest of the summer, so she's spending most of her time with me at Norah's Ark."

"Good for you, dearie," Auntie Lou said approvingly. "You work too hard lifting, cleaning…"

"…snuggling, petting. I love what I do."

She gave a sigh that seemed to come from somewhere in the vicinity of her knees. "I do, too. I just hope I can keep on doing it until the day I wake up in heaven."

"What is that supposed to mean? Of course you can! You live here. All you really need to do is turn the shop key and things practically sell themselves." No longer willing to search for vintage items herself, Lou has several shoppers with keen eyes who know just what she wants. They keep her store full to overflowing along with the new items she orders herself.

I looked at her sharply. "Are you feeling all right? After your fall…"

She waved a dismissive hand. "Fall, schmall. All that did was scare me a little. It made me think that without the store and all of you on Pond Street, I'd have nothing more to live for, no purpose."

"That's not…" I began to protest, but she held up a hand to stop me.

"Dearie, don't try to tell me that I have been living out my purpose with this shop. I know that. I have no doubt I was meant to be here, listening to people who come to the shop and recall their own childhoods. Why, I've been told a thousand stories about what people remember—and what they regret. I can't begin to tell you the times that people pick up an item in the store that reminds them of a loved one. Pretty soon they are talking about a relative who has passed on and end up pouring out stories of their joys and regrets. 'I should have spent more time with him…' or 'He died before I could apologize….' This little store has given me many opportunities to talk about God's grace, Norah. It is my purpose."

I stared at her, dumbstruck. I'd had no idea. "Auntie Lou," I said, laying my hand on her aged, spotted one, "if there's anything I can do to help you to stay on Pond Street, you know I will. But there's no use worrying about it now because, as long as you can get Arthur to behave himself, you're just fine."

Her twinkle returned. "You've got that right, dearie. Sugar?"

I was so deeply pondering what Auntie Lou had said that I nearly walked straight into Sarge's saddled midsection as I crossed the street. I stumbled backward. "Oops, sorry. You don't give out tickets for absentminded walking, do you? I didn't intend to T-bone your horse."

"He doesn't look any worse for wear. In our line of work he has to be accustomed to people." Nick scratched Sarge's withers right next to the saddle horn. "What's on your mind that took you so far away?"

He's a mystery, this new policeman. He's so serious and stern on the job that he has a bubble of ice encircling him. If anyone gets too close they bump off it. But sometimes, like now and when he was helping me with Auntie Lou, he's very different—tender, concerned and caring. I get the idea that both sides of him are completely genuine. He's definitely an enigma, cool and warm, aloof and friendly—a little like the stuff my dad uses on his aching muscles, Icy Hot.

"I've been talking to Auntie Lou. She's wondering about her future. She's all alone in the world. If someday she can't be at the shop…"

"She didn't get hurt, did she? Is she feeling any aches or pains from her fall?"

"Only her sense of security was damaged." I shrugged. "But Auntie Lou has to make her own decisions and, if she has any say in it, she and her antiques will be growing very old together."

Nick cleared his throat. I looked at him. He cleared it again. His closely shaved, finely drawn jawline looked tense. As did the rest of him.

"Something wrong?"

"I hope not." He looked unconvinced. I leaned forward a little, hoping to encourage him. It's a paradox really, a shy cop, but here he is.

"What?" I finally asked. He appeared poised on a precipice, ready to jump.

"You don't know me very well…."

I eyed him warily.

"…and I don't know many people in Shoreside yet but I have moved into my new place. I thought it might be time to start cooking…but I thought maybe, if you wanted, of course if you don't…"

"Cooking is good," I encouraged helpfully. "But wanted *what?*"

"...steaks, maybe. Or fish, if you prefer...."

"Nick, I may be a little dense. What are you talking about?" I put my hands on my hips and cocked my head.

"...dinner. Sometime this weekend. I work Friday and Saturday so Sunday would be best. At my place. Just to get to know each other...nothing else. But if you don't want to...I understand."

This was unexpected and terribly sweet.

It's not easy to be new in a close-knit community. It takes a while—and some effort—to fit in. The least I could do was be friendly.

"Thanks, Nick. It's nice of you to ask. It's not easy getting acquainted in a new place."

He smiled faintly. "Yeah. It gets pretty quiet. But I wasn't quite sure, being a stranger and all, I thought..."

True, but he has already passed one of my most important qualifying tests for friendship—kindness toward animals. I'm fully aware of how he treats Sarge and people who are truly kind to animals are usually kind to people. He'd won me over.

Then he flashed a brilliant smile, one that put even Connor's to shame. "Great. About seven? I live at..."

"I know. I have friends who live next door. They're snoopy. They'll probably be listening in."

He grinned. "You're not so reckless after all. See you Sunday."

After Nick disappeared around a corner I clapped my hands to my cheeks.

Wait until I tell Bentley about this. He and Nick are going to love each other!

We parted, leaving me to scratch my head and wonder how all this had come about. Little Pond Street had become a veritable smorgasbord of available men.

I thought about Nick's invitation for a while before I told Lilly. Although she knows about my conversation with Joe and agreed in a very fishy metaphor that his best chance for "reeling me in" was to "give me lots of play at the end of his line," I wasn't sure it was important enough to mention.

Finally, though, I caved in. Lilly and I don't keep secrets from one another.

"He asked you over?" Lilly asked for the third time, as if she couldn't believe her ears. "No kidding? I'm so happy for you!"

"I'm happy for me, too, Lilly, but not for the same reason you are. I'm going to get a good meal. And that's all."

Her lovely eyes narrowed. "What's Joe going to think of this?"

"Nothing, I hope. Because it's no big deal."

"Who knows, Norah? This may be the catalyst that pushes you either toward or away from Joe."

Hardly. Right now Lilly is hearing wedding bells. I, on the other hand, am more interested in the dinner bell.

Chapter Nine

❧

Bentley should be on the stage. He is so theatrical some-times that instead of Rodney Dangerfield, I think he might be W. C. Fields with a little Richard Burton thrown in.

As I locked the shop for the night, he came to me carry-ing his leash in his mouth. He sat down at my feet and looked up at me with mournful eyes that were meant to con-vey, "If you don't take me home now I'll perish on the spot." When I didn't jump at his ploy, he ever-so-slowly crumpled, allowing his back legs and butt to slide along the tile until his belly was flat on the floor and his front paws splayed out in front of him. His gaze remained locked to mine.

When I still didn't budge, he slowly began to tip to one side until he was lying flat, his stubby legs rigid, his normally wagging tail motionless. A single eye now captured and held mine. Every fiber and pore of his body looked dejected.

"Oh, all right," I muttered. "You win."

And, wonder of wonders, Bentley jumped to his feet like an Olympic gymnast, snapped to attention and looked as dignified as a dog can while drooling all over a hot pink leash with cartoon sketches of Deputy Dawg on it.

Bentley loves to walk by the water. There are bike paths all around the lake, little gazebos to rest in and always plenty of other dogs to sniff. Although the rest of him is timid and shy, Bentley does have an extroverted nose.

There's one dark spot about walking around the lake with Bentley. People on in-line skates. Bentley is terrified of in-line skates. He runs in a circle around my legs until I'm hog-tied by his leash every time a skater comes by. I haven't told anyone—for fear of being committed to an institution or something—but occasionally I wear my in-line skates around the house to help him get accustomed to them. I have a dream of the two of us someday sailing along the path ourselves. So far he'll walk up to me when I'm not moving, but the night I cooked supper in them he hid under my bed. Patience, I tell myself, patience.

Anyway, we got only a short way down the beach when I heard someone call to me. I looked around, but there was no one I knew on the path. Then I saw Connor waving to me from the bow of the *Zachary Zephyr.* He disappeared for a moment into the bowels of the ship and then reappeared on the dock.

He loped toward me with athletic grace. As he neared, Bentley backed closer to my ankles.

"Glad I caught you, Norah." Not a hair out of place and after all that running, too.

"Just walking my dog."

He glanced at my feet and, as if for the first time, noticed Bentley. "May I walk with you?"

"Sure, why not?" Bentley banged into my ankles as if to give me a reason to say no—he doesn't like sharing me—but I ignored him.

We walked in silence for a while, watching the gulls do their ballet over the water. Covertly I watched people staring at us. Actually, it was Connor who was attracting the attention. His raw physicality is hard not to notice. It's like walking with a movie star.

"Do you like it here in Shoreside, Norah?" Connor asked softly.

"How could I not? You?"

"It's fine for now." His gaze was unfocused as he stared into the distance.

"You look like you're a thousand miles away."

He smiled and his even teeth flashed white as his uniform. "What can I tell you? I'm a seafarin' man. But I'm hoping that I'll find what I need in Shoreside."

"And what's that?" Bentley stopped to examine a mound of rocks and I took it as an opportunity to sit down on a nearby bench.

"Contentment, happiness, a reason to stay in one place for a while."

"Big order." I was impressed with his openness and honesty and with Connor himself

"Shoreside is up to it, I think."

Only God is up to that.

"And you haven't found that anywhere else? I understand you've done a lot of traveling around the world." That, at least, was what Lilly had informed me along with a narration about how perfect they would be together.

"Parts of it, not all."

"What is the part you are still looking for?"

His face relaxed into a smile. "The love of a good woman, for one," he said lightly. I thought he was joking but was not quite sure.

Wait until I tell Lilly. This could be her chance.

"No kidding?"

"Well, yes, I suppose I am, but it wouldn't hurt, now, would it?"

Then a big gull made a belly flop landing on the water nearby and drew our attention. Bentley barked at nothing in particular.

I felt Connor's gaze on my back as I leaned down to scratch Bentley's ear. "I was on my way across the lake to have dinner at Ziga's when I saw you. Would you care to join me?"

He referred, of course, to the popular waterfront restaurant his family owns. Although I've been there several times, it has always been for appetizers on the patio overlooking the water or to share a dessert with Lilly. My finances do not lend themselves to eating entire meals at Ziga's.

He saw me hesitate. "I'm taking the Chris-Craft. Fifteen minutes across, max, something quick to eat and fifteen minutes back. What do you say?"

It was tempting and I was starving.

"What about Bentley?" I looked down at my feet.

"Take him home. I know you live nearby. I'll wait for you at the dock."

I looked across the glassy lake. Dusk was coming and the patio lights at Ziga's were beckoning seductively. "Oh, why not?" I said impulsively. "I'll see you at the slip." And before I could change my mind, I stood and started for home.

Bentley, when he wants to walk, can move out like an Indy car but when he doesn't want to go somewhere, he simply drops to the ground and refuses to move. That's why I had to half drag, half pull him home, like a thirty-five-pound log tied to the end of the leash.

"Come *on,* Bentley. This is my big chance. Dinner at Ziga's. I'll bring you a doggy bag. Would you rather have ribs or chicken? I'll even bring you the leftover bread if you'll just get up and walk."

Bentley has values and he wouldn't be bribed. I wrestled him into the house, fed him, put on a dab of lip gloss and hurried out again. As I turned back to see if I'd left my outside light on, I saw Bentley in the window. He stood on my couch gazing accusingly at me. Connor had made no points with Bentley on this particular evening.

Having dinner with the owner of a restaurant is a considerably different experience than ordering one dessert and two spoons off the luncheon menu. Ziga's is dark and embracing, especially by candlelight. I felt slightly out of place in my Norah's Ark attire, but Connor didn't seem to mind. Besides, anything Connor thinks is all right is acceptable to this staff. Most of the other tables were taken by couples, some in deep conversation, others gazing happily at each other through a candlelit haze. Me, I could hardly wait to get my hands on the bread basket.

It was dark by the time we returned to the boat, but rather than start directly across the lake, Connor took us close to the shore and we glided slowly along admiring the beautiful lake homes. Maybe I should have been an interior decorator. I certainly love to see the beautiful vignettes framed in large windows, as we passed by. Or maybe I'm just a latent nosy Nelly. Either way, I didn't realize how late it had gotten until we were tying up at the dock.

"One minute to midnight?" I stared in horror at the large clock on a black-iron lamppost by the dock. Pond Street was still but for Barney, who was just closing up Barney's Gas. "Thanks, Connor, for dinner, but I've got to run."

I think he spoke to me, but I was already racing toward home feeling like Cinderella running from the ball, her Prince Charming calling after her.

I heard the shop phone ring, but because I was immersed, literally, in cleaning fish tanks, I let the answering machine pick up. I listened as I worked.

Winky does a very nice job as my receptionist. "Norah's Ark, may I help you…awwk…" he squawked on my answering machine. When we were taping it, I had to cut him off before he could use any of his more ribald or insulting language. No point telling a customer to take a long walk off a short pier or to go play in the street. Winky's former owners endowed him with a unique vocabulary that makes him totally unacceptable for white-haired ladies who like to give teas.

"Norah? Norah? Is that you?" Connor asked. "Is something wrong?" Apparently Winky and I sound alike to Connor.

The only thing "wrong" was that I couldn't reach the phone to ward him off. By the time I finished the tank I was working on, Connor had arrived on the doorstep.

"Is everything okay in here?" he asked, looking genuinely concerned.

"Great. Sorry about the answering machine. I've never had anyone think that Winky was me before."

The blush crawled up his neck and spread across his entire face. "That…that bird?"

"He does rather well, don't you think? It took about fifteen tries to get it right though. He kept adding 'Stifle it' to the end of the message which, I thought, was counterproductive. Don't you?"

Connor looked a little like I'd hit him in the face with a two-by-four. Finally he began to smile. "I came to check on you because of that thing?" He pointed an accusing finger at Winky, who didn't even bother to quit preening his feathers or take his beak out of his birdy armpit. "I can't believe I did that."

"Did what?"

Neither of us had noticed Lilly come into the shop, but there she was, a vision in scarlet—a red dress and a red hat pulled low over her eyes, something out of a 1940s Vogue magazine. Joan Crawford or Bette Davis maybe.

Connor blinked as he looked from Lilly to me and back again. He could get fashion whiplash trying to make sense of the two of us.

"Did what?" Lilly insisted. She strolled inside with a lit-

tle more wiggle to her hips than usual, for Connor's benefit, no doubt.

"Connor called and got Winky's message on my answering machine," I said with a laugh. "Apparently he thought
I was having a terminal case of strep throat or something
because he came over to see what was wrong."

"Really." Lilly's tone was cool and disbelieving. When I
glanced at her, she was staring at me appraisingly.

"You tell her, Connor," I urged. Why was everyone acting weird today?

"Let's just say I'm completely embarrassed," Connor said,
chagrined. "I heard…I thought…oh, never mind." He
glanced at his watch. "Listen, I've got to go. Glad you're
okay, Norah. Lilly, nice to see you." And he escaped the
shop.

"You look lovely today, Lilly," I said. "Very red. Did they
move Valentine's Day to July this year?"

"Don't try to change the subject, Norah."

"What subject? Do we even have a subject to change?"

"Why was Connor here?"

"Because of Winky. I told you…." Then a lightbulb flickered in my dim brain. "Okay, what's wrong, Lilly? Spill it."

"I talked to Barney this morning."

"Yes. And?"

"And he said he saw you and Connor on the dock at midnight."

"And from that you deduced…"

"Norah, are you horning in on my territory?"

"Lilly, am I hearing a hint of the green-eyed monster in
your voice?"

"I *told* you I was interested in him, Norah. I don't get…"

"You certainly don't, you silly goose." I gave up getting the fish tanks cleaned anytime in the near future. "Connor asked if I wanted to ride over to Ziga's and have dinner. I went…."

"Ziga's?" Lilly sounded shocked. "That's the most romantic place on the lake!"

"It's also his family kitchen, and I don't think he views it as anything else. We had a bite to eat and came back." I stared her down. "And there was no funny business. I'd planned to tell you about it this morning."

For the first time, Lilly's shoulders relaxed and I realized how on edge she'd been as the tension drained out of her. "Sorry. I just…you know."

"You've got it bad, don't you?" I rubbed her shoulder and she leaned into the pressure.

"I'm used to guys falling all over me, Norah. Connor doesn't. He's pleasant and polite, but not, you know…"

Actually, I don't know. Men rarely fall all over me unless they've tripped on a crack in the sidewalk. Still, I tried to comprehend.

"And because he's not fawning over you, he makes you nervous. That makes you like him even more. Great psychological ploy if you can pull it off."

Lilly needed to see this wasn't just about Connor and me but was about her own self-esteem issues, as well. She was blowing this incident between Connor and me totally out of proportion.

Something must have rung a bell in her head. "I've never felt this way before. I'm even jealous of my best friend. I'm sorry, Norah."

Of course Lilly has never been rejected or overlooked, because it is virtually impossible to do so. It would be like ignoring the Statue of Liberty in New York Harbor.

"Is there any chance that the main reason you're interested in Connor is because he *hasn't* asked you out?"

Lilly tossed her head and I saw that some of her old fire was back. "Don't be silly." Then she faltered. "Well, maybe. I just felt something for him the first time I saw him and he really doesn't seem to know I'm around!"

"Give it time," I soothed. "And don't worry about me. You...and Joe...know better than anyone that I'm not in the market right now."

Lilly softened and threw her arms around me. "I don't know what got into me. Sorry. I'd trust you with my life, so I should certainly trust you with Connor."

The subject didn't come up again, but I felt an uneasiness in my stomach that hadn't been there before.

Chapter Ten

✧

Barney, it seems, is a highly efficient communicator. So effective, in fact, that he "communicated" all up and down Pond Street the news that he'd seen me with Connor on a Tuesday night. Fifteen years ago when I was living under my parents' roof, I wasn't any more heavily monitored than I am now. Small-town living—gotta love it, gotta hate it.

Joe gave me a speculative once-over when I entered the Java Jockey, but as I ordered a caramel mocha with an extra shot of espresso and heavy on the whipped cream on top, I put his mind at rest. "A spur-of-the-moment boat ride," I said, before he could even think of asking. "Innocent, innocuous, pleasant and definitely not worth the press that Barney is giving it. The man needs a new hobby."

Joe grinned and set my three-million-calorie cup of coffee in front of me. "Thanks, but I wasn't even going to ask."

I had a sudden urge to hug him. He, at least, trusted me.

"Lilly was upset," I confided. "She has her eye on Connor and I got into her line of sight."

"She told me. She also said she was feeling ashamed of herself for acting so silly. Now I think she's hoping you'll set her up on a blind date."

"Since when did you two become confidants?" I teased, surprised but nevertheless glad Lilly had Joe to talk to.

"Since yesterday." As Joe smiled his dark eyes warmed and with his forefinger brushed a curl from my eyes. "I know how she feels, Norah. When you're in love, you just act crazy sometimes."

I sighed and pulled a stool up to the counter. "How can you fall in love after one quick look at someone?"

He studied me with such intensity that I had to look away. "I did."

"Joe, don't…."

"Well, I did. How can you help falling in love with someone with so much curly black hair coming out of the top of her head that you mistake her for a fountain? Someone who smiles like a thousand-watt bulb? Someone who *carries* her dog to work because the pavement is too hot for his feet?"

"Only in August. When they were tarring driveways on my street," I reminded him. "And can I help it that Bentley likes it?"

"If I'm going to be jealous, Bentley is my target, not Connor Trevain."

"Now you're talking common sense." I pushed my cup toward him. "Put a little regular old plain Jane coffee in this, will you? I have to dilute the calories somehow." When I left, I surprised and pleased Joe by putting my arms around him and giving him a big squeeze. He's got to be one of the sweetest men on the planet.

Because Annie had everything handled at the Ark, I decided to stop at Auntie Lou's Antiques for a visit. There, I stepped into another world, one made up of painted crockery, sewing machines powered by foot pedals, platform rockers, Victorian settees, kerosene lamps, old framed pictures of somber-looking children and vintage toys. An antique bedstead, washstand, basin, pitcher, the hand-tatted linens and a selection of beautiful pillows were displayed in a vignette near the front of the store.

Though one wouldn't know it to look at her, Auntie Lou has a sharp eye for design and unerring good taste. She is, in fact, one of the smartest businesswomen I know.

"Lou?" I called. "Love the new sideboard. How old is it? Lou?"

The fat—and getting fatter—Silas was bathing on a rocking chair near the cash register—also vintage—but Auntie Lou was nowhere in sight. Calling her name several times, I went into the storeroom where she keeps extra inventory. The room appeared empty but for some garden statuary, a collection of birdbaths and stacks of boxes filled with items to sell. Then I heard a rustle in the far corner.

"Lou? Are you there?"

"Norah?" The voice was a whisper.

"It's me. Where are you and what are you doing?" I

headed toward the location of the voice. I passed several boxes labeled China and Linens before I saw Auntie Lou sitting on a spindly ice-cream-parlor chair rubbing her knee and sporting a black eye.

"What on earth?"

"Shh." She held a finger to her lips. "Not so loud. I don't want anyone to know."

"Know what? That you were mugged? Or had a fistfight with an unidentified stranger?"

"That I fell again."

That brought me up short. "Again?"

"I tripped on something, a broomstick lying on the floor. And on my way down, I connected with the corner of a box of lamp shades. Lamp shades! Of all things. No one gets hurt by lamp shades!"

"No one but you. You're developing a real shiner. Do you want me to get you some ice? Or a slab of red meat?"

"Ice, dear. I've given up red meat."

After I settled her in one of her many rockers and found a plastic sandwich bag to fill with ice for her eye, I took a seat across from her. "What happened this time?"

"Same as last. I think I can do something and then find out I can't." She looked furious with herself. "After I've fallen over like a silly old woman."

"You aren't silly," I advised her.

"No? But I am as old as dirt, dearie, and it's beginning to show." Her eyes flashed. "Why'd God save the hardest part for last, do you think?"

Old age isn't for sissies. My grandparents, once a robust farm couple, now have a social life that revolves primarily around doctor appointments and conversations that center on the price of prescription medicine. They hate it, but they keep going, fighting back. They also attribute their success to Friday night bowling and leading a group at church, counseling young marrieds on how to have the kind of life my grandparents have. They are as in love as the day they were married and they give God all the credit. Grandpa also gives a little credit to "selective hearing" which, he says, filters out nagging and complaining but amplifies loving words.

"What are we going to do about you, Lou?" I asked. "I'm beginning to worry."

"Pretend it didn't happen. Two little incidents do not a problem make." Lou looked at me intently. "Right?"

"But if you're falling…"

Auntie Lou put a finger to her lips. "Not a word to anyone, Norah. Promise? I don't want to be known as that stumbling old lady on Pond Street. What's more, I don't want anyone to think that I can't run this store or be left alone at night. Too many people think the words *old* and *incompetent* go together." Her voice pitched higher. "And because the only way anyone will get me to leave this store is feetfirst, when I'm already with the Lord!"

My mouth worked but no words came out.

Auntie Lou took my hand and I felt her warm, papery skin as she patted my wrist. "I don't want anyone thinking it's time for me to give up and go into one of those retirement homes."

"You, retire?" I must have looked aghast. "Never!"

"I'm glad you agree with me. Now, then, this ice reminds me there's no need to let it go to waste, would you like a glass of lemonade?"

* * *

When I finally got back to the store, Annie was sitting behind the desk, staring at a pile of mail.

"Why do you look so serious?" I picked up a kitten to give it a cuddle. His new owner would be in to get him later this afternoon.

"I can't figure something out." Annie picked up a bill and waved it in the air. "You got another bill from Fur and Feathers."

"The pet food supplier? I paid them a couple weeks ago."

"I know. But they don't indicate that it has been paid. It's marked Past Due."

"Maybe the check and bill crossed in the mail." Annie loves to do bookwork and I'm lukewarm about the numbers thing, so I appreciate her help. "I remember signing the check. We could call and see if there's something we need to straighten out...."

"I did already. They say that they never received the check, Norah. They're insistent upon it."

"Then where did it go?" I put the kitten down. "Lost Letter heaven?"

"I wish." Annie's lips pulled downward.

"You do?" I took the bill from her hand and studied it. I've never had trouble paying my bills on time. In fact, I pride myself on being prompt.

"I called the bank and the check has cleared."

"Then send a copy to Fur and Feathers so we can get this straightened out."

"Norah, the check that cleared isn't written to Fur and Feathers. It's written for Cash to a bank in the city."

"What does that mean?"

"They asked if we mailed our letters from the post office."

"Why do that when we have a perfectly good mailman pick them up outside our door?" I like the little cast-iron mailbox hanging by the front door. I found it at Auntie Lou's. It makes me feel as though we've stepped back in time when I raise the little red flag to signal to our postman to stop for a letter.

"The bookkeeper for Fur and Feathers suggested we quit using the box. Apparently it's not a good idea. Check stealing, identity theft, that sort of thing."

"What's becoming of this world!" I blurted then stopped cold. Was that my mother's voice coming out of my mouth? How many times had I heard her say that over the years when calamities and tragedies happened around the country? And now it was me saying it, because it's not safe to use my own mailbox outside my own store on a street full of neighbors who watch out for one another. Too sad.

Instead of voicing the opinions that would put me out of Annie's age bracket and into that of my mother's, I said, "So what do we do now?"

"Call the police?" Annie offered hopefully. "Or the FBI?"

"Or stop payment on that check."

"Can't. It's too late. It's cleared, remember? You'll still have to pay Fur and Feathers whether you get that money back or not. Do you want me to write another four-hundred-dollar check?"

I felt a rush of blood to my ears. I work hard for my money. Harder than most, considering that the items I stock in my store need feeding, brushing and major cleaning up after. Four hundred dollars to me is a healthy piece of change.

"I need to report this to someone," I muttered. "I can't afford to have this happen again."

"Looks like you're in luck." Annie waved a hand toward the window.

I turned to see Nick on the sidewalk outside the Ark, talking to Chuck from the grocery store. They were both waving at the ice-cream truck, which was already chiming its musical tune as it drove down the street. I stomped out to join them.

"Morning, Norah," Chuck greeted me. "Nice day."

"It was."

They both turned to stare at me. "What happened?"

"My supplier says my last payment never arrived yet the bank says the check cleared." I blathered out what Annie had told me, my face getting warmer by the second. The sun wasn't terribly warm or high in the sky, but I felt my skin burning. Finally it occurred to me, I was *blushing*.

It certainly wasn't caused by my proximity to Chuck, who smelled of soap and raw meat, so that left Nick as the source of my reddened condition. Maybe it has something to do with the fact that he, unlike Chuck, smells faintly of musky shaving lotion and leather. Normally my body doesn't form opinions without bringing my brain up to date on its status, but it certainly was happening now.

"Why are you two looking at me like that?" I took the defensive as Nick and Chuck stared at me.

"I've been having mail trouble, too," Chuck said. "Officer Haley tells me that we've got to stop using our mailboxes. Apparently someone's filching the checks we mail and washing them."

"Washing?"

"Removing the ink, rewriting the check to cash and pocketing the money," Nick explained.

Washing laundry, yes. Washing checks, no. If criminals would spend their time putting their cleverness toward good behavior rather than bad, we'd have cures for everything from mosquitoes to world conflicts.

Nick noticed the distress on my face and followed me into the shop after Chuck had gone. Annie, upon our arrival, scooted to the B and B to put out fresh water.

"I'll take the information, Norah. We've had several reports of this type of thing in the last couple days. We're working on it."

"You'll probably never 'work' that four hundred dollars back into my bank account, will you?"

"I'll do my best." Then he stood awkwardly rooted to my floor like he was standing in a puddle of spilled soda pop, his dark blue eyes darting side to side.

Little sparks of electricity ignited the air between us. It snapped, crackled and popped, like milk on Rice Krispies but far more potent.

"Nora, ah, I…I'm sorry about your check."

"Thanks. Me, too." I leaned forward a little, hoping to encourage out of him whatever it was he wanted to say.

"I just wanted to tell you I'm looking forward to this weekend."

Me, too!

Chapter Eleven

❧

Sunday is still a long way off and a lot can happen in a week. It can be aeons, in fact, between Wednesday and the following Sunday.

I didn't have the opportunity to talk with Lilly the next day about my unexpected dinner invitation because her part-time helper was minding the store. Lilly hadn't told me she was going to be gone. It's odd. Lilly and I usually talk several times a day and neither of us makes a move more significant than cutting our fingernails without the other knowing about it.

It was Julie Morris who greeted me on the sidewalk this morning looking almost happy.

"Ready for your grand opening?" I inquired.

"I think we are. We've already had more business than we expected. Pond Street has been good to us."

"It's good to everyone. Very few stores change hands here."

"I can understand why." She took a breath and sighed deeply. "I've dreamed of a place like this. Somewhere small and peaceful yet urban, a place where people are friendly and things are…more manageable."

Manageable. Who or what was more manageable? Bryce?

Come to think of it, I haven't seen Junior the Defiant much since they arrived. No loss really. He is likely the kind of boy who skulks inside all day playing video games and slinks out at night to hang with his friends. Or perhaps that's not fair. Maybe I'm underestimating him. Lilly said she's seen him helping out at the store. Imagining him behind the counter ringing up the purchase of a Barbie doll translates into a King Kong–Faye Raye image for me.

From across the street, Auntie Lou beckoned me over. She was wearing a thick black skirt and a print blouse overlaid with a ruby-red hand-knitted cardigan. Her shoes were white lace-ups with cushiony bottoms and good arch supports, "nurses' shoes," I call them. Her knee-high nylons were rolled to little sausages around her ankles and she wore a flower in her thinning hair. In other words, Lou was all dolled up.

"Don't you look nice today." I gave her a hug and took the chair beside hers. "Are you going somewhere special?"

"Nowhere. I've decided to change my image and start dressing up. What do you think?"

"I think your image is perfect as it is, any way it is."

"Don't be kind, girl. Tell me the truth."

"You look great. Younger, even."

"'Younger?'" Auntie Lou beamed at me. "Now that's what I like to hear! It's not easy to think of yourself as old. Seems to me they're making adults much younger these days.

"I wish I weren't so stiff and achy." Her eyes began to twinkle. "Of course, I like to think that if God really wanted me to touch my toes these days, He would put them on my knees."

"Are you still concerned about those tumbles you had? Young people trip and fall, too, you know."

"A little." Her expression told me it was much more than just "a little."

"You've got lots of years left in this shop, Auntie Lou. Don't let this get you down."

My stab at being a cheerleader didn't do much to encourage the home team.

She looked at me sympathetically, as if I were a poor, misguided child. "You're young yet, dearie. People don't interpret my stumbling on a broom handle the same way they might if you'd done it."

"I don't see…" Then I stopped because, of course, I *do* see.

"Ignoring the facts doesn't change the facts," Auntie Lou continued. "I'm an old lady and it shows."

"What better kind of lady for an antique shop than an 'old' one?" I countered. "I never heard you say a word about old age until recently."

Auntie Lou gazed toward the street, fixing her eyes on nothing in particular. "It's like this, Norah, I've begun to realize these days that life is like a roll of toilet paper."

She snagged my attention with that one.

"At first, the roll goes down very slowly, but the nearer you get to the end, the faster it goes. I'm afraid I may be getting to the end of my roll, Norah. And I'm going to fight back."

Still processing the toilet paper metaphor, I could only echo, "Fight back?"

Auntie Lou's button eyes took on a cagey expression and she leaned toward me so her mouth was close to my ear. "I want you to assure me of something."

"Yes?" I ventured cautiously, wondering what was coming next.

"I want you to promise that you'll make sure no one kicks me out of my home before I want to go."

A tickle of anxiety fluttered in my stomach. *Me?*

"I don't have any family, Norah, except you and that fat old cat, and both of you have been adopted into my heart. I've fallen twice in the past few days and I'm not happy about it. I want to know that someone—you—will be my advocate…just in case."

"In case *what?*"

"I don't know. I can't predict the future." Her eyes clouded. "I saw that lovely Mazie Henderson the other day. Her children are forcing her to move out of her home. They say it's 'too much for her' and that she'll be 'safer' in a place near them." Lou snorted so loudly I flinched. "What they *don't* know, because they refuse to listen, is that by moving her away from her home, her garden, her church, her friends and her routine, they're going to hasten her death." She shook her head gloomily. "Mark my words."

"You're blowing things out of proportion, Lou. You

tripped on a broomstick. You fell out of bed. You aren't going anywhere. Okay?"

"Just remember what I said, dearie." There was a lively intelligence in her eyes. "Life is tough, but I'm tougher. Me and my Maker are in charge of it and no one else."

With those cryptic words, she patted my hand and said, "Now why don't you run into the back of the shop and get us some nice iced tea."

After leaving Lou's, I spent the rest of the afternoon getting very little accomplished except wondering where Lilly was and what had gotten into Auntie Lou.

I diverted myself for the afternoon by ordering freeze-dried liver and pooper-scoopers but it wasn't until I was heading for home that I saw Lilly.

She flagged me down as she drove past in her little yellow Miata.

"Hop in, we're going for sushi."

Sushi is my least favorite food, but I was too curious to turn down her offer. Why anyone wants to eat raw fish is beyond me. That would be like swallowing one of the guppies out of my fish tanks. If I wanted to do that, I'd leave a little wasabi and soy sauce in the fish section for an afternoon snack.

It was difficult to talk with the wind whipping through our hair so I sat back to enjoy the ride. Lilly is a good driver but a fast one. She's had dreams of racing cars. She even went to high-performance race car driving school and she can talk about cars with 800 horsepower and V-8 engines with the best of them. Beneath her fluffy exterior beats the heart of a fierce competitor. Lilly simply doesn't like to lose—at anything—ever. When Lilly can't have something, she wants it even more. For me, not being the competitive type, it's a little difficult to comprehend, but it works for her. She's built her business from scratch with pure determination.

We pulled into the parking lot of the fashionable new hot spot Lilly had chosen. That's another skill of Lilly's, scoping out the newest and trendiest of everything from clothing to dining.

After we'd ordered crab meat with wasabi mayonnaise and karei shio-yaki—she says it's flat fish with salt—for Lilly and vegetarian sushi and miso soup for me, I could finally ask the questions that had been burning in me all day. "Where have you been? I was getting worried about you!"

"I had the most wonderful day." Lilly's faced softened with a rosy glow. "I went sailing with Connor."

No wonder she was radiant. "No kidding? I didn't know he'd asked you. Details! Tell me all about it. I want details."

Lilly frowned for the briefest second then broke into a smile again. "He didn't exactly 'ask' me. I just put myself in a position so that he almost had to ask me."

"You stowed away on his boat?"

Lilly ignored that. "Early this morning, I saw Connor at the slip where he keeps his sailboat. I casually walked over and started a conversation. I told him how much I *love* sailing and what a *beautiful* day it was. And he asked me to join him!"

How could he help it, without looking like a real jerk? I wondered. But I'm the least aggressive woman I know when it comes to men. Growing up, I was always a tomboy and had all the male friends I wanted. Now, when I meet a new man, if I don't hear a hint of those bells I'm waiting for, I'm not all that interested. And, of course, I reminded myself, I have Joe.

"Well, you certainly go after what you want."

"I think he likes me, Norah." Though Lilly is always beautiful, her porcelain skin glowed. The last time I remember her being this excited was when she found a Vera Wang gown at the consignment shop for only thirty dollars.

"How could he *not* like you?" Sometimes Lilly's lack of self-esteem blows me away. I felt like I was back in junior high.

"We ate lunch on the boat. He had a basket of breads, cheeses, fruit and chocolate. Ziga's packed it. He does treat the place as his kitchen. I can see now why he thought it was no big deal to take you there."

Well, thanks a lot.

Still, I was glad to hear relief in Lilly's tone. The idea of me and Connor together had bothered her a great deal—that competitive spirit of hers rearing its ugly head.

Lilly rambled on for several minutes before I asked, "When will you be seeing him again?"

She dismissed the question with a little flick of her hand. "We didn't get around to discussing that. Soon, I'm sure." Then she took both my hands in hers. "I am so happy, Norah. And I'm so glad I was wrong about you and Connor."

"Trust me, you were *very* wrong about that."

Reminding myself never to go after the same man as Lilly even if he were Adonis or George Clooney, I bit into my faux sushi and wished for a juicy burger with fried onions and a side order of waffle fries.

I heard a raucous squawking from the front of the store and ran out to find Bryce Morris and a boy I didn't recognize standing by the desk eyeing Winky. He clung to his perch, flapping his wings and chattering in birdspeak. Winky threw his head around and complained loudly. I can't remember ever seeing him so upset. Bryce didn't look so good, either. He was pale and there was a grim set to his mouth. His friend, however, dressed in even more outlandish garb than Bryce, seemed perfectly at ease, with the air and confidence of a smarmy politician at a baby-kissing contest.

"What's wrong with your bird?" the junior politico asked. "We walked in here and he started squawking, just like that."

Bryce stepped back, shifting so that he was turned away from the other boy and buried his chin in the collar of his T-shirt.

"I have no idea. I'm sorry if he bothered you. It's not like him. Are you okay?" I had one eye on Winky and one on the boys, not knowing who to tend to first.

"Yeah. No dumb bird's gonna get me." He scowled at Winky.

Bryce snapped out of his trance to remember why he was here. "My mom is having a dumb tea party and I'm supposed to give you this dumb thing." He thrust an invitation across the counter and sneered.

This, I thought, had become a very *dumb* conversation.

Though Julie has stopped by to chat a few times, I don't see her as the party-giving type. I also hadn't expected that she could get her sullen son to do anything as mundane as deliver envelopes.

"Thank you, I…"

"Whatever." Bryce turned his back to me and sauntered

toward the door, the hems of his black denim pants dragging on the floor. His friend followed, then turned back to give a parting barb. "You should probably put that stupid bird in a cage so he doesn't hurt somebody. You could get sued if he hurt a little kid."

I reached out to stroke the agitated Winky who was still squawking and fluttering his wings. "Why'd you do that, Wink? You talk big but you don't scare people. I don't want you to get us in any trouble...." My words trailed away as I saw a bright splash of color on the floor beneath his perch. Slowly I leaned down and picked up the feathers. They were Winky's no doubt and, much to my horror, they were tipped with fresh blood. These hadn't fallen from Winky's body, they'd been *pulled.*

I was still troubled about Winky the next morning when I stopped by Auntie Lou's to return a book she'd loaned me.

Auntie Lou had mentioned that Bryce Morris occasionally visited the store, seemingly fascinated by a very old pinball machine she had on sale. She hadn't seemed bothered by his brooding ways. "Kids," she'd said, "and their phases," as if that explained everything.

I might have told her my suspicions about Bryce but when I arrived she was already upset and I didn't want to add fuel to the fire.

"I'm missing twenty dollars from the till!" she announced when I walked in the door.

"Are you sure?"

"Of course I'm sure. I know what I took in yesterday and twenty of it is missing."

"Maybe you forgot…."

She gave me an admonishing look.

"Okay, so you didn't forget. Then what happened?"

"I have no idea…." She rummaged around the many papers near the till and then held up an envelope. "What's this?"

I recognized the pastel floral envelope. "Julie from the Toy Shop is having a tea. It's probably your invitation."

"When did it come? There's no stamp on it. Why would it be just sitting here?"

A sudden sinking sensation torpedoed through my stomach. Bryce delivered it, of course. Had he pulled out Winky's feathers *and* a twenty-dollar bill out of Auntie Lou's cash?

Feeling thoroughly depressed, I slunk back to the store wanting to go home, crawl into bed and pull the covers over my head. I hate being disappointed by people. Now I had to figure out what to do about Julie's son, Winky's tail feathers and Auntie Lou's twenty-dollar bill.

I walked into the store and Annie greeted me with a squeal. "Look what came!"

A dozen flawless yellow roses sat on the counter between fungus medication for fish fin rot and bagged catnip. Fortunately roses look good in any setting.

"Where did they come from?"

"The deliveryman just left." Annie pointed to the card but before I could take a step, Lilly flounced into the store carrying a hatbox.

"You've got to see this, Norah, it's perfect for you…oh, roses! Who are they from?"

"I don't know. I just got here myself."

"Well, it's not your birthday." Lilly put the hatbox down

and headed for the roses. Before I could make a move, she plucked the card from the bouquet and opened it.

As she read the inscription her face crumpled. Without another word, she dropped the card on the counter and walked out.

Annie and I exchanged a startled glance. She picked up the card and handed it to me. As I read the inscription, I felt my insides implode.

Norah—
I hope you're having a wonderful day.
Connor

Chapter Twelve

I followed Lilly into The Fashion Diva but she wasn't happy to see me. She looked at me as if I'd tried to slap her in the face.

"What's this about?" she demanded. "'I hope you're having a wonderful day' signed *Connor?* What's going on between the two of you?"

I wanted to shake her for even *thinking* that there was something between Connor and me, but the evidence *was* condemning. What on earth had the man been thinking…or fantasizing? Suddenly I wanted to shake him, too.

Lilly's expression told me what I already knew. She was terribly, terribly hurt and had already made up a story about the roses and drawn a not-so-pretty conclusion.

"Nothing is going on between us. Absolutely nothing. I

don't even know why he got it in his head to send these. Maybe it would make sense if I'd stuck around and talked to him after we went to Ziga's but I raced straight home to walk Bentley."

"You did?" That seemed to console Lilly somewhat. "You didn't, like, you know…"

If she said the word *kiss* I was going to barf. Me and Connor? After Lilly's vocal "staking her claim" where he was concerned? No way, no how. I'm a loyal friend and it hurt that she'd even question that.

Still, there were these incriminating flowers….

"He's just being friendly, Lilly. No big deal. I'll talk to him…."

"No!" Her eyes got wide with alarm. "Don't you dare tell him that I asked about them. You're probably right. No big deal. But I just can't see…if what you say is true…why…"

If what I say is true? My stomach landed somewhere around my knees. Could a bouquet of flowers annihilate a friendship?

"He has every right to send flowers when and where he chooses," Lilly said, her voice controlled. "I'm sorry. I can see you're as surprised by this as I am. Maybe I'd better get used to it. Connor is such a generous man—he probably does this all the time."

I watched her talk herself into a new frame of mind, all the time wondering what was really going on in Connor's head and wishing that he'd sent the flowers to Lilly and not to me. By the time I'd left, she was feeling much better and there was even a spring in her step a few minutes later as she made her way across the street to the Java Jockey and to Joe.

Fluffy as Lilly appears and acts, she's a realist at her core.

I don't blame her for being upset. If I were in her shoes, I'd be disturbed, too. But if things were the other way around, I'd also believe Lilly if she said she'd had nothing to do with the attention Connor was paying her.

And if the flower fiasco wasn't enough, I had to go to Julie's party. Attending a tea party and trying to be pleasant when I knew Julie's son had intentionally set out to hurt Winky is not my idea of a good time.

On my way back to the store, a tinny sound caught my attention. Nick and Sarge came around the corner. Nick was leading Sarge who now had a sleigh bell attached to his headstall.

"What's this?"

"Auntie Lou gave it to me. Said she couldn't hear me coming and Sarge scares her so she wants some warning when he's around." Nick smiled and scratched his horse's ears. "Not regulation, of course, but I'll keep it in my pocket so I can humor her once in a while."

My heart warmed. "You're a good guy, Nick." When he's around I feel comforted, as though he can take charge of any troubling situation and turn it around.

I wonder if he's a Christian.

"I didn't mean to keep you," he said with a tip of his hat.

"It's okay," and I told him where I was going, but he said little. I guess he's just not into ladies' tea parties, either.

As it turned out, I couldn't go to Julie's party anyway.

Annie met me at the door of the shop. "Joe called. Everyone has called in sick but him. He's desperate and asked if I could please work there this afternoon. I told him I thought it would be okay. Is it?"

I hadn't mentioned Julie's party to Annie, so, rather than cause Joe any more disruption, I let her go.

Fortunately, Julie was very understanding. And, by the sounds of talking and laughter in the room, the rest of her guests had not disappointed her.

"You'll have to come sometime and just have tea with me, Norah. I'd love that." The new lilt in her voice was unmistakable. "I'd like to get to know you better."

"It's a deal." I paused before adding, "You sound happy."

"I have high hopes for this place and our move. Things are going better than we expected."

Far be it from me to ruin her day by telling her about Winky's tail feathers.

It was after six when I got home. Bentley and Hoppy were sitting in the window, their heads and paws visible on the back of the couch. Hoppy gets on the sofa using several graduated stacks of books that make a little staircase for him. Bentley just flings himself at the furniture and hopes for the best. He's not terribly agile or graceful. Poor fellow has an overdose of neuroses and few physical gifts. Fortunately, his personality makes up for his shortcomings.

The phone on my answering machine was blinking so I grabbed a soda, pushed the play button and flopped onto the couch to listen.

"Norah? Is that you? I hate these answering machines. Who invented them anyway? People should just stay home and answer their own phones…." Auntie Lou ranted for a few more seconds about technology being the demise of civilization before she got to her point.

"You can call me crazy if you want, but I'm not. Remember that jewelry display that was in the case at the back of the store? Well, it's gone. Not everything, but the good pieces. That old diamond ring, a pair of ruby earrings and a gold watch. I can't figure it out. How could anyone have gotten in there? I don't think I left it open, I—" The machine cut off the rest of Lou's message.

I closed my eyes and put the cool soda can against my forehead. Everything had been going so nicely on Pond Street and now things had gone topsy-turvy. There was the influx of eligible bachelors to cause needless trouble and misunderstanding between Lilly and me as well as tension with Joe, a rash of disappearances from newspapers to diamonds, not to mention Auntie Lou's falls and black eye….

Bentley padded over to stand on my lap and gaze at me with soulful eyes. Then he dipped his head and licked my arm as if to say, "It's all right, Norah."

I put down the can and gathered the goofy dog into my arms. His warm, solid body felt firm and comforting against my chest as he nestled in. Animals don't make up stories, get offended, cause trouble between people or open display cases to remove jewelry that isn't theirs. No wonder I like them so much.

I was grateful to wake up to such a beautiful Sunday morning. Not only did it put a finish to a tumultuous week, it gave me a chance to go to church, the place I can reconnect not only with God but also with myself. Sometimes He gets a little lost in the hustle and bustle of the week. If I don't take daily time to spend with Him, my issues grow bigger and bigger and push Him to the back burner. I know from experience that this is a recipe for trouble. As long as I'm focused on Him, I'm fine, but the minute I start trying to do everything by myself, my peace disappears. It had happened this week. Between Auntie Lou's issues, Winky's tail feathers and the Lilly-Connor fiasco, I'd spent too much time in worry and not nearly enough in worship.

And something else brought a smile to my face. Today was the day I was invited to Nick's.

"What do you think he'll be like when he's away from work, Bentley?"

Bentley yawned and rolled into my spot in the bed. He often sleeps flat on his back with his hind legs stretched straight out, his head thrown back and his front paws crossed in a corpse-like position over his barrel chest, sort of like I do, actually.

"Oh, no you don't. You aren't sleeping in without me." I returned to the bed and scratched his belly. "I need your opinion on what to wear."

After my shower, I walked into my closet where Bentley was waiting. He knows the program. I pulled out three skirts and held them up for his perusal. Bentley stood up, walked over and sat down again by the frothy floral skirt.

"Okay. Camisole or cotton sweater?" He pointed his nose toward the rosy pink camisole I held up.

"And shoes?"

Bentley went to my shoe rack and gently with his teeth extracted a single waffle-bottomed hiking boot. Bentley has never been good at picking out shoes.

Bentley and I interact like this daily. He, unlike Lilly, is never offended when I say I don't like his choices of clothing.

Of course, the fact that I let my dog choose my wardrobe might have something to do with the reason that Lilly's always telling me I need to be more fashion conscious.

Lilly.

I can still see the hurt and confusion in her eyes when she read the card with those roses. I couldn't blame her. How would I feel if I thought she was pursuing a man for whom I'd fallen head over heels?

Dressed, I twirled once for Bentley's approval. He'd done well. I felt very feminine. I clapped my hand over my belly which was doing excited little flip-flops. Surely that wasn't from the idea of seeing Nick today? Nah. No doubt I needed oatmeal.

My church, like everything else in Shoreside, is picturesque. It has clapboard siding and a steeple pointing toward heaven which hearken back to the little old country churches that still dot the countryside in the Midwest. I've always believed that it's built of some amazing expandable material because its walls stretch to hold as many people as want to come. On Christmas Eve, when God is looking upon us, I imagine He sees a little white church with a bulging belly, full of worshippers and love.

No matter how early I start out for church, I arrive late. So, as usual, I was hurrying up the steps at the last moment and nearly collided with a broad male back standing just inside the doorway. He was jiggling the coins in his pocket and waiting in line to find a seat.

"Sorry, I didn't mean to run you over." The man turned around. "Nick!"

He smiled. Though his lips move, he smiles mostly with his eyes, I've realized. Those mirrored sunglasses are a shame, really, because they hide something so beautiful.

Before we could say any more, the usher beckoned us forward. "I have seats for a couple in the front. Follow me."

Obediently Nick and I fell into step behind the white-haired gentleman.

Couple? An interesting mistake.

When he meant "in front" he meant in *front*. Nose to nose with the pulpit where Pastor Gregory could keep an eye on us.

As a holdover from my childhood, I feel duty bound to sit very still and not turn my head in church. After all, I didn't want the preacher to think I wasn't paying attention. I was eight years old then, but the habit remains. Today it was easy. He was talking my language—stewardship and animals.

"Then God said, 'Let us make humankind in our image, according to our likeness, and let them have dominion over the fish of the sea, and over the birds of the air, and over the cattle, and over all the wild animals of the earth, and over every creeping thing that creeps upon the earth.'" Genesis 1:26

Dominion. Power over, control, authority. In my book, that also means *responsibility for.* Not much. God created us to be responsible for His other creatures. And He gave me the gift of nurturing those creatures—which I take very seriously.

Christ was humbly born in a stable, with animals as witness, privy to the most miraculous birth of all time. Though I may never know why, no one will ever convince me that this happened by accident.

Afterward, we were expelled from the church with the rest of the parishioners like frosting out of a pastry tube. As we spread across the lawn like sugar roses, people gathered into little groups to visit.

"There's a potluck picnic today," I said after introducing Nick to everyone in the vicinity. "Are you going?"

"I didn't bring anything to contribute."

"Are you kidding? Potlucks are like Matthew fourteen, verses twenty and twenty-one. 'And all ate and were filled; and they took up what was left over of the broken pieces, twelve baskets full. And those who ate were about five thousand men, besides women and children.' There's bread and fish for everyone no matter how many come. More than once I've seen people ordering pizza to be delivered so that the food never runs out."

"I *am* entertaining later today and I still have some food to prepare." There he was again, crinkling those smile lines around his eyes.

"You aren't supposed to fuss. I'm not company. I'm just me. I'm flattered, though."

"Then why don't you come to the farmers' market with me? I need to pick up onions, tomatoes and avocados. I'll buy you a hot dog at the food cart."

"Great. I'd love to."

"Good. My car is in the parking lot. Come on."

And that was how I came to be squeezing avocados, sniffing melons, picking out perfect strawberries and discussing the freshness of tortillas with the friendly neighborhood cop. Not only that, I was grateful to Bentley for choosing a pretty outfit this morning.

Nick, I discovered, is a different person away from Shore-side and from work. I would never have expected him to buy me a tambourine with a hand-painted parrot on the calf-skin drum and colorful jingles.

"You didn't have to do this." I bumped the drum with the heel of my hand. "But I love it."

"How could you resist something with a perfect likeness of Winky on it?"

He's right. The bird on the tambourine is without a doubt, a lory identical to Winky. He even has the same ro-guish, up-to-no-good twinkle in his beady eye.

"I don't believe I've ever heard you laugh so much," I com-mented as we examined a display of vegetables with novel shapes—a carrot with a protrusion like Jimmy Durante's nose, a zucchini like a boomerang and a bulbous potato with the profile of the wicked witch in the Wizard of Oz.

"I'm off duty."

"You take your job very seriously."

His expression grew shuttered. "I have to. It can be a risky occupation."

I wanted to ask him more, but there are invisible No Tresspassing signs posted around that part of his life.

As we sat at a picnic table in a tiny park eating hot dogs smothered in sauerkraut, I said, "I thought sometimes you were on duty at the market."

"Sometimes, when they expect unusually large crowds."

He looked at me with warm eyes and I felt my insides grow shivery.

Not an acceptable reaction to a man I barely know, so I

decided to bring up Auntie Lou. She's a safe and unromantic subject.

"Have you talked to Auntie Lou about…"

"The jewelry? Yes. She called me right after she talked to you."

"Good. She was a little hesitant, thinking you might believe…"

"That she's old and forgetful and the jewelry would turn up somewhere later, like inside her stove or behind the china?"

"Something like that."

"My grandparents' biggest fear was that someday, someone—my father, most likely—would decide they were 'incompetent' and force them out of their home and into a nursing facility. Grandma refused to admit that she'd lost something and Gramps would never 'fess up to forgetting a detail. They thought that would be the beginning of the end with my father."

"And would it have been?"

Nick frowned and his tanned forehead wrinkled. I wanted to reach up and smooth away the lines in his brow. "Maybe. With my father."

"Why did you stay with your grandparents so much?"

"My parents should never have married. They loved each other, I think, but they couldn't live together. Sometimes the arguments would escalate to a point where I'd beg to go live with my grandparents."

"I'm sorry."

"Me, too. You don't know how many times I've wished that my parents had never met or married."

"But then you wouldn't be here."

He looked at me with unhealed pain in his eyes. "I know. As a child, I thought many times that not being here would have been better than what I was going through." He paused. "I never thought that way again until an incident when I was with narcotics."

He'd wanted to die. Whatever it was, it must have been nasty.

We were quiet then, except for a squishy chewing sound of the hot dogs disappearing. Life is so complex and people come with such thorny baggage that there's no way to get through it in one piece without God.

"Sorry. I didn't mean to bring you down. Life is better for my parents now. They've made some peace with each other."

"They're still together?"

"Incredibly, yes. God is good."

I leaned forward. "He is, isn't He? Amazingly good."

Though Nick only smiled, a sensation of lightness and pleasure fluttered within me. Completely of its own accord and without my permission, my brain put a little check mark by "Christian" on the mental list of qualities I want in a partner. Nick is already halfway to filling the bill.

I was so startled by this act of mental mutiny—*Score one on the marital checklist for Nick!*—that I felt a flush head up my neck and onto my cheeks.

I'm not looking for a guy. I've got Joe who wants to marry me and Connor who gives me too many roses. I hardly need another one to complicate matters. I gave my brain a good scolding and started to pick up the food wrappers and put them in the trash.

"I'd better let you get your groceries home," I offered, feeling flustered and desiring to regroup.

"If you don't have any commitments for the next couple hours, you can come over and help me cook. We can eat a little earlier than we'd planned."

"Ah, well, I have to…" I could hardly admit that I'd planned to spend the afternoon sorting my underwear drawer, polishing shoes, taking a brush and some TNT to the toilet bowl and generally giving my closet an overhaul. There was nothing on my list glamorous or important enough to beg off until later.

"I suppose I could," I said reluctantly. "But I'm not much of a cook."

Nick held out his hand to take mine. "That's okay. I'm a great one."

Chapter Thirteen

❧

Nick lives in a small but picturesque house across the street from the lake, a former guesthouse for the mansion-like home next to it. I have to admit, my curiosity ran rampant. The way people decorate their homes says a lot about them and I want to know more and more about Nick.

I was pleasantly surprised. His home is a high-tech country cottage with stainless steel appliances, a plasma screen television, computer wires and a dining room set that looks as if it came off the Starship Enterprise. These twenty-first century accoutrements shared space with an inviting fireplace, portraits of racehorses, overstuffed chairs and heavy footstools, like those in an old-time private men's club. He watched me as I gazed from high-def and TiVo influences to snuggly wool throws and healthy-looking houseplants. There were wind chimes outside several windows and I could hear their delicate tinkling on the breeze.

"Eclectic. I like it."

Nick gave me a lopsided grin that reminded me not to underestimate his charm. "My decorating has a split personality," he acknowledged. "When you're looking at a fifty-two-inch plasma HD screen, you still have to be comfortable, right?"

The man knows about comfort.

And cooking.

"Did you actually make these?" I held up a grilled shrimp-and-vegetable combination on a skewer. "Your appetizers are better than most full-course dinners." I sat, swallowed up in one of the large chairs, watching him move easily around his kitchen. He also knows how to use a wicked-looking chopping knife, which I suppose isn't too surprising considering he's an officer of the law. Maybe they take a course in knives and hand-to-hand combat…or he's an escapee from a culinary school.

He pushed a chopping block filled with fresh vegetables my way. "Do you want to peel and slice the avocados or chop tomatoes?"

"Both. If you trust me, that is. My idea of the perfect kitchen is a vending machine for every food group."

I was joking, but not much. My idea of a balanced diet really is popcorn in one hand and a soda in the other. "Besides I don't want you to quit working on whatever it is you have going there."

"Flan. I thought we'd go south of the border tonight. Custard *al baño* Maria."

Custard baked in a water bath.

I'd never met a man before who actually knew what flan was, let alone could cook it. I could be interested in a guy like this…. I nearly severed my index finger from my left hand at the thought. I've definitely been hanging around Lilly too much. I've begun to think like her.

"Hurt yourself?" He frowned as he noticed me sucking on the tip of my finger.

"Just a scratch. I wasn't paying attention." *I was looking at you.*

"Maybe I'd better have you watch the beans instead." He gestured toward the stove.

"You even make your own refried beans? I'm impressed."

"Takes a little longer, but it's worth it." He handed me a tall cold glass of sweet tea.

"Where'd you learn to cook like this? Cordon Bleu?"

"Actually, I did take a few classes. Sometime I'll cook pan-seared sea scallops with soba noodle salad or cedar-planked salmon with horseradish dill cream, two of my specialties, for you."

"A cooking cop. Making the world safer one meal at a time."

While he worked, I drifted around the kitchen. The man owns his own cookware, gourmet cookbooks and even a spice rack. The kitchen was immaculate but had a cozy, domestic feel I didn't expect. It was a real kitchen, not just a stopping-off place when one wanted to use the microwave. I could get used to this.

"I was on leave from the police force for a few months

and thought I'd go crazy if I didn't do something. I wasn't able to do anything too physical, but I could still manage a cooking pot, so I tried it."

"Medical leave?" I ventured.

"Yes." The way he said it did not invite more questions.

He was quiet a long while before adding, "Injury on the job. When I was in narcotics."

His broad shoulders had gone rigid and I could see it cost him to say that.

Okay. Bad home life. Injured on job. Time to find a cheerful subject.

"What do you think of our little church? And of Shoreside?"

I saw the tension slide from his features. "So far, so good. I feel well accepted." He straddled a stool across the counter from me and sat down. It occurred to me that Nick managed to look even more masculine in this kitchen.

"I do have a question for you, however."

"Ask away."

"How…sound…is…"

"Auntie Lou?" I felt a twinge of anger at the question. "She's fine. Sound. Sane. Rock solid. She's just old, not senile."

He held up a hand. "Whoa. I didn't say she was, did I?"

"No," I admitted, chagrined. "But a lot of people seem to think that *old* and *out of it* go together. Her body might be stiff and sore, but there's nothing wrong with her mind."

"Good. I'm glad to hear that."

"She's very worried that if she tells anyone about the jewelry from her store being missing, they'll start to say she's too old to be running the store any longer. Auntie Lou is a proud woman."

"I can see that's true. But even though she doesn't feel old or vulnerable, someone thought she was defenseless enough that they could get into that case and out again without being caught." Nick stretched out his long legs and put his palms on the counter and stood. "I'm going to keep a close eye on her place for a while."

I felt a surprising bit of relief at his words. I've been feeling a lot of responsibility for my elderly friend's welfare.

The hours passed like minutes before I found myself announcing, "If I eat another fajita I'm going to start speaking in Spanish."

"More guacamole? Salsa?" Nick handed more food my way. The table was littered with near-empty dishes and there was a glob of sour cream and drizzles of salsa decorating the tabletop.

"Stop! You'll have to rent a cart to roll me home if you don't quit feeding me."

"Does that mean you aren't quite ready for dessert?"

"Just aim me toward a couch and let me rest awhile. Even my jaw is tired from chewing. That was far and away the best meal I've eaten in recent memory." *Even better than Ziga's.*

I glanced at the clock and was surprised to see it was nearly 7:00 p.m. We'd managed to cook, talk, eat and laugh the day away. "I should probably go home."

"Without dessert?" He reached out a hand. "I've got a surprise for you."

"For me? I'm a sucker for surprises."

In the living room he handed me a videotape.

"An old movie. *The Thin Man,* the first of the Nick and Nora series. Remember them?"

"I don't, but I've heard of it. There are always clues for their dog, Asta, in the crossword puzzles."

"I haven't seen them, either, but it seems appropriate somehow. Want to watch it?"

He'd gone to all that trouble just because our names were Nick and Norah? Touched by the thoughtfulness, I curled myself into a ball at the end of the couch while he started the video.

Nick took the other end and put his long legs on the leather ottoman he used for a coffee table. "You don't have to hide in that corner, Norah. Make yourself comfortable."

So I did.

Boy, did I ever.

I awoke as the end credits rolled across the screen and realized that I'd seen little more than a minute of the movie before I'd dozed off. And, as I always do when I sleep, I'd hogged as much space as I could. Most of the couch, in fact, leaving Nick about eighteen inches in which to sit.

I bounced upright so fast I gave myself a brief headache. "I'm sorry! I didn't mean to…"

"That's all right. I wasn't much interested in the movie, either, but I had a great time listening to you snoring. I had a speedboat once that did that *putt…putt…putt…*thing when I didn't have the gas mixed just right."

I tried to think of something more embarrassing than this but I couldn't. Snoring and drooling in front of a man I'd just met is at the top of the list. I was about to apologize profusely when I saw the grin on his face.

"I did not!" I eyed him cautiously. "Did I?"

Then I threw a couch pillow at him. "You tease!"

He caught the pillow in one hand and shook it at me. "You're very easy to tease."

Funny, until now, I wouldn't have thought of that as a compliment.

Nick walked me home after our flanfest during which we nearly finished an entire flan made up of eggs, milk and sugar.

"I should keep walking until I've worn off all the calories I ate today," I said as we reached my yard.

"You'd end up in New York City," he pointed out reasonably, "and besides, you could use a pound or two. You work hard in that store of yours."

I could? I do? How nice of you to notice.

"Would you like to come in?" I asked as we stood on my front step. "There's no food but I could probably rustle up a soft drink."

"Thanks. Can I take a rain check for another time?"

"Sure. I had a great day." I reached out and squeezed his hand. It was meant to be a purely friendly gesture but he held it until the heat of his skin warmed mine.

"Me, too, Norah. I'll cook for you anytime." He tilted his head and stared into my eyes. A rush of blood flooded my cheeks with color.

Is he going to kiss me?

When he didn't, I wasn't sure if I was disappointed or relieved. Still, I floated blissfully into my house and scooped Bentley into my arms. "Just wait until you meet Nick. You're going to love him."

My buoyant moment didn't last long.

Bentley, in my absence, had entertained himself by removing every pillow and cushion from all the chairs and dragging them to the middle of the room. I could see by the fresh body imprints that he and Hoppy had made a sleeping nest there for the afternoon. To his credit, Bentley had not made a tooth mark in any of the cushions.

It's not easy to have a dog who demands so much time and attention.

It's also difficult to have a demanding man in one's life. I decided that when I opened the door to my deck and found another bouquet of flowers there with a note.

Norah,
Sorry I missed you. Am going out of town for a few days. I'll see you when I get back.
Connor

This time I shredded the note and put it in the wastebasket before anyone—especially Lilly—could see it.

Then I stared at the flowers, a riot of tulips, lilies and irises, and scratched my head. Now what? I glanced across the room to a photo of Lilly and me on her birthday, the one we'd celebrated at Belles & Beaus. We had blue masks on our faces, cucumbers for eyes and our heads swathed in white terry towels. We were grinning widely and toasting ourselves with bottled water. No matter what, I couldn't let Connor—rich, handsome, urbane—cause trouble in a friendship like Lilly's and mine.

After allowing Asia Mynah to tell me what a "pretty bird" I was and tell me he loved me a few times, cuddling Hoppy and having Bentley fling himself into my lap, I felt a little better. I can see storm clouds forming on the horizon over Lake Zachary and I don't like it. Lilly is chasing Connor, Connor is chasing me. Joe is waiting for me to come to my senses about love and marriage even though I think my senses are perfectly fine already. And if that weren't difficult enough, there's Nick who, despite my efforts to the contrary, has lodged himself inside my head and won't come out.

Lake Zachary is turning into a romantic swamp of noteworthy proportions.

As always, both when things are going well and when life seems far more complicated than it should, I turn to Scripture. Being a practical, down-to-earth type, I've always gone to Proverbs first. Pithy, to the point, no-nonsense Proverbs is the book that always snaps me back to my senses. And, as I've come to expect, it did so today, too.

I know the Holy Spirit directs my reading material. Otherwise, why would this particular verse leap out at me now, when my friends are first and foremost in my mind? *"Many will say they are loyal friends, but who can find one who is really faithful?"* Proverbs 20:6.

That's the question, isn't it? Who do you trust? Who, in this case, should Lilly trust? Me? I hope so, but I saw the doubt in her eyes and it hurt me to the core. It's easy to trust people when there's no trouble brewing, but when things look dicey, the question always comes up. It makes me terribly sad to think I could lose my friend over a misunderstanding about a man. No way. I can't let that happen.

"It's harder to make amends with an offended friend than to capture a fortified city. Arguments separate friends like a gate locked with iron bars." Proverbs 18:19. I used to think those

were terribly harsh words, but I know now that they are true. Whether Lilly realizes it or not, Connor isn't worth it, not to me even though I could be attracted to him in other circumstances.

But how can I pull this back without damaging my friendship with Lilly or Connor, Lord? I don't want to alienate one friend in order to appease another.

And the Holy Spirit answered in the words of Proverbs 11:9. *"Evil words destroy one's friends: wise discernment rescues the godly."*

Well duh! Keep your mouth shut, Norah. Think before you speak, look before you leap. Pure common sense. I love Proverbs.

But the Holy Spirit wasn't done with me yet, I realized when my eyes fell on Proverbs 17:9. *"Disregarding another person's faults preserves love; telling about them separates close friends."*

I closed my Bible and my eyes.

Lord, is that how You want me to handle this Lilly-Connor-me triangle? To watch my tongue, be smart and don't make too much of Lilly's faults? I want to build and keep her trust even if her suspicions are chipping away at our relationship. I'm going to need Your help with this, You know. Like everything else, I can't do it alone. You provided me with Lilly's friendship and now I ask that You protect it—and me—as only You can. Amen.

Life was definitely easier before Connor arrived on the scene. Then my big decisions were whether to treat the parakeets with lettuce or cucumber and give Bentley a pig ear or a nice juicy bone. It is men who are the problem. They aren't satisfied with the human equivalent of a pat on the head or a doggie biscuit.

Which reminds me…it's time to order more snacks for the Bed and Biscuit. All this relationship stuff has distracted me. No doubt my customers think I'm neglecting them.

Chapter Fourteen

❧

"Where do you think he went, Norah? Surely he told somebody."

I bit my tongue and kept restocking shelves. Lilly had already been over twice this morning to speculate on Connor's absence and his oversight of not telling anyone—particularly her—where he had gone. I'm beginning to feel trapped in a remake of *Grease,* propelled backward in time to my teenage years when boys, makeup, fashion and mean teachers made up ninety percent of our conversations.

Finally, after her third "But we had such a nice time together," I scowled at her.

"Lilly, you're fixated on a man. A *man*. You've got better things to do than that."

Lilly sighed and sank down on a pile of fifty-pound sacks of dog food. "You're right. I am. It's just that he's so…"

I held up a warning finger.

"…that *I'm* so ready to help you. What do you want me to stack first, the canned cat food?"

"Much better," I said. "Help me get these bags out of the way and I'll buy you a quick cup of tea when the store closes."

"Quick" turned into leisurely, late afternoon which turned into evening and finally Joe, Lilly and I decided to have dinner.

We were sitting on the deck of The Waterfront overlooking the lake and scraping cheese out of the bottom of what had been a huge basket of nachos when Joe announced that his sister was getting married.

"When's the big day?" I asked, wondering if I'd be invited to attend.

"Not until next summer. It's a good thing, too. I'm not sure if he's the right guy for Ellen. She thinks he is—most of the time—so she's decided to go through with it."

"That doesn't sound promising." I thought about those bells I'm waiting to hear. Or maybe Ellen is right and I won't get to hear them until I'm going down the aisle. I don't want to believe it.

"Ellen loves him, of course, but she's got some questions. I suppose they'll have this year to work it out."

"Has she given him the Pet Test?" I swirled the dregs of my iced tea in the bottom of my glass and wished the waitress would come around to give me more.

"The Pest Test? What's that?"

"Not Pest, *Pet*. The Pet Test."

"Okay, I'll bite, what are you talking about?"

"Does your sister have any pets?"

"Two dogs. A black lab and some sort of yappy white thing."

"Yappy white thing" is not a normally acceptable description of a dog in my book, but I let it pass.

"How do the dogs like Ellen's fiancé?"

"Like him? How should I know?"

"Ask her. See what she says. It will tell you a lot about the guy, you know."

"Explain that, please," Joe said doubtfully. "Maybe I've missed an angle on attracting a beautiful woman. Is it possible to flunk the test?"

"Absolutely. I dated a guy in college who, I thought, might be The One, Mr. Right. Then I visited him at his home."

"What happened?"

"He came to the door and his dog followed him. He started yelling at it to get away and pointing his finger. Finally he kicked at it with his foot to get it away from me."

"Uh-oh," Lilly muttered.

"We broke up on the spot. Finis. Whatever made him think his behavior was acceptable is beyond me."

"That's a pretty dramatic example," Joe said doubtfully. "I doubt Ellen's fiancé kicks at anything. He has a dog of his own. Ellen says it's a big annoying thing that wants to put its head in her lap when she's eating."

Boundary issues. Can't discipline properly. Owner has desperate need to be liked.

"He treats it very well, in fact. Sometimes too well, according to Ellen. It's a strange breed. He paid a lot of money for it and he's always taking it in to be groomed. He likes the attention it draws when he walks it in the park. That's how they met, in fact."

Uses pet as date bait. Needs to be noticed. Ego issues.

"Sometimes the dog jumps all over her and he doesn't do anything about it. She says he thinks it's 'cute' and that the dog 'likes her.'"

Doesn't watch out for her. Doesn't help dog with its negative behavior. Not thoughtful. Wishy-washy.

"If he treats Ellen like that now…" Joe frowned. "I'd better talk to her about this."

Maybe I should be a dog psychologist someday.

"There's Julie and Frank Morris." Lilly pointed out the couple from the Toy Store being seated across the room.

"She's all right, but he's not very friendly and that son of theirs." Lilly wrinkled her pert nose. "What a rude boy! I saw him near Auntie Lou's with another kid and, when she couldn't see them, that friend of his began imitating her walk and he made no effort to stop him."

"Her walk?"

"Haven't you noticed? She's been hobbling all week, like her hip hurts."

Come to think of it, I hadn't seen her outside much lately other than to sweep the sidewalk in front of her store. Maybe that tumble in the back room had taken more of a toll than I'd first suspected.

"She's showing her age," Joe commented.

"Shouldn't somebody be taking care of her?" Lilly's brow furrowed. "Does she have any family?"

"Not that I know of," I interjected, "but I think she's doing just fine."

Joe looked skeptical. "Lilly, have you told Norah what you told me?"

"I was in the store yesterday," Lilly began, "to see if she had some small bills. Lou had to go in the back to get them. She told me that she wasn't using the cash register because she'd set a *booby trap* around it. Can you believe it? She showed me how she had it hooked up with wires tied to some of those sleigh bells she always has in that bowl on the counter. If anyone tried to open the till without knowing about the wires, a whole batch of bells would fall on the floor and make a terrible racket."

Oh, no, Lou! That's not a good idea.

"Then what?" Joe asked, amused. "She'd call in a reindeer to stomp all over the burglar?"

Lilly giggled. "I think she planned to hit whoever it is over the head with a broom. I think she's a little—" she made circling motions near her temple with her index finger "—loony."

"She is not! She's fine. You just don't know…"

"She's not young anymore," Joe said. "She probably shouldn't be living alone over that shop."

"So you think she's loony, too?"

"Maybe not loony but I do have questions about her ability to run the store much longer."

"What would she do without the store?" How could they discuss Lou and what they perceived as her problems so nonchalantly?

"I don't know. Lou would have to decide that."

She already has, I thought to myself, and it made me very uncomfortable to hear others take her so lightly.

* * *

"Why," Annie asked when I walked into the store the next morning, "do banks charge for insufficient funds when they know perfectly well that we don't have enough funds already?"

I dropped my purse on the counter and grabbed the notice that had come in the mail. "Again? I thought we had this all straightened out."

"That missing four hundred dollars messed us up, Norah. I'll call the bank again, but they aren't inclined to be understanding."

"Bad girl! Bad girl! Awwwk!"

Even Winky is on my case. I felt tears sting the backs of my eyes. I want nothing more than to close and open them again to have Pond Street as it used to be—friendly, safe and calm, a haven in the storm. With all the stupid misunderstandings, suspicions, speculation and gossip going on, I might as well stay home and watch soap operas.

Nothing smells better than a horse. A close second, however is the pad of a Siberian husky's foot. Don't ask me how I know this, but take my word for it. Maybe I do spend a little more time with animals than I should....

That's why every time I see Sarge, the big sorrel gelding entices me out of the shop and into the street.

Sarge turned his head to nicker at me when he saw me start across the street. That sound is music to my ears. I interpret it as, "Hello, darling, I'm so glad to see you." Who wouldn't fall for that?

I stroked the broad side of his neck and he nudged at me

with his nose, completely ignoring Nick. He was wearing Auntie Lou's sleigh bell on his headstall again. When Nick turned around, there was a smile already on his face. "I figured it was you. Sarge doesn't get lovesick over just anyone."

"Oh, I'll bet you tell that to all the girls."

"I don't, but you should know there is a pretty little filly that has her eye on him. She's a buckskin with great flanks and a saucy flick to her tail."

"How can a mere human compete with anything like that?"

"Just warning you not to get your hopes up. She hangs out in the same pasture and she's tough competition."

"Where do you keep, Sarge? I've been curious about that."

"All the mounted police horses are kept together at a boarding facility where they're trained and cared for. It's a great place. Every horse should be so lucky."

"So you don't ride him when you're off duty?"

"I have my own recreational horse."

"You do? That surprises me. I thought you and Sarge were inseparable."

"He's my partner and as professionally trained as I am. We work together and rely on each other for our safety. Sometimes it's okay for us to get away from each other."

"I hadn't thought about it that way." The sun was warming my back and Sarge was smelling deliciously of saddle leather and fresh hay. I could have curled up and napped right here in the sunlight. That's what animals do for me. They make me calm. They are perfect as God made them and they never try to be anything but themselves. Humans could take a lesson or two from them.

"If you'd like, I can introduce you to Cocoa sometime."

"Cocoa? That's nice."

"I grew up riding her mother, Duchess, and I raised Cocoa from a colt. Would you like to meet her?"

"I can't think of anything I'd rather do." I felt my chin draw down and I stared at the pavement. "I have to admit, though, that I don't ride."

"You don't? I thought surely…"

"City kid," I said by way of explanation. "My extracurriculars were soccer, tennis, French horn, choir, cheerleading, volleyball, ballet…"

"Ballet?" Nick cocked his head in a way that told me he'd buy into anything but ballet.

"Let's just say my toe shoes never got off the ground, okay? I was a big disappointment to all involved, but Mother kept pushing because 'all the other girls love ballet, dear.' Now if she'd signed me up for clogging…"

"It sounds like you are way past due for a riding lesson, Norah. What do you say?"

"Yes." *Emphatically, unequivocally, undeniably, Yes!*

But before I could do anything else, I had to have a conversation with Auntie Lou.

Chapter Fifteen

I heard Joe loping after me as I headed down the street.

He was panting by the time he reached me and his perfect black forelock was mussed a little. "Where are you going in such a hurry?" I slowed and he took me by the arm.

"To visit Auntie Lou. What are you doing? Practicing for the Olympics? You have a great sprint."

"I'm chasing you. Do you want to go to the theater on Saturday afternoon? *Romeo and Juliet*. My sister asked me to use their tickets because they'll be out of town."

"I'd love to but I can't. I just made other plans for Saturday."

"Anything you can cancel?" He looked charmingly hopeful.

"I don't think so." If I were a hundred percent honest with

myself I might have said, "I don't *want* to." The idea of spending Saturday learning to ride was just too tempting. I like Shakespeare well enough, but even he can't compete with a horse.

I saw the look of disappointment on Joe's features. "I'm sorry. Could you take someone else?"

"There's no one else I *want* to take. You know that."

"Maybe Lilly could sub for me this once," I suggested and was surprised at how quickly Joe took to the proposition.

"Good idea. Do you want to mention it to her? I'll stop by her store later and see if she's up for it." He smiled widely and it occurred to me that I took Joe too much for granted. He's an incredible-looking man, sweet, thoughtful…everything a girl could want. Except, of course, for a horse.

Auntie Lou was standing on a ladder, ubiquitous broomstick in hand, straightening pictures. Today, in a black crinkle-fabric skirt she'd purchased from Lilly, a long-sleeved sweater with pearlized buttons that went right to the first of her chins, a little black chiffon scarf tied around her head and that broomstick in hand, it wouldn't have surprised me much if she'd launched herself out for a sail around the room cackling, "You'd better watch out for your little dog, Toto, my pretty."

"You're looking frisky on top of that ladder." I bit my tongue to keep myself from adding, "Don't fall."

That sort of warning annoys Auntie Lou as much as it exasperates me. "Don't fall" is a ridiculous suggestion, really. After all, no one gets up on a ladder with the express idea of falling off. In fact, most people take extra precautions to see that they come off the ladder the same way they got on—

one rung at a time. Since Auntie Lou is touchy about her age these days, I don't want her to get the idea that I'm worrying about her—even though I am.

"Here, take this." She swung the broom toward me so that I had to duck as I grabbed it. Then she navigated her way off the ladder and dusted her hands on her skirt.

I'm sure Lilly didn't mean to have Lou wear that skirt with crocheted bedroom slippers, I thought to myself. Where are the fashion police when you really need them?

"I sold that pair of frames over the fainting couch this morning. A few minutes ago the lady called and says she wants the couch, too."

"Productive morning." I followed her to the back of the store and helped myself to a cup of Lou's coffee. I've always speculated that Lou has a little side business with the city providing them with tar to repair the streets—and she cooks it up in this very coffeepot. "Do you have any cream?"

"You hate my coffee, dearie. Why do you keep trying to drink it?"

"To be sociable, I suppose."

"I don't eat fish food when I come to your shop. You don't have to be polite. We're beyond that." Auntie Lou cackled. "I'm way beyond being polite. That's one thing about being my age. You can be honest, instead. Last month when that furniture salesman tried to sell me a new couch that looked like a casket, I told him what I thought about it. Forty years ago I would have tried to be polite." She snorted. "Who wants a sofa that looks like a casket, anyway?"

No one I know, that's for sure.

"I'm sure there are lots of benefits to being your age."

"Maybe. I'll let you know when I think of them," she quipped before adding, "I've finally quit lying about my age and started bragging about it, instead." Her eyes held a foxy twinkle. "My bad knee is more accurate about predicting a change in the weather than the weatherman and I'm getting more men in my life all the time."

"Men?" I choked.

"You know Arthur and his friend Rhuma because they've landed me on the floor a time or two. Now I've met someone new, two fellows, in fact, Charlie and Ben."

Puzzlement obviously showed on my face.

"Charlie Horse and Ben Gay!" Lou chortled, slapping her weather-predicting knee. Then she looked at me slyly through lowered lashes. "Not too bad for an old thing, eh?"

"You are incorrigible, do you know that?"

"Nicest thing anyone's said to me all day." Lou whipped off the little black scarf she was wearing and looked in the mirror that hung beside the coffeepot. "Do you think I'd look good if I got a facelift?" She stretched her jaw from side to side and lifted the folds beneath her chin with the top of her hand. "Or is there just too much to lift? I wonder if I could find a doctor who works with a crane instead of a scalpel."

"Behave yourself, Auntie Lou. What's gotten into you?" Much as we were laughing at her barrage of jokes, I knew there was something more behind her words that she wasn't saying.

"Nothing that rewinding the clock wouldn't help." Heavily, she sat down in her chair. "Getting old isn't for the fainthearted, Norah. I do not like it very well."

" 'You're only as old as you think'—isn't that what you always tell me?"

"And I believe it. I'm just having a little trouble convincing this body of mine."

"Then I have a great idea. Come with me to church on Sunday. We'll walk. It's not far and it will be good exercise. Then we'll find somewhere to have brunch. What do you say?"

"What does she say to what?"

Our heads swiveled toward the door. Neither of us had heard Nick come in. He was appearing around town more and more often when he wasn't on duty.

"To church and brunch."

"Sounds nice."

Before I could say another word, Lou popped in, "Will you join us?"

I don't know who was more surprised, me or Nick.

Caught off guard, Nick stood there openmouthed. "Sure," he finally managed. "Why not?"

Why not, indeed?

"Lou," he began, "I'm wondering if you have an antique price list book of items between 1920 and 1940. A buddy of mine inherited his grandfather's estate. There are a lot of things in the house that were purchases during and around the Depression. Carnival glass, milk glass, depression glass, Fostoria, anything like that. He's trying to get some idea of their value."

Auntie Lou scrunched up her face into a prunelike pucker. "Now where might I have put those books? I haven't looked at them recently but I think they're on the third shelf in the storeroom, left-hand side, right next to my

books on Chippendale furniture." She did that little rocking motion she uses to build momentum to get out of her
chair. That's another thing Auntie Lou says about aging, it
takes more tries to get herself off the couch.

She scurried into the back, leaving Nick and I together.

"Third shelf, left-hand side, next to Chippendale, huh?
She may have a little trouble with mobility, but there's nothing wrong with her mind," he observed.

A rush of warmth and appreciation flooded through me.
"At least you see what I see when I look at Auntie Lou—a
sharp, savvy forty-year-old mind trapped in a weakening
body. Sometimes life just isn't fair…."

"Sometimes you're the dog and sometimes you're the hydrant," Auntie Lou said as she triumphantly exited the
storeroom with a book in hand. "If you get to be the dog
most of the time, I suppose you should count yourself lucky.
Here's your book."

We were all laughing when a well-dressed couple entered the store. Lou thrust the book into Nick's hand before
toddling to the front to greet her customers. "If your friend
decides to sell some of his items, have him call me. I'm a bit
of an expert on the Great Depression, having been a child
in those days."

Nick and I wove our way through the maze of antique
baby buggies, rocking chairs, trunks and footstools to the
front. Outside in the sunlight, we stared at each other, neither of us seeming to know quite what to do or say.

Nick broke the silence. "I thought I'd head to the Toy
Store next. My buddy wondered if they'd know anything
about old toys that an antique dealer might not."

"I'll walk with you," I offered. "I don't know them very well. It wouldn't hurt to act friendly." *And keep an eye on Bryce.*

I wasn't quite ready to tell Nick my suspicions, mostly for Julie's sake, I suppose, but I couldn't wait much longer.

"Do they keep to themselves?"

"Let's just say that if the shopkeepers on Pond Street are family, they're distant cousins who don't seem to like their relatives very much."

"I see." Nick's eyes took on a faraway gaze that made me wonder exactly what it was he did see.

To our surprise, it was neither Julie nor Franklin behind the counter but Bryce himself. He was plugged into so much equipment that he looked like a bionic man recharging. He wore a headset attached to an iPod, a watch so complicated it could probably tell him what time it is in every time zone on Mars. He had his hand on the joystick of a Nintendo, a cell phone clipped to the pocket of his signature black T-shirt and more earphones draped around his neck. The orange tips of his hair had been replaced by pink and green. He was so engrossed in his music and the game that he didn't even see us until Nick reached out and waved a hand in front of his down-turned eyes. A shoplifter could have made off with every baby doll in the store without having him notice.

When Nick did get his attention, however, he had all of it. Bryce scowled at him as if he'd interrupted a delicate bit of brain surgery instead of *Barbarians meet Godzilla* or some other weird game.

"Are your mom or dad around?"

"Nah. Mom's at the market and Dad took the car to the garage. He'll be back in an hour or so."

"You don't happen to know anything about antique toys, do you?" Nick said conversationally, obviously not expecting an answer.

"I used to collect PEZ dispensers and Matchbox cars when I was a little kid. Does that count?"

"Further back than that, I'm afraid. I'll write down what I'm looking for if you'll give me a piece of paper. Your dad can call me if he can help."

When Nick was finished, Bryce took the slip of paper and carefully taped it to the cash register. "I'll tell him as soon as he gets back. Is there anything else I can help you with?" So he could actually be polite when pressed.

Then the telephone rang.

"Toy Shop, can I help you?" His expression slid from faintly cordial to surly in a nanosecond. "Can't. Dad's out. No. Don't. I don't want…" He then resorted to a series of one-syllable grunts as whoever was on the other end of the line took over the conversation. When he slammed down the receiver it was clear his cordial phase was over.

Without another word, Nick nodded at the now-brooding boy, took me by the arm and steered me outside.

"What do you think that was about?" I asked once we were clear of the doorway.

"Hard to say. He's not a happy kid. I'll keep an eye on it."

"Do you think Annie is right? I don't want to point any fingers, but…"

"Is he responsible for all the things that have turned up missing lately?"

"I don't want to think he took the check out of my mailbox, but…"

Nick looked down at me with those intense, mesmerizing blue eyes. "I'll take care of it, Norah." He paused. "I'll take care of you."

I'll take care of you.
The words stayed with me for the rest of the day. In fact, I made up an entire fantasy around them involving me, Nick and Sarge, who had, for my daydream, turned pure glistening white and wore a flashing silver saddle to match Nick's new clothes. I don't dream small. If I'm going to be carried off by a knight in shining armor, the guy definitely needs a white horse.

Unfortunately the lovely fantasy only made me feel guilty as I watched Joe come and go from the Java Jockey. I'd promised myself to give *him* a serious chance in my life and he hadn't even gotten his own flight of the imagination. I tried to make one up to match the one I'd concocted about Nick, but the closest I could come was Joe on the back of a donkey in the Andes looking like Juan Valdez and drinking Colombian coffee.

Winky is the guy demanding most of my time. He's taken it into his head to exercise his vocal cords by making the most hideous screeching noises. When he's not shrieking, he's blurting all the bawdy words he's ever learned and cackling delightedly at his efforts. Otherwise, he sits on his perch mumbling to himself, having a secret conversation with his armpit.

At closing time, I wandered over to Auntie Lou's as she was giving her sidewalk a final sweep for the day. "Are we on for Sunday? Church and brunch? I'm taking Saturday off so I won't be seeing you around. Shall I come by about nine?"

To my surprise, Auntie Lou looked at me with such an expression of love and gratitude in her eyes that it nearly took my breath away. "You're a good girl, Norah. I wish you were my daughter."

Impulsively, I put my hand on her arm. "Then consider me such. Or at least a sister—we're all children of God, you know."

She took my hand and held it tightly. "Whether you like it or not, Norah, you're all I have."

Chapter Sixteen

❧

I'm all she has.

"Bentley, I can't get it out of my mind." Bentley and I were face-to-face across the patio table on my deck. He sits there sometimes, rump on a chair, paws on the wrought-iron filigree of the table, listening to me. I know he's listening by the way he cocks his head and his one black ear goes up attentively. Sometimes his expression even changes as I talk. And when I mention the word *veterinarian,* he growls.

I know I'm wacky over this dog, but Bentley represents all that's both wrong and right with people and pets. What kind of person considers it acceptable to abandon, injure or torment anything vulnerable?

It's easy for me to get on a soapbox about this. I suppose

that's why I love Bentley so much. He obviously—from the scars on his sturdy little self—has had some of the worst kind of treatment, yet he's still a creature full of love and hope. Fearful as he is of anything new, he keeps trying and learning. There are people who shall remain nameless who could take congeniality lessons from Bentley.

Nick, however, is not one of them. He, I'm discovering, is about as congenial as they come. He's quiet but not aloof, solid but not stodgy. It's weird of me to say this, but I feel safe with him. Not that I've ever felt unsafe, but he has that effect on me. Nick, like Bentley, is becoming one of my favorite people.

But today I don't have time to wax eloquent about my fanciful thoughts of Nick, because I have too much to do— like getting ready for a riding lesson. I've changed clothes three times since my shower. My most slimming, and snuggest jeans didn't allow me to lift my leg more than a foot off the ground—not nearly enough to get me astride a horse and my baggy jeans are not the most slimming things on the planet. After I'd tried on a third pair, the kind that ride below my waist and make the flesh around my hips look like the overflow on the top of a cupcake I accepted the fact that I was not going to be glamorous today any more than I was going to suddenly become tall and leggy. I would just have to look like someone going to muck out stables.

When Nick arrived he was wearing denim jeans and a T-shirt, too, but it all looks better on him. I can't even remember the last time I fussed or worried over how I looked. Lilly would be proud that I'd started to care if I impressed anyone with my looks or not.

* * *

Mulberry Farms, a horse boarding facility tucked cozily into several wooded acres, is as pretty as its name. As we walked through the main barn I noticed that many of the horses have box stalls with padded flooring and their own trainers. Some even had their own wardrobes.

"What's this?" I held up an oddly shaped piece of stretchy plaid fabric. "And this?"

"A hood and a fleece-lined turnout. And that's a regular stable blanket." Nick moved along a wall displaying foreign-looking equipment. "Martingales, breastplates, curb straps, lunge lines, tail bags…"

"Tail bags? Never mind. I don't think I want to know."

Nick's horse Cocoa, however, is fairly modest in her needs—she eschews a box stall and her only wardrobe is a well-polished saddle and some impressive tack. She is also tall. Very tall. Especially when you are five foot four and plan to climb *gracefully* onto her back sans a ladder or even a stirrup.

"It's good to get the feel of a horse riding bareback," Nick assured me as I eyed her shiny, *slippery*-looking back. "That's how I learned to ride. Hop on and I'll lead her around the arena for you."

"Hop? Do I look like a grasshopper to you?"

"Just get a handful of her mane and swing yourself up. Here, I'll help." Nick bent to give me a leg up. I imagined myself a graceful nymph floating lightly onto the horse's back. My reality was slightly different. As I clung to a hank of the horse's mane and flailed my right leg around I realized that I have structural flaws that prevent me from doing the splits while hanging midair. I oozed down the side of the horse like a glob of grape jelly sliding down a wall. Twice. Then Nick took matters into his own hands and hoisted me into place in the least ladylike manner possible. I felt his handprints burning on my backside as he calmly handed me the reins.

Now I could float around the arena like that nymph of my imagination…*not*. Cocoa's wide, slick back offered little in the way of grips and her spine beneath me felt as if it had been sharpened on a whetstone. With every step I slid to one side or the other until I finally gave up on the reins, leaned forward and hung on to her neck for dear life.

Then she actually started to move out.

"Nick…ouch…I don't…eoww…think…aurgh…this is… ooowww…working."

"You're doing fine. I didn't realize you'd never been on a horse before, Norah. You should have told me."

"Don't…ouch…carousels count?"

"Just relax. Feel her move. Be aware of her shifting weight as she walks. It will help you later when there's a saddle under you."

I would have wiped the grin off his handsome face, but I didn't dare let go long enough to do it. After a few minutes I realized I was enjoying the rocking motion, the warmth seeping into my legs from her sun-heated coat and the smell of fresh-cut hay that seems to be her signature scent. I closed my eyes, tightened my grip, ignored the pain and tried to enjoy the moment.

"What are you doing, falling asleep up there?"

"As long as I can avoid having her backbone slice me in half, this is nice."

"Want to try her under a saddle?"

"Is she tired of me yet?"

"Hardly. She barely realizes you're there. You're a featherweight compared to me. Slide down and I'll toss a saddle on her."

Nick's idea of "tossing" a saddle is different from mine. What he'd really meant was "I'll teach you to saddle this horse even if it kills you." And it almost did.

"I had no idea saddles weighed so much," I gasped, the stirrup clunking me in the head for the third time as I tried to lift the saddle onto the horse's back.

"That's as light a saddle as I have, Norah. If you want to be a rider, you'll need to know how to do this."

"Who said I ever wanted to do this again?" I gritted my teeth and shoved. A cinch slapped me in the face.

"Just wait. You will."

The only one not frustrated by the whole affair was the horse, who was gazing patiently into the distance as if she had clumsy, incompetent riders do this to her all day long.

I love this horse.

I was still waxing eloquent three hours later while we sat in the shade of a huge umbrella drinking iced tea and Cocoa had fled to the back of the pasture faster than a getaway car at a bank heist.

"I want one. Just like Cocoa only a little narrower. I feel like I've been doing the splits all afternoon. And shorter, too. How tall is this horse?"

"About sixteen hands," Nick said.

I lifted my own hand. "Like this?"

"There are about four inches in a hand."

"Whatever. I've fallen in love."

"I can see that, Norah. Love becomes you."

I was taken up short by that comment, but when I looked at Nick I couldn't read anything out of the ordinary in his expression. "It does?"

"*Life* becomes you, Norah. You have a knack for getting the most out of every moment, don't you?"

A pleased blush heated my cheeks. "Thank you. That's one of the nicest things anyone has ever said to me. I do love life. God is good, Nick. I take pleasure in every bit of His creation."

He studied me without speaking. Finally he lifted his hand and brushed a stray curl off my cheek. "I envy you that."

"What do you mean? You enjoy life."

"In my work I see a lot of the dark side, too. It's a little overwhelming sometimes."

I thought of how it must have been for him before tranquil Shoreside as a detective with the narcotics division. Dark, indeed.

"But that's in the past, right?"

He looked away. "Most of the time. At least when I'm awake it is."

"And when you're sleeping?"

"You can't do much about your dreams, now can you?"

He shifted slightly and the jagged scars on his arm seemed to make him wince.

"Is this what you dream about?" I gestured toward his injured arm.

His eyes flickered before he smiled. "Less and less all the time."

"What happened? Can you tell me?" I didn't realize

until I'd asked the question that I was leaning forward, holding my breath.

"Happened on a drug bust. It was a bad time for me." He drew a deep breath. "I nearly bled to death before anyone could get me help." His expression darkened at the memory. "It was about that time that I realized I'd better be square with my Maker." He smiled grimly. "So one good thing did come out of it."

"A very good thing."

"That's what I try to remember—and to forget the rest."

Clear enough. Conversation over. Subject closed. I didn't need any further direction to see that this was a subject Nick did not like to dwell on.

Okay, so maybe it's not just the horse I'm a little in love with.

I scooped up Bentley and took him for a twirl around the living room. He sighed and went limp knowing that trying to squirm out of my arms when I was in a dancing mood would only make me cuddle him more tightly.

"He is so sweet, Bent," I crooned. "You're going to love him. We'll have to have him over soon."

Granted, people may have been institutionalized for less than planning a dinner party with a dog but he was the only one available.

Until Lilly stopped by, that is.

"You look happy," she said without preamble when I opened the door. "I'm glad one of us is."

"Hello to you, too." Before I could stand back she breezed by me like a trade wind.

She was already in the kitchen getting chocolate syrup

out of the refrigerator and digging ice cream out of my freezer. Without a word she concocted from canned pineapple, strawberry preserves and two overripe bananas, a couple of wicked banana splits.

"Do you have any whipped cream in a can?" she asked as she stood in the cooling breeze from my refrigerator door.

"No, but I have the shaving cream I use on my legs, will that do?"

"Nuts? We should have nuts."

"We *are* nuts, Lilly. You, at least."

"Here it is." She pulled the whipping cream from the back of the refrigerator. It was as though I'd never spoken or maybe didn't even exist.

Fortunately for Lilly, I'd stocked up on maraschino cherries only last week, so her creations were complete. She finally seemed to realize I was present when she carried the banana splits to the table and pushed one toward me.

"Trouble?" I asked. "You never come here and make banana splits, malts, sundaes or root beer floats unless there's trouble." Lilly doesn't keep anything fattening in her refrigerator. If I had my refrigerator stocked the way she does, I'd be a waif. I'd certainly be too bored to eat anything she purchases.

"I haven't heard from Connor."

"Were you expecting to?"

"I don't see why not! We had a lovely time…." Her eyes narrowed. "Have *you* heard from him?"

"Not a peep."

She seemed to relax.

"I just don't get it, Norah. He should…others do…I don't understand!"

I'm great at playing fill-in-the-blanks where Lilly is concerned. "He should be more attentive and considerate? Other men call you when they leave town? You don't understand why he doesn't fall all over you?"

"It sounds rather crass when you put it that way, but yes. I'm not used to being ignored!"

"Lilly, if Connor were behaving like most men do when they meet you, would you like him as much as you do now?"

"I…of course…I think so…sure."

Probably not, I thought. If he'd fallen all over her, her conquest would have been complete and she'd feel obliged to leave him in her wake and move on. Lilly the Conqueror, like Napoleon or Attila the Hun.

My heart goes out to her. Connor has her all wound up in knots like a pretzel. Maybe she actually does like him for other reasons than that he seems to be playing hard-to-get.

"Lilly, forget about him. You know how sailors are, a woman in every port. You can't go crazy because there are one or two men on the planet who don't fall head over heels for you the first time they meet you."

She thrust her spoon into her ice cream so forcefully that I thought the whole thing would go flying. Bentley did, too. I saw him jump to his feet and ready himself to catch the ice cream as it fell.

"I can't help it. I don't know what it is, but he feels right for me. And if he doesn't reciprocate, I don't know what I'll do!" She stamped her foot on my kitchen floor.

"You can't make someone love you, Lilly. Not if they don't want to."

"But *I* want him to! It's different this time. It really is."

I have no idea if Lilly is in love or in love with the idea of being in love. Either way, she's worked herself into a state. It took not only the banana split but half a jar of fudge ice-cream topping and three-quarters of a bag of chocolate chips to calm her down.

Imagine, then, my shock and surprise when Connor Trevain showed up on my doorstep only a half hour after I'd packed Lilly off to her own apartment.

Chapter Seventeen

❧

"What are you doing here?" That was a little abrupt to be a warm and friendly greeting, but I wasn't feeling all that benevolent toward Connor after Lilly's visit.

Connor seemed oblivious to my coolness and strolled into my house as if he belonged there.

He is one good-looking man. I seem to forget that when he's not around. It's that "out of sight, out of mind" thing, but the minute he comes back into view I am surprised anew at his good looks. I can hardly blame Lilly for getting twitterpated around him. I'm not much better.

Bentley, who had obviously thought we were done with guests for the evening, trotted into the room carrying my bedroom slippers in his mouth. It's his sign that he wants me to go to bed so he can cuddle with me. Some days he has my slippers in his mouth from morning until night. How can you not love a dog like that?

He skidded to a halt at the sight of Connor. I could hear a low rumble building in his stocky chest. Bentley doesn't like strangers, men in particular. Connor looked at the dog and dismissed him entirely.

"Nice place you have here. Great location. Nice view of the lake."

"Thanks. I like it."

What are you doing here? I got a cold chill thinking how close he and Lilly had come to crossing paths tonight. That would have hurt Lilly terribly.

Then, to my amazement, Connor turned and took my hands. "I had to come by and tell you that I've missed you this past week."

"Me?" When did my voice begin to sound like a squeaky dog toy?

"Do you mind?" He indicated the couch in the living room. Stupefied as I was, I gestured for him to sit. He didn't even notice that Bentley, who, when he saw his scare tactics had failed, rolled over and played dead.

I have got to consider getting a watchdog. As it is, the only way Bentley would protect me is if a burglar tripped on him and broke a bone in the fall.

There, in my cream-colored living room, Connor looked like a movie star as he leaned back against the red sofa cushions. Like a magnet, he drew me in.

"Can I get you something? I have…er…banana splits?"

"Only if I can help you make them."

Sure. Why not? I've got a regular Baskin-Robbins thing going right now.

My skepticism vanished, however, as he pitched in and made even more elaborate concoctions than Lilly and I had done earlier. When he handed me my second sinful indulgence in less than two hours, I smiled weakly. I learned from my mother that a good hostess always joins her guests to eat, and does not hover in the kitchen being a martyr and taking all the leftover scraps. Lettuce and water tomorrow.

Bentley had fallen asleep playing dead on the carpet so I left him where he was and joined Connor on the couch.

"We missed you around town," I commented. Truer words were never spoken. We, of course, meant Lilly.

"I'll be traveling off and on. I have interests in several places. That's one of the challenges I see living here in Shoreside, but I believe it will be worth it."

"Why *are* you here, Connor? Hawaii would have been a hard place for me to leave."

"I don't think of it as leaving permanently, but the business here needed my attention. And—" he hesitated slightly "—I'm tired. Being here makes me think of a simpler life. A main street, shopkeepers, friendly people, all tucked inside a metropolitan area. It's very appealing."

"Trying to kick back, in other words." Now that's something I can understand. Still, it surprised me. "I assumed a man like you would be bored in a place like Shoreside."

"I guess it's my age," he admitted honestly. "I've had a busy life, lots of travel and excitement. The idea of settling down is becoming more and more appealing."

You, too? I thought. He sounds like Joe. This must be a

symptom of the twenty-first century, men being ready to nest before their female counterparts. Lilly excluded, of course, but that was new since Connor had come to town.

"I thought that someone like you would have a dozen women ready to settle down with you." I stirred my ice cream into sludge as I spoke, unable to eat any more.

"It has to be the right one."

Something in his voice made me look up. Connor was staring at me with a strange light in his eyes.

"Someone natural and real. Not a woman concerned about how she looks and how much jewelry she has. Someone who doesn't check the mirror in her compact at every opportunity to see if her lipstick has faded. Someone whose main hobby isn't shopping."

Uh-oh. That would make me exhibit number one and Lilly exhibit number two.

"There's nothing wrong with people who shop," I offered hopefully. "Just because someone is concerned about how they look doesn't mean they aren't nice people. In fact, I'm probably a little too careless." I flicked at my wild curls. "Taming this is like taming the wind."

"Exactly what I mean, Norah. I like things natural and real. Like you."

This is not going at all as it should. Connor should be coming here to ask about Lilly. He should be enamored with her and frantic to know how he can make her fall in love with him. He should think the sun rises and sets on her beautiful face. He should not be looking at me like this—like I'm something much more delicious than ice cream and that he's a very hungry man.

"That's nice. I like things natural, too, like…him." I pointed at Hoppy, who had just bounded into the living room.

A fourteen-pound rabbit can be a useful diversion, especially when he heads right for Connor's shoes and begins to gnaw on the laces.

Connor tried to shoo Hoppy away, but Hoppy is not easily shooed. He, like Bentley, feels very secure in the cocoon of my household. He looked up at Connor, wriggled his nose and went for the laces again.

Connor jumped up to get away from über-rabbit and startled Asia Mynah out of a doze.

"Great balls of fire!" the bird screeched. He flapped his wings and glared at Connor. Then Asia Mynah made some smooching sounds and said, "Gimme a kiss, will you, baby?"

I swear he and Winky have been getting together and teaching each other things when my back is turned.

As he backed toward the door, I quashed an urge to sing a verse or two of "Talk to the Animals" but even all this pandemonium didn't seem to deter Connor.

"You see what I mean, Norah? You're real, down-to-earth." Instead, he looked inordinately pleased. "And these animals, well…you're really something."

I was not about to pursue what that "something" might be, but I did have to take a stab at pointing out that Lilly was "something," too.

"You should get to know Lilly Culpepper, Connor. She's a fabulous person. Salt of the earth. Lilly has a great business head and she's funny."

"Lilly's a nice person, but she's nothing like you."

Before he could say more, I nudged Bentley with my toe. Startled, he jumped to his feet and started growling again, more out of fright than protective impulses. That, it seemed, helped Connor decide that it was time to say his goodbyes.

As I held Bentley by the collar pretending I was keeping him from attacking Connor—fat chance—Connor let himself out. When he was gone, I sank to the floor next to Bentley and put my head in my hands.

"Now what am I going to do, Bent? He can't fall for me! It would just kill Lilly. She'd never understand."

Unfortunately Bentley didn't have any more answers for this sticky situation than I did.

I have become paralyzed in the night. The lower half of my body is no longer functioning. I lie in bed imagining how it will be for me to live in a wheelchair. I consider the importance of handicapped-accessible buildings. I wonder what potent painkillers will do to my delicate insides. I grieve over the fact that I will no longer be playing tennis, jogging, in-line skating or horseback riding….

The light comes on through my fog of stiffness and pain. Horseback riding. Having one's hip joints manipulated by a horse as wide as a Volkswagen. Using every muscle in my back and shoulders to hang on for dear life. Sitting on an animal that has a backbone like a razor blade.

And all in the name of fun. Perhaps next time I want to have "fun" I will have my tonsils removed…or my toenails. It can't be any worse than this.

As I rolled to the side of the bed, it occurred to me that this is the way Auntie Lou feels every morning. I looked over the side and realized how far it was down to the floor when one's limbs are frozen into a permanent V shape. I recall Arthur, Rhuma-tiz, Charlie and Ben. I vow to treat Auntie Lou with the utmost respect and love. She says growing old isn't for sissies and now I know why. If this is her lot every day, then I have even more to thank God for—joints that usually work.

By the time I actually flailed and shimmied my way out of bed, I had gathered quite a crowd. Hoppy and Bentley were sitting in the doorway staring at me suspiciously. I suppose the thrashing of bed linens and muted groans made them apprehensive. "She got into that bed," they're probably thinking, "but where'd she go and who is that mess that's replaced her?"

I managed to stand up and waddle stiff-legged to the shower where I stood for nearly half an hour soothing away the kinks and aches in my legs. The other benefit to the shower was that I didn't know if it was just water or tears of pain streaming down my face.

By the time Nick called to see if I was ready for church, I could almost laugh about the situation.

"Talk about humbling! I've always prided myself on being somewhat of an athlete but pride, obviously, does come before the fall."

"You'll work it out. Riding takes a little getting used to. If you wanted to get on Cocoa again this afternoon, it might help loosen you up."

"Are you kidding," I retorted. "I have to wait until my hip bones return to their sockets before I do this again."

I'm not sure who needed more help getting up the steps into the church sanctuary, me or Auntie Lou. At least *she* wasn't walking bowlegged.

We were only halfway to the car after church when Auntie Lou announced, "Now that I've been spiritually fed, where do we eat?"

"Don't beat around the bush, Auntie Lou, cut to the chase."

She chuckled. "I'm too old to be tactful, I'm afraid. Ever since I turned seventy I've been speaking my mind and I like it." She tittered again. "I'm not sure anyone else likes it, but it suits me fine."

"I admire straightforwardness," Nick said tactfully. "Especially when I'm hungry, too."

Fortunately for both of them, there was no waiting line at the restaurant and we were seated immediately.

"Brunch buffet or would you like to order off the menu?" the waitress asked. "The buffet is outstanding today. Eggs Benedict, smoked salmon, waffles, omelets…"

Nick and I both ordered the buffet. Auntie Lou looked wistfully at the vast tables loaded with food on the far side of the room and then at the menu. "Pancakes, please."

"Pancakes? With that food over there?" Nick was surprised. "Where's that appetite, Lou?"

"It's not that." She hesitated. "But my legs are bothering me today and it's quite a walk over there."

"She'll have the buffet," I ordered. "And I'll dish it up for her."

"You don't have to bother…."

"Auntie Lou," I scolded, "if you won't order the buffet because you can't walk back and forth a few times, then you aren't so honest as you think you are. I saw you look at that food. Pancakes, my foot. It's your pride that's pinching you."

Nick got wide-eyed and silent. His reaction told me that perhaps I had gotten a little stern. But how else could I get through to this woman and let her know that we're here to help her?

"I'm sorry, I didn't mean to scold you like I was your…"

"…daughter?" Then I saw that Lou had tears in her eyes. "You read me like a book, my dear. You make me feel like I'm family. Thank you."

A lump formed in my own throat. How lonesome was Lou? How long had it been since anyone was concerned for her welfare? "I'll fuss over you any time you want. Just call. Now, do you want to start with a salad or the breakfast entrées?"

"That was interesting," Nick commented as we walked to the buffet to fill our plates. "I thought she might smack you, not thank you."

"I don't know what's with me lately, but I'm in nurturing mode and I can't shake it."

"I think you must always be in that mode, Norah, you're a nurturer from your cells on out."

And that, I realized, was exactly who God had made me to be. I'm glad Nick appreciates it.

Chapter Eighteen

❧

I knew something was wrong even before Joe walked into Norah's Ark. His shoulders were rounded forward and his eyes studiously on the ground.

"Hey, big guy, what's up?"

He looked at me curiously, as if I should be in the same mood as he.

"I haven't seen much of you lately."

Aha. He's feeling neglected. I'm surprised. Joe is usually approving of my independent ways.

"It's been crazy," I admitted. "Why don't you come over for dinner tonight? We'll fire up the grill and make brats and corn on the cob."

He perked up immediately. "You mean it?"

"Of course I mean it! Can you pick up something wonderful at the bakery for dessert?"

He smiled that devastating smile of his and I wanted to hug him. "You're so patient with me, Joe, I can't believe you put up with me."

"You're worth the wait, Norah."

I felt a troubled frown forming between my eyebrows. "Joe…"

"I know, no promises. You've never led me to believe anything else. That doesn't change how I feel about you." He leaned forward and kissed me gently.

After he'd left, I sat down on the stool behind the counter and put my head in my hands. It was beginning to ache. Nine chances out of ten, if I'd been ready and looking for a marriage partner, the man well would be dry as dust. Because I'm not in any hurry, however, I'm attracting them like bees to honey. Joe, Connor…I can't really include Nick on the list, because though he's friendly, he's aloof, like there's a bullet-proof shield around him. Makes sense for a cop, I guess.

A wolf whistle in eardrum-shattering decibels only added to the pain in my head.

"Hey, good-looking, who's your daddy?" Maybe Winky was once owned by a politically incorrect construction worker.

I looked up cross-eyed to see Lilly charging through the door in a pale mint jogging suit and a snug T-shirt covered with bling. She blew Winky a kiss on her way by and he made some wet, smooching sounds and then something so high-pitched that I expected the neighborhood dogs to come running.

"I love that bird," Lilly said cheerfully.

"He's yours. You don't even have to pay me. I'll take his

cost out in merchandise. When do you want me to deliver him to your place?"

"I'd get a big head if I had someone whistling at me like that all the time. No, I'll just come in here for a pick-me-up." She plopped onto the second stool behind my counter and stared at me coyly from beneath lowered lids. "I saw you at church yesterday." She made a few silly noises of her own. "That Nick is awfully cute."

I ignored that part. "You were in church? Why didn't you come and say hi? I didn't see you." Lilly isn't exactly a regular, although she has gone with me a time or two.

"I was feeling a little down and I remembered that you said you always felt better after going to church, so I thought I'd try it."

There are certainly worse things she could try.

Thanks, God. I see Your hand in this. Anything You want me to do or say here?

"A little down? Could this have anything to do with Connor?"

Lilly's face told me all.

"Don't get depressed over a man, Lilly! You're smarter than that. If it works out, great, but if it doesn't, then he was never the one for you. Why would you want a man who's not truly into you?"

"It's different for you, Norah. You believe because God's going to take a hand in your love life that things will work out as they should. Frankly, I'm not as sure about that as you are. Besides, I'm not getting any younger."

Lilly's perfectly shaped lips drooped in her exquisite face with its practically poreless and wrinkle-free skin.

"Lilly, it doesn't matter. You still look like you're eigh-teen years old. Besides, thirty-one is not exactly over the hill. You haven't even reached the foothills yet. Where's your self-esteem?"

Lilly looked down at her feet. "Maybe I didn't have as much as either you or I thought I did. That's why I went to church, to get a new perspective."

"Here's my view. That's why Jesus came, not to invent a cure for wrinkles on a face but wrinkles on your soul."

She looked at me with such affection that it made my throat tighten. "And that's what you're worried about, isn't it? The unforgiven wrinkles on my soul?"

"The others are inevitable, those aren't."

"I can always count on a new angle from you, Norah. I come in worrying about my age and a man who's not head over heels over me and end up talking about forgiveness and wrinkly souls."

"Keep your head, Lilly. Connor's a nice guy but he's not the be-all and end-all of men."

"It's easy for you to say, he's a lot more relaxed with you than he is with me."

"Maybe he's relaxed because I'm not pushing to have a relationship with him."

Just the opposite, in fact.

"So your advice is to ease up?"

"Is that what you heard me say?"

"Close enough." She stood up and gave me a quick hug. "I'm so glad you're my friend." And she swept back out of the shop to a chorus of wild noises from Winky.

* * *

I was wearing my red-and-white checked cook's apron when Joe arrived. Bentley was in his matching red-and-white bandana. Hoppy has one, too, but he's not much for dressing for company. Bentley, on the other hand, is a bit of a show dog. Or maybe he's a show-off dog that's frightened of people. An odd combination, that Bentley.

"I just put the brats and corn on." I waved a pair of tongs in his direction. "Salad's ready."

Joe put a box of pastries on the counter and rubbed his hands together. Ever practical, he announced, "Let's pray before the corn starts to burn."

After dinner we sat on the deck in companionable silence, gorging ourselves on pastries and watching sailboats glide ghostlike through the water. Bentley enjoys boating. Actually, he enjoys watching boats. I've had him out on the water a couple times and I think he gets seasick. I can't think of any other reason his eyes roll and, honest, his lips get a green tinge.

"I like this, Norah."

"Me, too. For once there aren't any of those annoying little watercraft ruining the peace and quiet."

"That's not exactly what I meant." He wagged his index finger between himself and me. "I like *this*. You and me. Together. Doing nothing but enjoying each other's company."

"Of course. That goes without saying."

He turned and looked at me with a gauging expression. "It certainly does. Go without saying, I mean. By you. You never tell me that my company is enough for you."

Not now, Joe. Please? Don't start this now!

But of course, not being a mind reader, Joe did.

"Sometimes I get the idea that I'm hopelessly infatuated with a woman who's only mildly fond of me, Norah. Is that true?"

"I can't respond to the hopelessly infatuated part...."

"Norah," he warned, "I'm serious."

"And I'm much more than 'mildly fond' of you and you know it. I'm just not sure I'm..."

"...ready," he finished for me. "I want to know what will get you ready?"

Bells.

But I could hardly say that. If I didn't even know how to explain this feeling, there was no way I could expect Joe to understand it. Besides, it makes no sense. I've always believed that God will show me the "who" when the time is right but it's not Biblical to think that He is going to do it through the handbell choir at church.

"If I knew, I'd tell you," I said honestly. And I would. The thought of Joe not being in my life is devastating, but for right now it has to be as a friend rather than a fiancé.

He swung his long legs off the chaise longue and stared at me. "You're worth the wait, Norah, but I don't want to be sitting in my wheelchair on this patio with you in forty years asking when you'll feel ready."

"I can't expect you to. I wouldn't."

"I know." Then he repeated almost verbatim one of our previous conversations. "If God wants us together, we'll be together."

"Exactly." This just kills me. Part of me wants to say, "Yes, Joe, let's give it a whirl," but another, more cautious part says, "A relationship is not about 'giving it a whirl.' People's lives are at stake—one of them being yours."

Of course I've never believed relationships are all about *bells,* either, but I'm certainly hung up on it anyway.

Bentley and I were curled up on the couch doing my Bible study when the doorbell rang.

"Again? Who could it be this time, Bent?"

For a dog, Bentley does a pretty good job of shrugging his shoulders. He didn't look elated at the prospect of more company, either. He'd just gotten me all to himself. Even Hoppy was off somewhere, probably sitting in his litter box thinking about the good life he lives.

I almost didn't answer, but the light through the small transom windows in my door was a giveaway that I was at home. I shlepped to the door and checked to make sure my hair, which I'd put up in a bun and fastened with a pair of unsharpened pencils, wasn't making a prison break from its confines.

When I opened the door, it was déjà vu all over again! Now it was Connor at my door. Lilly, Joe, Connor, are all sweet roses as friends, but when the *R* word—relationship—starts to complicate things, it makes for a very thorny bush.

I put on my hostess smile and invited him in.

Chapter Nineteen

❧

"Am I stopping by too late in the evening?"

"No, not at all. Come in."

If this is how things are going to be, I'm going to install a revolving door in this place.

For once Connor wasn't dressed in white. He still looked like a seafaring man, however, in a navy cotton sweater with a rolled neck, cream-colored trousers and good, sturdy shoes just right for standing at the wheel of the ship in a gale wind. All he needed was a beard, a pipe and a captain's hat and to start yelling, "Batten down the hatches."

"I was at the office doing some paperwork and I lost track of time. I meant to stop by an hour ago. I'm sorry to disturb you so late, Norah."

I'm not. Just over an hour ago, Joe and I were knee-deep in conversation. Connor arriving on the stoop, hat in hand, hopeful look in his eye, but one hour earlier would not have been useful.

"It's fine. What can I do for you?" Hoppy landed on my foot with a thud and I picked him up.

Connor looked disconcerted and his mouth worked a little, like a gasping goldfish vacuuming the top of the fishbowl for oxygen. Maybe it's disconcerting to have a conversation with a woman in bunny slippers who's also holding a bunny in her arms. Or maybe it's the SpongeBob Square-Pants motif on the sweatshirt I changed into after Joe left. Hard to know. All I can say is that if my fashion statement bothers him, he should march right down the road to Lilly's.

I led him to the kitchen table and indicated that he should sit down. There were still a half-dozen pastries left. I put on the coffeepot—decaf—because I don't even ask at this time of night and put out the pastry plate.

We made small talk about the weather and the folks on Pond Street for several minutes before Connor got to the reason for his trip.

"I want to invite you to dinner on the *Lady of Lake Zachary.*"

"The *Lady?* Really?" Everyone on Pond Street knows about the *Lady* even though not many have been on her. She's the little jewel in the crown of Connor's fleet. She's the boat bigwigs request for the VVVIPS—very, very, very important people—they entertain. Ziga's provides food for all the cruises, but the *Lady* has a chef on board until moments before she sails, putting the finishing touches on the gourmet meals to be served. I'd been itching for a ride on the *Lady* ever since I opened Norah's Ark, but my VVVIP's are usually just as happy with a dried pig's ear or a bone as duck à l'orange.

"I'd love a ride on her!" I'd briefly wondered once why all seafaring vessels are referred to as "she" but it's actually pretty clear to me—boats provide smooth sailing, keep you above water on rough seas, rock you to sleep at night to the lullaby-gentle waves and provide all kinds of fun and entertainment. What else *could* a boat be but a "she"?

"Are you free on Friday evening?"

"Yessss…" Then a frisson of alarm shimmered through me. "We won't be alone, will we?"

"Of course not!" Connor laughed. "For one thing, I can't sail the *Lady* all by myself!"

That was all I needed right now, to be out sailing with Connor while Lilly and Joe were watching me so carefully. I'm not all that keen to have Nick think there's something romantic between Connor and me, either. A party suits me much better.

"You have such wonderful, old-fashioned charm, Norah." He looked at me as though I'd just hatched a chick or grown a daisy out of my ear or something equally fascinating.

Not knowing what to say to that, I, for once, did the wise thing and said nothing.

Connor took that as a signal of satisfaction with the arrangement and stood up. "Friday then? You can board any time after seven."

"Perfect. I'll be at the dock at seven."

After he'd gone, I fed the pets. Asia Mynah was itching to have a conversation.

"What's shakin', baby?"

"Just my head, Asia. My life's getting way too complicated."

"Overworked and underpaid," he intoned.

"You've got that right."

"Gimme a kiss, will you?"

"Sorry, I'm not in the kissing mood tonight, Asia."

"Naughty girl."

"You could say that." Why, I wonder, do I enjoy talking to this bird more than with my friends lately? Maybe because when Asia Mynah talks, there are no surprises.

"I love you."

Well, maybe a few.

By the time I got to bed, my dreams were a regular circus of activity—Bentley, wearing a sailor suit, was steering the *Lady*, Asia Mynah was screaming, "Avast ye matey!" and Connor was in my kitchen with Joe cooking a gourmet meal. Lilly stormed in and out of my dream as if she was modeling in a fashion show and Nick and Sarge were staring at me through a window, just outside the insanity of my life.

The door chime jingled, signaling that someone had entered.

"I'll be right back," I told the big German shepherd I was brushing. I pamper each of my "guests" during the day. Today is massage and brushing day. Tomorrow will be belly scratching and ball tossing. Saturdays are for a long walk around the lake.

"Can I help you…?" I hurried to the front brushing dog hair off my clothing—a fruitless task if there ever was one. "Oh, it's you."

It was him, all right, Nick, in jeans and a sweatshirt. No uniform—maybe he was tired of wearing it all night in my dreams.

"What can I help you with?"

"Maybe the question should be 'what can I help *you* with?'"

"Nothing, unless you do windows. There are hundreds of fingerprints on the outside windows. That would be from the day I put a basket full of kittens up there."

"Actually, I do. Did you see me doing Auntie Lou's?"

I glanced across the street. Auntie Lou's windows were sparkling. "When did this happen?"

"Yesterday. I saw her struggling with a squeegee and a bucket of water so I offered to do the job for her. Took twenty minutes, tops. It could have taken her half the day."

"That was very sweet of you."

"So do you really want me to do yours?" He looked, if not hopeful, at least willing to take on the job.

"No. I just think it's sweet. I need the exercise. I haven't used my in-line skates much lately and I don't want all this food I've been eating to head south."

His expression was blank.

"Head south." I patted my hips. "And land here."

"I see." He grinned. "Although I don't think it would be a problem."

I left that open for interpretation.

Just then, Lilly, in orange jeans, a sunshine-yellow top and lime-green accessories, burst out of The Fashion Diva like a bottle rocket. She came to me, threw her arm around my shoulder and said to Nick, in no other persona than her own, "Isn't she a darling?"

"Wendy and her brothers were *Darlings*, Lilly. And since Peter Pan is not a close friend of mine you don't need to call me one, either."

Lilly looked over my head at Nick. "She's modest, too."

Then, as if her work here was done, Lilly turned on her three-and-one-half-inch stiletto heels and reentered her store.

"Matchmaker, Matchmaker" from Fiddler on the Roof played in my head.

"Ignore her," I advised Nick. "Too many hair-spray fumes. Her brain is muddled. She doesn't know what she's saying."

"She's pretty astute for being under the influence of hair spray," he commented. "I have to agree with her."

Fortunately I didn't have to respond because there was a terrific clatter coming from Auntie Lou's. Saved by the bell. She was hammering on a big old dinner bell she had for sale in her store.

As we dashed across the street I admired Nick's long, muscled legs. He took the trip in half as many steps as I and was already in the store with Auntie Lou when I trotted in.

Auntie Lou was seated in a platform rocker upholstered in garish orange-and-yellow-paisley velvet—some fabrics just should never have been born—holding a rubber mallet in her hand. Her complexion was pasty and her breathing short. Nick was interrogating her like the policeman he is.

"How long have you felt this way?"

"It started about forty-five minutes ago. I had some dizziness and trouble walking. I picked up the phone to call you, but my speech was garbled so I just sat down for a few minutes until the weakness passed."

"What's going on right now."

"I'm still dizzy but it's improving. I'm sure it wasn't anything. I shouldn't have rung on this big old bell, but for a moment there…." Her voice trailed away.

Nick glanced over his shoulder at me. "I've already called an ambulance, Norah." He turned back to Auntie Lou. "Is there anything you want Norah to get from your apartment?"

"I'm not staying in any hospital, if that's what you're insinuating. You just call those ambulance people and tell them to go back where they came from if that's how it's going to be."

Nick ignored her. "Norah will pull together a couple things for you just in case you need to stay."

I immediately started for her apartment. Auntie Lou's voice followed me up the stairs.

"But what about Silas? And the store? I can't just leave it like this…."

I heard Nick promising that I would feed the cat and lock up the store as the wail of a siren could be heard coming down Pond Street.

"So what's the scoop on Auntie Lou?" Lilly asked. She, Joe and I were sitting outside the Java Jockey as we often do, debriefing our day.

"Her blood pressure was 'unacceptable' according to her physician. They're keeping her for observation and some tests." Auntie Lou had listed me as her "next of kin" and given me permission to consult with her doctor, leaving me, I'm afraid, with a very large sense of responsibility where her case was concerned. "Frankly, I think she probably had a small stroke, but that remains to be seen. Nick believes the same thing."

"I'm so glad you two heard her," Lilly said. "I was in the back unpacking a new shipment of clothes. You know how I am when new styles come in, I lose track of everything else."

"And I was at the bank making a deposit," Joe added. "You and Nick were right there for her. If it weren't for you, it might have been a customer who found her."

"And Nick's a cop. He's used to acting in emergency situations." Lilly put her chin in her hands and her lovely brow furrowed. "I hope she's going to be all right."

"She's not young," Joe said gently. "This may be the beginning of the end for her."

"And what's that supposed to mean?" I demanded.

"You know perfectly well what it means. Lou may have to give up the shop and find someplace to live where she can be taken care of, that's all."

"Joe's right," Lilly concurred. "She's been old forever, but now…"

"She felt dizzy and called for help. She didn't keel over in her pudding at dinner. There's nothing wrong with asking for help when you don't feel well."

"Of course not, Norah, but when you're old…"

Though Lilly and Joe didn't know it, they were pressing on one of my hot buttons. My *hottest* button, perhaps. When did we quit respecting age and begin making old people disposable, like tissue or paper cups? Why is it that when an elderly person has something happen to them, we immediately start talking nursing homes or care facilities?

Granted, the elderly don't have the resilience that younger people do, but they should be given a chance to decide for themselves if they're capable of carrying on with their own lives. Age and illness make us uncomfortable, I think, and many of us work on the premise "out of sight, out of mind" where the elderly are concerned. I want the elderly to be given the chance to make their own decisions as long as they can. Why? Because if I can't do that when I get to be Auntie Lou's age, I'm going to be fighting mad, that's why. So I'd better start now to make sure that's in place when I get as far over the hill as Auntie Lou is.

The elderly, animals, little kids, those are my passions. God made me a nurturer and gave me a couple extra doses of the nurturing serum. I can't help myself. I'm the only person I know who started a Goldfish Rescue Program when she was nine years old. It's my little secret, but I still have friends in the banquet industry who call me if a wedding party decorates their tables with bowls full of goldfish. Those fish rarely go home with the partygoers and rather than having a group flush, they call me and I dole them out to people who want them.

Granted, it cuts into my own goldfish selling business, but I don't care. I just carry more guppies and neon tetras to make up for it. I've even thought of only handling rescued animals and just selling animal food and accessories....

Then I realized that both Joe and Lilly were staring at me, waiting for me to say something.

"Don't get me started on this," I muttered. "For now we just have to think about Auntie Lou and her best interests."

As I watched Joe and Lilly's expressions I realized that

something I'd said didn't fit for them. "We" have to think about Auntie Lou's welfare. Was that the rub?

"What about her family?" Lilly wondered. "Shouldn't they be notified?"

"She doesn't have any."

"No one?" Joe, he of the massive family tree, sounded surprised, too.

"We're not all as lucky as you, Joe," I reminded him gently.

He grinned. "True, but there's a price to pay for a large extended family, you know."

"Piano recitals," I groaned.

"And don't forget band concerts, boxcar derbys, 4-H demonstrations and junior high science fairs. And my youngest nephew," Joe said with a shudder, "has just started *violin* lessons."

"Whatever night his recital is, I'm busy. Far too busy to come. Give the family my regards and tell them how sorry I am not to be there."

Joe regarded me fondly. "Coward."

"I like to think of it as Auditory Safety, something that should be taught in every music class and lesson."

And the conversation drifted on to more cheerful things than Auntie Lou's next step.

Chapter Twenty

❧

Auntie Lou and hospitals do not get along. She doesn't like the bed, the food and the clothing, especially not the clothing.

Nick and I walked into her room to find her huddled in the bed in her floor-length nightgown with cotton ruffles that stand so high around her neck they obscure her chin. She held the sheet close to her face as if she might have the need to dive under the covers on a moment's notice. A hospital nightie—the kind with air-conditioning in the back—lay discarded at the foot of her bed.

"Don't these people have any sort of propriety?" was her greeting. "They wanted me to go for tests in that…that…bikini!"

Nick and I both stared at the offending garment. A bikini on an elephant, maybe, but we weren't there to argue.

"How are you feeling, Lou?" he asked gently.

"Like going home. These doctors don't know what to do with me. They say I'm a hopeless case."

"Hopelessly stubborn," said a warm voice with a chuckle and Dr. Chase Andrews walked through the door. "Hi, Norah, how's the Ark?"

Dr. Andrews is daddy to Mr. Tibbles and Scram, two cats who, thanks to him and their mommy, Whitney, have more toys, collars and paraphernalia than a team of Clydesdales. All, I might add, purchased lovingly at my store.

"When are you going to let me out of here?" Lou demanded. "You're the only pretty scenery in the place and you're taken, so I might as well go home."

I choked back a laugh. Apparently that was Auntie Lou's idea of flirting. Maybe that's why she never remarried.

"Did you want to discuss this with me while your friends are here?" Dr. Andrews asked. "Or would you rather we do so in private?"

"Nothing's private from those two. Norah's like my own daughter and policemen don't talk anyway." She peered at Nick. "Do they?"

"Not when they're not supposed to."

That seemed to satisfy Auntie Lou which in turn satisfied the doctor.

"You've had a small stroke, Lou, a TIA. We'll get your blood pressure down with medication. It was very high and probably the reason you had trouble. You will also have to look at areas in your life that are giving you stress and try to resolve them. I can send you home tomorrow if I have

your promise that you'll take the medications I give you and
have your blood pressure checked frequently."

"That's good news, Auntie Lou."

She harrumphed at me. "Tomorrow? Why not today?"

"I need to make sure you're regulated. Besides, this is your
chance to put your feet up and rest. Enjoy it."

"Enjoy it? That's like the executioner telling the con-
demned man to enjoy his last meal." She crossed her arms
over her chest and she reminded me of an irate capuchin monkey.

"Think of me as your cruise captain, Lou, I'm just telling
you we aren't going to dock until tomorrow so you might as
well find a nice book and sit on the deck for one more day."

Cruise captain? I nearly groaned out loud. I'd almost for-
gotten about Connor's party tonight.

I stewed for nearly a half hour about what to wear, spread-
ing clothes on the bed to study them. Too bright. Not bright
enough. Too casual. Too formal. Too…too. Finally Bentley
came to my rescue. He'd been sitting in the door of my closet
holding a pair of black velvet slippers as if he knew exactly
what I should wear with them. I might as well ask, I thought
to myself. He knows me better than anyone else.

"You pick it out, Bent. What should I wear tonight?"

He stood up, walked deliberately around the bed and sat
down in front of a black velour pant suit. The jacket is
quilted in a delicate Oriental design and the pants are trim
and fit like a glove. It is one of the few things in my wardrobe of which Lilly approves.

Why not? It would be cool on the water and a jacket

would feel wonderful. Besides, it matches the shoes Bentley held in his mouth.

"You're right. It's perfect for a party on a cruise boat. More points for you."

Bentley dropped the shoes in front of the outfit where it lay on the bed and looked up at me with hopeful, pleading eyes.

"Yes, you can have a bone. Come on."

Bentley led the way into the kitchen. He has a funny little walk, a side-to-side waddle that shows that he's well fed and reveals some Staffordshire bull terrier in his bloodline.

I know I anthropomorphize animals, attributing them with human characteristics, but God created and gave us authority over them so whatever helps to make them more endearing to me can't be all bad. Besides, I'm around Bentley and the other animals more than I'm around people.

I have definitely got to get out more.

Just for the fun of it, I unleashed my long curly hair and let it float mysteriously around my face. I even gave it a little pump of glitter hairspray—a gift from Lilly, of course. That, and some eyeliner and sparkle around my eyes made a picture that surprised even me.

"Not bad for a lady who just came off the Ark," I murmured to the reflection in the mirror. "And here I am, ready to get onto another boat."

My place is only a brief walk to the dock and the streets were deathly quiet. Shoreside is one of those little towns that roll up their streets at night. We have more than our fair share of events on the water—races, triathlons, art fairs— but the nights when nothing big is planned, it morphs into a sleepy little cove town.

Tonight is the kind of night that Bentley loves to go for walks. Since everything alarms him—cars, motorcycles, people, noise, fire hydrants and the like, a quiet evening is perfect for him. I'm working on acclimating him to the real world a bit at a time. It's funny really, for a dog who is often mistaken for tough, to be soft as a fresh marshmallow on a sunny day.

I glanced at my watch and was surprised to be early for a change. I'm usually the last one to a party, hoping there is food left and that all the good gossip hasn't already been re-hashed. Fortunately I'm a terrible gossip. My mind is like a sieve where hearsay and rumor are concerned. I wasn't *too* early however, because the crew members were waiting on the dock to greet guests.

They were dressed in white and looked very official. "Welcome to the *Lady of the Lake,* Miss Kent. We hope you have a wonderful evening on board. Please step inside. There are refreshments waiting."

First I had to take a good look at the *Lady.*

I stepped onto the main deck and was taken aback by how sleek and lovely she was. Rich dark cherry paneling on every surface, large windows overlooking the water, intimate tables set with white linen and fresh flowers, a granite-topped bar with small plates of escargot, shrimp and canapés. It didn't get much better than this.

Then I checked out the ladies' restroom.

If I had a powder room this lavish in my home, I'd sit in there just to enjoy the view. It was hard to believe I was actually on a boat. The sink rested in an antique cherrywood chest. There were mirrors and fresh flowers everywhere and something was pumping both classical music and a delicious floral scent into the room.

I was making my way aft to the stairs to the sundeck when I felt a small lurch. I grabbed for the handrail and peered toward the dock to see what had happened.

We were backing out of port! Why hadn't we waited for the rest of the guests?

It took a few minutes for the light to come on in my befuddled brain. Nothing had gone wrong. In fact, everything had gone exactly right. Me and my assumptions had walked into this with my eyes wide open.

I stormed up the stairs to confirm my suspicions. There it was, proof that I am an all-time innocent idiot.

On the observation deck a single table was set in linen and with roses. A wine cooler filled with ice sat on the table with the label of the bottle turned conspicuously outward, sparkling grape juice. Connor even anticipated my kind of drink.

Instead of regular deck chairs there were two, believe it or not, wing chairs for opulent leisure as we sailed the lake. How could I be so obtuse? I'd assumed this was a large party and had never asked otherwise. Connor hadn't said he was inviting others, though I'd assumed it to be so. If I'd thought for a moment that I was going to be alone with the man Lilly has convinced herself she's in love with, I'd never have come. Now it was too late to abandon ship. The *Lady* was headed directly for the middle of the lake and, even as athletic as I am, I can't swim that far.

Besides, Connor was coming toward me in a suit and tie, looking like the world's richest investment banker—and delighted to see me. Things were going to be sticky.

"Norah! You look wonderful. Is that a bit of sparkle I see in your hair or is it fairy dust?"

Had I walked right into this one, or what?

"Connor, what a lovely…surprise." I hoped the frog in my throat would jump out soon. "I didn't realize this party was just for me. I'd expected…" I waved my hand in the general direction of shore—and of people.

"I've wanted a full evening alone with you ever since we ate at Ziga's. You're very hard to pin down so I took matters into my own hands. How do you like the *Lady?*"

"She's beautiful. I had no idea—" clueless, that's me "—that she was this lovely. And elegant. And glamorous." There was no way the word *romantic* was going to squeeze its way through my lips.

He took my hand in his. "So are you. Beautiful, elegant, glamorous…"

I've never been so flattered to be compared to a boat. Especially when he could have used words like *barge* or *tug*.

Deftly, I retrieved my hand. "Connor, I have something to confess."

Those personable smile lines appeared around his eyes. "A confession? This sounds serious."

More than you know.

I thought of Lilly's reaction if she found out about this charming little tête-à-tête. Since Connor had come to town, I'd learned just how insecure even a beautiful woman like my friend could be. One more reason she needs God. It's very helpful to get your worth through Him, not yourself.

"I thought you were having a larger party tonight. I assumed I'd be one of several on board. If I'd known…" I let my voice trail away. I was sounding like a real stuffed shirt and not the least bit grateful for what might be the most romantic dinner of my life.

"You wouldn't have come?" He didn't look offended. In fact, he looked rather pleased. "I admire a woman who has principles and stands by them. You're in no danger of a compromising situation here with me. And there is a crew of three on board."

Frankly, it wasn't my honor or my reputation I was worried about. I can take care of myself. It was Lilly's reaction. How could I steer Connor's interest away from me and toward Lilly without hurting either his or my best friend's feelings?

Chapter Twenty-One

✣

I mulled over my conundrum all through the dinner that Ziga's chef had perfected before we left dock.

Some of the homes on Lake Zachary are so large and ostentatious that I would have been content to live in their accompanying boathouses. Although my father was successful, our lives were simple. There was always more than enough of what I cared about—love and pets. Maybe it's a good thing I can't afford to build one of the beautiful homes on the lake. It would probably look suspiciously like a barn. Or, if I actually knew what a cubit was, an ark.

Connor is a perfect gentleman. Not an ounce of impropriety in his bones. That, however, didn't delude me into thinking that his interest in me was purely platonic. I've been around enough to recognize the look in his eye. If only his gaze were directed toward Lilly instead of me.

Because fools go where angels don't dare to tread, I took a stab at diverting Connor from his original goal—me.

"Connor, this is wonderful. You should invite Lilly Culpepper to do this."

Subtle as a wrecking ball, that's me.

He looked at me with something akin to sympathy. "But it's not Lilly I'm interested in, Norah. It's you."

"But Lilly…"

"She's a lovely person. There's no doubt about that. But I can't force myself to be attracted to someone. That just happens." His expression warmed. "Like the first time I saw you."

I recalled that day trying to remember what had made me such a devastating and desirable woman. It might be useful to recreate that bit of magic again sometime but unfortunately nothing came to mind. I'm not a conscious femme fatale, either.

"You are all eyes and smiles and curly black hair, as exotic as some of the creatures in your shop."

Imagine that. I had no idea that I—in walking shorts and Norah's Ark sweatshirts, the kind with a big, rollicking boat filled with pairs of grinning critters—could be so alluring. Apparently the cliché is true. Love is blind. And deaf. And bewildering. Look what it had done to Connor's brilliant mind. It had made pudding of a perfectly good brain. Such a waste.

"That is flattering, but I'm not exactly looking for…"

"And Lilly is?"

"You could say that."

"Do you believe you can love on command? Or even be attracted to someone?"

"Of course not!"

"Then why do you assume it could happen for Lilly and me?" He snapped his fingers. "Just like that. Besides…"

I hadn't realized before that he had dimples—masculine slashes of gorgeous dimples. I love dimples.

"I like a challenge, Norah, and you are a definite challenge."

So even my hesitation was a come-on for him. Was there any way I could worm myself out of this situation without hurting Lilly? I like Connor—a lot. In another day and time maybe we…but knowing how Lilly felt about him made me very cautious. Besides, there's Joe.

A pang knifed through me as I realized that Joe had been almost an afterthought. He was anything but and deserved more. Then my head started to ache. Maybe I should just give up waiting for bells. Not every woman hears bells when they meet the men they are going to marry and they still have a perfectly nice life.

But Christ came that we might have life and have it *abundantly.* I don't think He planned for us to skimp in the love department, either.

With that in mind, I decided to enjoy the ride. Maybe I'll just give up on the idea of hearing bells altogether.

By unspoken agreement, we didn't talk of Lilly or of love again. As we relaxed on the top deck the breeze gently brushed my hair away from my face and cooled my skin. It couldn't have been more perfect.

"There's my house." I pointed to a small dot of light on the shore. "I wonder what Bentley is doing right now."

Connor looked at me strangely, unaccustomed to women who speculate about their dog's welfare while on romantic shipboard dates. Maybe there just aren't that many of us. Still, I think of Bentley a lot. He depends on me for life. And I depend on him for fashion advice.

It seemed perfectly natural for Connor to move his chair closer to mine and I barely realized that he'd taken my hand as we sailed slowly across the lake. I felt a little like Auntie Lou's cat. Had I been Silas I would have started to purr.

"Connor…"

"Hmm?"

"This is lovely."

"It could be like this all the time, you know. Us, sailing together. Here, Hawaii, anywhere there's water and good weather."

"I can't imagine."

"Just say the word."

Say the word? That shut me up. No way am I going to say a single word that might make Connor think I'd go sailing off into the sunset with him.

After the *Lady* docked, Connor walked me home. The night was so hushed and perfect that it was easy to imagine that we were alone on the planet. At my door, he took my face in his hands and looked somberly into my eyes. "Thank you, Norah, for a lovely night. Next weekend?"

He took my astounded silence as a positive sign, pressed a gentle kiss on my forehead and glided like an apparition into the night.

I walked woodenly through my front door, past Bentley,

who was at the door with my bedroom slippers, hardly aware of my surroundings until a harsh voice accosted me.

"Feed me. I'm starving."

"You are not. I fed you before I left."

"I love you."

"Flattery will get you nowhere."

"Naughty girl," Asia Mynah scolded.

Without a second thought I dropped the cover over his cage. The last thing I needed tonight was a lecture from a bird.

I woke up Saturday morning feeling as guilty. I also felt as though my pillow and I had engaged in a fistfight and the pillow had won. Fortunately I'd arranged for Annie to watch the shop today. I was in no shape to deal with customers—two or four-footed or even finned.

Lord, what am I going to do? I'm in agony here. I had a dream date last night, yet I feel as though I betrayed my best friend. Lilly's in love and I'm the one who gets the guy. Where's the justice in that? I don't want to hurt anyone but my choice seems to be deciding who to hurt first!

I reached for my Bible, eager to find some word of wisdom to guide me. I can read the same verse in scripture over and over again and each time, depending on where I'm at in my life, it speaks to me in a different way. Today I Peter 3:8 jumped at me from the page: "*…have unity of spirit, sympathy, love for one another and a humble mind.*"

I may be reading between the lines, but this feels like a warning. If I'm being directed to seek unity of spirit, maybe that means there isn't going to be any unity for a while—not between Lilly, Connor and me, at least.

I splashed water on my face, pulled on a pair of shorts and a T-shirt and staggered to the Java Jockey for a triple espresso latte with sugared hazelnut flavoring and whole milk to desperately throw all the chemicals at my disposal into my system at once.

I sat on the terrace allowing the heat of the sun to seep through my shirt and warm me. Gradually the fuzzy feeling in my head and chest subsided. Unity, sympathy, love and humility, I kept repeating to myself. My watchwords for the day.

I might have dozed off if I hadn't felt warm, moist breathing down my back. Then the tinkle of Auntie Lou's sleigh bell on Sarge's halter clued me in as to who and what was behind me.

I turned slowly and came nose to muzzle with Sarge. He wobbled his lips in that way horses have, then yawned in my face. Evidently he'd not slept well last night, either.

"Good morning." Nick sounded amused at Sarge's and my silent dialogue.

If Sarge and I were tired, Nick was nauseatingly fresh and crisp-looking in his uniform. "You're out early," I muttered, sounding cross.

"There's a parade later this morning. Sarge and I are on duty in half an hour." He swung off the horse in a single graceful movement and I felt a twinge of jealousy. When I'd tried to dismount Cocoa, I'd tumbled clumsily into Nick's arms. If that horse boycotts me next time I try to ride her, I won't blame her a bit.

I've never been particularly attracted to men in uniform, but Nick looked appealing today. He was crisply pressed and spit-polished to a sheen. I, meanwhile, was masquerading as an unmade bed.

"A little overtired today?"

Why is it that men always notice me when my hair is electrified, my nose has a bright red blemish on the tip or I've put on my shoes in the dark of my closet and one is brown and the other black? I can work for hours to be a knockout and no one notices. Then I accidentally forget one little tiny thing—like untucking the hem of my skirt from my waistband or putting my sweater on backward and I get far more attention than I need.

"I got to bed later than usual, that's all." I didn't have time to comment further because Lilly and Joe walked out of the Java Jockey together and spotted us.

"Hey, what's up?"

Lilly peered at me, her brow wrinkled in concern. Even in jeans and a simple T-shirt, Lilly looks glamorous. Maybe it had something to do with the silver and rhinestone pendant earrings and three-inch silver heels with which she combined them.

"She's tired. Had a late night," Joe offered.

That started a barrage of questions and then led into their own evenings, the weather and what everyone had had for dinner.

I was not in the mood for a crowd and, after a few unintelligible grunts in response to questions, I hoped to take my leaded coffee and slip away somewhere to wait for it to kick in.

No such luck. The perky little steward from last night, already in her perky little uniform, prepared for some perky early-morning cruise, perked her way toward the door of the Java Jockey.

I slid down in my seat and tried to divert my gaze, but there is no force field that can divert perky.

"Hi! Norah! How are you this morning! It was so cool having you on the *Lady* last night!" Miss Perky talks in exclamation points. "Didn't you love the duck à l'orange? It's my favorite of all the things we serve! Very romantic, too! Well, see you!" And she perked her way into the coffee shop leaving pandemonium behind for me to clean up.

"Last night?" Joe began.

"The *Lady of the Lake*? Connor's boat?" Lilly demanded.

"Duck à l'orange?" Nick echoed. But Nick was the least of my problems.

"You didn't tell me you were going sailing on the *Lady* last night," Joe said. I could hear confusion and hurt in his tone. Not that he would have tried to stop me, but I could tell he would have appreciated being informed. I don't blame him, of course, but I thought he was going to be on board and that there was nothing to tell! Silly, deluded me.

Lilly looked positively wounded. She stared at me as if I'd taken a knife to her heart. Which, of course, I had. That it was completely unintentional wasn't counting for much at this moment.

"Who else was there?" The words cost her something to choke out, especially in front of Joe and Nick, but she obviously had to ask them.

"The crew—" I waved my hand in the direction of Miss Perky "—Connor, of course, and…" I waved my hand again, fluttering my fingers toward the universe hoping that she'd fill in the blank with the names of dozens of close friends.

"You were *alone* with Connor?"

"Of course not! I just told you…"

"The staff. Right." Lilly's expression clouded. Looking into her eyes, meteorologists would predict a massive cold front to come with snow to follow. "And you didn't tell me?"

"I thought you were all going to be there…." My voice sounded weak in my ears. Why wasn't this caffeine working? Why wasn't I being swallowed into the bowels of the earth? Why hadn't I decided to close the shop and take an extended pleasure trip to Siberia instead of getting up this morning and making my way here?

"I didn't get invited," Nick said helpfully. "Of course, I'm new here. I wouldn't expect to…."

"He didn't want us," Joe said slowly, "Apparently it was a private dinner."

"And maybe Norah is keeping other things from us, too." Lilly said the words slowly, with great gaps between each one, gaps big enough for me to fall into and be lost. She pushed away from the table. "If you'll excuse me, I have things to do this morning. And I don't have the excuse that I partied all night."

And, as Lilly does, she swept across the street and into The Fashion Diva and slammed the door behind her.

Joe, not so given to dramatics but obviously disturbed, stood up. "Guess I'd better get back to work, too." He glanced at me. "Come by later, Norah, if you want to talk."

To explain, you mean? Well, there's nothing to explain!

Nick, sweet and out of the loop, turned to me. "What's with them?"

"Got out on the wrong side of the bed? There's a lot of that going around."

"Obviously." He scratched Sarge beneath his headstall and made the bell tinkle. Then he looked me straight in the eye and said, "Connor's a lucky guy, Norah." And he turned and walked away.

One minute I had friends, the next I felt like a flea on a dog, a louse on a chicken, a tapeworm in a tummy. No one wanted me and it could be that some of them were willing to take active measures to stop me in my tracks.

I stumbled back home tired and teary-eyed. I *knew* I should have taken Bentley's recommendation and stayed in bed today.

Chapter Twenty-Two

❧

Lilly hasn't spoken to me in three days; Joe has been suspiciously absent from the Java Jockey; Nick has been doing crowd control for large events downtown; someone soaped several store windows along Pond Street and dumped the garbage cans upside down. And, to add insult to injury, Connor sent me roses again.

I'm just sick about Lilly. She obviously, and not without reason, feels betrayed by me and is steering clear. Not that I blame her. I feel like avoiding me myself. I don't know how I got into this mess but somehow I think I should have known better.

The only one who's really glad to see me lately is Auntie Lou.

"You're looking as blue as Elvis's shoe," she said as I walked into her upstairs apartment after work. She had tea steeping in a pot cuddled into a tea cozy, shortbread cookies on a plate and some egg salad and tomato sandwiches—a horrible combination but they are her favorite—at the ready.

"I feel like a leper. You and Bentley are the only ones talking to me and Bentley doesn't know English."

"There is a little good news," Auntie Lou said calmly as she poured me a cup of tea. "Matthew chapter eight, verse two."

"And that is…"

"*There was a leper who came to him and knelt before him, saying, "Lord, if you choose, you can make me clean."*"

"You're right, of course. This is one for God." I paused. "They all are, aren't they?"

"Lilly will have to run into you eventually. Then you can tell her what happened with Connor on the *Lady*."

"Nothing happened! Nothing."

"She doesn't know that, now does she?"

"Lou, she's been making a play for Connor, full throttle, and he's barely noticed. Can you imagine how she must feel? I'm sure she's embarrassed and humiliated. Poor Lilly." I couldn't even be angry with her for trusting me so little in the friendship department. The evidence against me was stacked pretty high.

"I know she won't listen to an old biddy like me, but I could tell her what a loyal friend you are." Auntie Lou gestured toward our little supper. "You keep coming back even when I feed you egg salad and tomato sandwiches. You don't seem to mind that there are decades between our birthdays or that you're pretty as a picture and I could break a mirror with my looks." She pushed the plate my way. "Sandwich?"

Silas entertained us after dinner with the fresh catnip mouse I'd brought him and it was after seven when I left Lou's building and noticed that the lights were still on in The Fashion Diva. That meant Lilly was either unpacking stock or doing paperwork. Impulsively, I followed my feet to her back door.

"Lilly? Are you here? It's me, Norah."

Her pale face appeared from around the corner of a clothing rack. "What is it?"

"I want to talk to you."

"There's nothing to talk about."

"I don't agree. Lilly, you have to listen to me."

"I don't *have* to do anything. I certainly don't want to hear how you betrayed me and stole Connor out from beneath my nose."

"I didn't do any such thing." *Unity, sympathy, love for one another and a humble mind.* "I didn't think I'd be alone with him. I thought there was a dinner party…"

"I expected more of you, Norah. You, of all people! You wouldn't have said anything at all if that woman hadn't spilled the beans when we were at the Java Jockey."

She caught my hesitation and misread it completely. "I thought so! What other things haven't you told me? How long has our friendship been on such a shaky foundation? Is our whole relationship a lie?"

"No, no, no! How can I make you understand…?"

"And you're the big 'Christian,' too!" She made annoying quotation marks in the air with her fingers. "Now I'm really getting to see a Christian in action. If that's what they do to their friends, then I certainly don't want to be one."

The kick I felt in my gut made me want to weep. "Don't

make this about being Christian, Lilly. I didn't do anything to intentionally hurt you or 'go after' a man you're interested in. It was a comedy of errors, nothing more. I have no control over Connor's feelings, emotions or actions. If I did, I'd make him madly in love with you."

"I don't need your help, thank you very much. I need you to step out of the picture."

"Gladly. I'm out. I've always been out. I had no idea…"

"Maybe it's a good thing this happened. You almost had me convinced that Christians were different from others— trying to do the right thing, loving their neighbors. It was a close call, Norah. You almost tricked me into believing it, but now I know you aren't any different from anybody else."

"Of course I'm not. That's the point about being Christian. We're as flawed as they come. It's through Christ we're forgiven for being so imperfect."

"I'm glad He can forgive you because it's going to be hard for me to forgive and forget. I thought you were my best friend. I don't see how you allowed all this to happen, knowing how I felt."

Me, either. That's the whole point. It shouldn't have happened. I didn't intend to take Connor away from Lilly. He was never hers to begin with but I didn't want to be the one to cause her heartache and yet I seem to be dealing it out in big doses.

"Don't confuse this with what it means to have faith in God, Lilly, please."

"How can I help it? You're the one who talks about God all the time…and now this." She turned away. "I need to go home, Norah. I'll lock the back door behind you."

I've never felt so helpless. *Lord, instead of being a good wit-*

ness for You, I've suddenly become Your worst worker in the
kingdom. I ask that You turn this around. Show me what I need
to do—or not do.

I walked home feeling both miserable and grateful. At
least God has the power to mend this shattered friendship.

"You look like you just lost your best friend."

My head snapped up and I saw Nick peering over the
hedge into my postage-stamp-size yard. I tossed my trowel
to the patio stones and waved him in. My garden isn't much,
but I enjoy it. I grow perennials like irises and lilies and fill
the gaps with annuals. This year I went overboard in the im-
patiens and begonia departments but I like the riot of color
around my wrough-iron table and chairs.

"How'd you know?"

Nick is so attractive that when we're apart I convince myself that I am mistaken, that no one can be that good-looking. Then I see him again and realize that, yes indeed, he is
so handsome that it should be illegal. And wouldn't that be
a fine predicament for a cop?

"I didn't mean it. It was supposed to be a joke. What's
wrong?"

I dropped into one of the wrough-iron chairs. "Do you
really want to know?"

"Of course."

Nick is the kind of straight-shooting guy who always
says what he means and means what he says. So if he wants
to know about my miserable life, I'm happy to tell him.

He remained quiet until I had exhausted my story. Every
time I think about this mess I feel depleted and helpless.

Then his silence began to annoy me.

"Aren't you going to say anything?"

"I'm trying to figure out what that might be, other than 'I'm sorry.'"

"Don't you have any brilliant suggestions?"

"Time?"

"I'm impatient, Nick. I want this fixed *now.*"

"Prayer?"

"Are you kidding? I haven't stopped."

"Patience?"

"You are no help whatsoever."

"See why I thought it was a good idea to be quiet?" He smiled a little and even though I didn't think I'd smile again for a very long time, the corners of my mouth twitched in response.

"Okay, so you're a smart man in a lose-lose situation. Thanks for listening."

"That I can do any time." He reached across the table and took my grubby hands in his clean ones. "I like listening to you, Norah. More than you might realize. You're a very special woman."

Whoa. Tingly feeling. Breathless. Blushing. Nice.

Then I felt tears come to my eyes. Just when I wanted to be appealing, I was going to look like an allergy sufferer before she takes whatever drug is touted on television. Just my luck.

"You're even beautiful when you cry."

That opened my waterworks. If he thought I was beautiful before, what must he think now? Red nosed and dazzling?

"Nick, I feel so terrible!"

"I see that."

"And there's nothing I can do."

"Obviously."

"And you keep sitting there agreeing with me. That's no help. Do something!"

"Okay." He stood up and pulled me to my feet after him. Then he cupped my cheeks in his hands and kissed me.

I suddenly felt wonderful all over. My condition improved even further when he gathered me into his arms.

I closed my eyes and felt his nonjudgmental, unconditional acceptance pour through me and I hung on for dear life. I laid my head on his chest and heard the steady thump of his heart. My body, which had been far more tense than I realized, began to relax.

He tucked me under his arm and we moved slowly toward the gliding swing on my deck. Then, before we got there, I felt him stiffen and heard the sharp intake of his breath. It's a quick jump from bliss to a bombshell.

"Nick?" I pulled away and was startled to see that he was white as a sheet. "What is it?"

His body was rigid. "What's that?" he said through gritted teeth.

I braced myself and turned to see what had caused that sort of response in him. All there was in front of me was my deck filled with flowers and Bentley leisurely licking one paw, his tail moving like a metronome on a piano teacher's baby grand.

"Did you see something? Out on the lake?"

"That." He lifted a finger and pointed toward Bentley.

The dog, sensing he was the object of speculation looked

up, saw Nick's pointing finger, took offense at it and growled.

Nick took two steps backward and nearly fell over a terra-cotta pot full of geraniums.

Bentley stood up to turn tail and run.

Nick moved to do the same.

"Hold it! Freeze!" I yelped, feeling like something out of a cop show.

Bentley dropped and rolled. I grabbed Nick to make sure he didn't do the same. Still, I couldn't prevent him from backing himself around to the front of my house and half-way out my front yard.

"Nick?"

"You didn't tell me you had a dog."

"I got him from the Humane Society. He's a sweetie, but he still has a few issues."

"What kind of 'issues'?" Nick sounded sharp as if he were chewing on glass.

"He's frightened of people and most everything else. He was abused as a puppy. Sometimes he's a little unpredictable…."

"You shouldn't own a dog that's unpredictable. He should be put down."

There are very few things that a person can say to me that will fuel my anger, but Nick just uttered one of them.

"Are you crazy? Bentley? He's the sweetest, most lovable, most gentle…"

"He's part pit bull, isn't he?"

"Who knows? My guess is Staffordshire terrier. They look a lot like the American pit bull. And he definitely has some bulldog and a little beagle because of that sweet face.

Pit bull? No matter how he looks, his personality is absolutely angelic... Nick?"

He was methodically stepping backward, forcing me to keep up with him until suddenly I found myself on the sidewalk.

"Sorry, Norah, but I don't like dogs."

"How could you not like..." I thought back. When had Nick ever stepped fully into my store? Certainly not when the mastiff puppies were in their cage up front. Come to think of it, he'd never been inside the store when there were dogs around at all. Had there been some connection I missed? "You really don't like dogs?" I blurted. "How can that be?"

"Sorry, Norah. I just don't." His color was returning but he still looked ghastly. There was a finality in his step that alarmed me.

"Nick, are you coming back?"

An emotion I defined as sadness washed across his features. "I can't. Not as long as you have that dog. I'm sorry, Norah, but that's just the way it is."

"But I'll always have Bentley!" I wailed.

He looked as though I'd kicked him in the gut. "Then I'll see you uptown." With that he spun around and strode up the street, a tall, athletic receding figure. I reached out my hand toward him but he didn't turn to look back.

Chapter Twenty-Three

❧

Now what?

Perplexed, I stared after Nick's retreating figure until I felt Bentley bump my ankle.

Bentley doesn't like the street, either. It's too noisy for his taste, so I was surprised that he'd ventured out to find me. I picked him up and held his stocky body close to mine. He laid his head on my shoulder and gave a contented sigh. How could anyone not like Bentley? And how could I like anyone who couldn't like him?

"He just doesn't know you, buddy, that's all. You shouldn't have growled at him even if you were scared. You'll charm him, won't you?"

The dog looked at me as if I were speaking a foreign language to him, which, of course I was.

When I got to the store the next morning, Annie was already there and fuming.

"Did you see Nick outside? Is he coming?"

"No. Is he supposed to?" He was the last person I needed to see right now. All night I'd dreamed that Nick was stealing Bentley from my apartment and I was chasing him, trying to discover where he was taking my dog.

"I called him." Annie held up a piece of broken glass. "Someone tried to break into the shop last night and I've got a hunch who it might be."

Before I had time to process that, the bell on the door rang and we looked up to see Nick standing in the doorway. His eyes darted from side to side and I recognized the behavior. It was how he'd always come into the shop, glancing at the kennels at the front of the store to see what they held. How had I missed it before now?

But I didn't have time for self-recrimination because Annie bolted past me waving the glass at Nick. He stood his ground as if crazed women with shards of glass attacked him daily. And yet he'd panicked at the sight of Bentley?

"It's that kid at the Toy Shop," Annie said flatly. "I've seen him snooping around here with his scuzzy-looking friends. He stops in sometimes and talks to Winky. I'd bet money that he was trying to steal him."

Break windows? Steal Winky?

"Annie, those are pretty strong words."

"He never comes in when you're here, Norah. I think he watches to make sure you're gone. Who else could it be?"

"Any number of people."

"And who of 'any number of people' would leave this?"

She pointed to the floor by the back door where a familiar leather wristband lay.

"Bryce?"

"His name is on it. Tell me that's a coincidence."

"Did you touch anything other than that glass?" Nick asked.

"No. Just the telephone, to call you."

"I'm going to get somebody in to see if we can pick up fingerprints."

I grabbed Annie by the arm. "Let's get out of here and let him work." It was a relief to get away from him to regroup. I felt uncomfortable in Nick's presence after last night. Surely it was all a misunderstanding.

Annie and I walked dazedly across the street and settled on the patio at the Java Jockey so we could watch the comings and goings at my store. Neither of us bothered to get coffee, so Joe and Lilly were surprised to see us when they came out of the building.

"What are *you* doing here?" Lilly asked, as if I were trespassing on Joe's property.

Apparently I wasn't even welcome to breathe Pond Street air anymore.

Fortunately Annie had no such sentiment. "Somebody broke into Norah's store and I think I have an idea who it is. They broke the window in the back door…"

I let Annie have the floor. I didn't want to talk. I doubt that if I were a camel, I'd be able to take one more straw before this spine of mine fractured. I saw shock and sympathy grow in Joe's and Lilly's eyes, but it changed nothing. Too many weird things had happened in the last few days. Even God, who I *know* is out there, has been silent.

Joe and Lilly were concerned and considerate but as help-less as Annie and me. The one thing that would have helped didn't happen. Lilly didn't tell me she no longer blamed me for her problems with Connor. That would cure a basket-ful of ills. If Lilly understood that I hadn't gone after Con-nor and if Nick liked dogs, life would be good....

Nick and dogs.... No one reacts to Bentley like that! It's like having a fear of powder puffs or feather pillows. But Nick had made it very clear that he disliked my dog. Un-fortunately I can't make Nick like Bentley any more than I can force Connor to fall in love with Lilly.

Nick finally came to talk to us.

"What did you find?" Joe asked.

"Not much. It's strange. There's not a fingerprint any-where, not even Norah's or Annie's. Wiped clean." Nick frowned. "I think you all should start taking extra precau-tions until we find who's doing this."

"Talk to that weird kid at the Toy Shop," Annie grumbled. "Norah, you need to take Winky home with you until this is settled."

Just when I thought things couldn't get worse I had to adopt Winky as a roommate? I almost started a pity party right there in the street.

"And that boy hangs out at Auntie Lou's Antiques. She lets him play the pinball machine," Annie continued. "We should warn her, too."

"Auntie Lou! Has anyone talked to her today?"

We began to stand, but Nick held up a hand. "Let me check on her."

"I have her spare key," I offered, holding up my key ring.

"Then you come with me. If someone's been around her place, we don't need any more people tramping around."

I was on my feet in a heartbeat.

She hadn't opened the front door of the shop. That isn't so unusual as to be worrisome, but I would rather have seen her in the back, puttering with the china or sitting in her rocker stroking Silas.

Nick strode around to the back of the shop. I found him there standing with his hands on his hips, staring at the disarray before him.

Every bit of garbage had been pulled out of the Dumpster and strewn around. Two galvanized tin trash cans had been stomped on until they were nearly flat and a garden hose was looped over the edge of the Dumpster where it had been left to run, making the ground behind the store a sodden mess.

"You'd better go around to the front. I'll get the guys to see if they can pick up any prints, but I doubt it will happen. Whoever is out causing mayhem doesn't want to be caught."

I opened the front door and made my way through the gloomy collection of old furniture and books to the stairs to Lou's apartment.

"Auntie Lou? It's Norah. I'm coming up."

Nick caught up with me as I reached the bedroom. I rapped on the door and heard a faint "come in."

"Hi, I'm sorry to barge in on you like this…Auntie Lou?"

She'd tried to get up. That was apparent by the tangle of blankets around her legs. Her alarm clock was on the floor, along with a now-empty glass of water. I hurried to her side.

"I can't believe this," she muttered, sounding irate and

anxious at the same time. "My legs aren't working properly. I should have stayed off that ladder yesterday."

I started to help her up but Nick stopped me. "Leave her, Norah. I'll call an ambulance."

"No need for an ambulance, young man. You just put that phone down."

He smiled at her with a gentle amusement. "Are you sure? Really sure?"

To my amazement, Auntie Lou backed down. "You're a silly boy even if you are a policeman. Go ahead, call. You'll see that I'm just fine."

"Thank you." And Nick began to dial.

"How did you do that?" I whispered as we waited for help to come. Auntie Lou did look terrible, but probably nothing that teeth, a wig and makeup wouldn't cure.

"Years of practice and irresistible charm."

"Of course, how could I miss it?" I know I have a hard time resisting him.

Within minutes paramedics were making their way up the stairs and set about moving Lou gently from bed to gurney. As they rolled her toward the door, she waggled a finger at me. "Take care of Silas and the shop. I won't be gone long and this smarty-pants young man will see he's not as clever as he thinks he is."

Then she shook that same finger at Nick as they moved her through the door and toward the stairs. "Then you can quit worrying about me so much."

"What did she mean?" I asked after the ambulance had pulled away.

"Oh, nothing," he said with a chuckle. "Although yesterday she did threaten to have a restraining order put on me if I didn't quit coming into the shop to check on her."

"You've been doing that?"

"I try to stop by during the day. I didn't like that fall of hers in the back room and I want to make sure she doesn't take a tumble like that again. I know you check on her, but I thought another pair of eyes couldn't hurt."

"That's very sweet of you." *Very sweet.* I even felt a little choked up to think that this man, new in town and a complete stranger, was watching out for Lou. Maybe it was my fragile emotional state, but it touched me so much that I wanted to cry.

Of course, everything makes me cry—the trouble with Lilly and Connor, the hurt looks Joe has been giving me, Nick's reaction to Bentley and now Auntie Lou. I feel like pulling a shade down over my face and hanging an Out To Lunch sign on my forehead. Anything to get away and think things through.

"Maybe I should follow Lou and see what's up," I suggested. "Annie can watch the store and I'll give Lou a ride home when the doctors prove that you had nothing to worry about."

"Fine. I'll finish downstairs. Want to meet later today and fill me in?"

I almost suggested we meet at my house. A little time with Bentley would change his mind about everything, but the words out of my mouth were, "I'll stop by your place about six."

"Burgers okay?" he asked, assuming I'd stay for dinner.

"I'll bring chips."

And that, I realized later, was a date. Apparently Nick thinks that liking me and hating my dog are two mutually exclusive sentiments. Little does he know....

By the time I got back to Nick's, I was so tired I could barely hold the sweating glass of lemonade he handed me.

"Long afternoon?"

"You have no idea. At the rate it took us to get to a doctor, do the necessary tests, consult with him, determine that Auntie Lou had to go back into the hospital and then convince her that she needed to be there... I love her, Nick, but Auntie Lou can try one's soul."

"I can imagine."

"Dr. Andrews didn't have much to say because the tests won't be back until tomorrow, but he looked very serious."

"And Lou?"

"Frankly, I thought she'd be more resistant. I think she's scared."

"And that makes you scared."

"Yes, it does. What if..."

"No need to go there," Nick said calmly. "The burgers are just about done. Want one?"

"I forgot the chips. I'm sorry. There was so much happening..."

"I figured you would, so I bought some. Sorry about the salads and baked beans but I bought them, too. Not enough time to make it all from scratch."

My life was falling apart and he was worrying about baked beans? I opened my mouth to say something and then shut it again. I'd told Nick about the rift between Lilly and me but he didn't realize how hurt Joe had been by my going on the boat with Connor. He didn't know that I'd promised to help Auntie Lou stay in her home as long as possible or that I was going to have to bring a trash-talking bird home to live with me. And then there was the Bentley thing. He had no idea how last night had shaken me.

I looked up to see him standing before me with burgers in one hand and the offending store-bought beans in the other.

Nick, you'll make someone a perfect husband.

I quickly reached for a burger to hide my distress.

That's a dangerous thought considering Nick's reaction to Bentley.

Chapter Twenty-Four

❧

"What's wrong, Norah?" Nick put his finger beneath my chin and lifted it gently. I thought of resisting, but I had to look at him sometime. It might as well be now.

"You've been staring out my window for twenty minutes."

"Nice garden." And it is. Nick's no slouch in that department, either. It also explains his calloused hands. He's been wielding a rake and a hoe.

"Not that nice. What's going on?"

"Nick." I mustered up my nerve. "What happened last night?"

"The business with Auntie Lou, you mean?"

"Not that. Later. With my dog."

He grew deathly still. "I didn't know you had a dog, that's all." He looked down at the floor. "I don't like dogs."

No kidding.

"You said he should be *put down,* that he was growling and aggressive."

"I wouldn't have an animal like that in the house."

"An animal 'like that'? What's that supposed to mean?"

"Dogs can be dangerous, Norah. You don't want to endanger yourself or your visitors."

"'Endanger?' Bentley? Nick, the only thing in danger from Bentley is his dinner! I've got a *rabbit* with more aggression than Bentley."

He had a very stubborn set to his finely shaped jaw. "I don't agree with you."

"Well, that's too bad, because you don't know my dog. He's the sweetest, most gentle, lovable animal on the planet."

"He growled at me. I don't call that lovable."

"You scared him!"

"I pointed a finger at him."

"Exactly. Bentley was abused. We are working through that. When a man, any man, raises a finger to him, he becomes terrified."

"And growls."

"It's his way of showing fear."

"The dog is part pit bull, Norah. Do you *know…*"

"I know the vet says he's Staffordshire terrier, beagle and a half dozen other things."

"You aren't being reasonable about this," Nick said with studied patience, the patronizing kind of patience that makes my skin crawl.

"Me? Not being reasonable? You came into my house, upset my dog and then said he should be destroyed. Nick, no one has ever insulted me so deeply."

Not even Lilly, but I didn't say that out loud. It wasn't until I'd started to express my frustration and upset with Nick that I realized how deep it went. "How could you?" I wanted to scream. Instead I did the adult thing—I crossed my arms over my chest and pouted.

"I don't want you hurt by that dog."

"You be careful, Nick. The only way I'll be hurt is if you keep threatening Bentley. I love him. He's one of my best friends." My *only* friend at the moment.

"Norah…"

"Thanks for dinner, Nick. And for help with Auntie Lou. I need to go now."

"Will you come back?"

"Not until you come to my house and get to know how loving and gentle my dog is."

His face hardened and for a moment he looked as though he'd been chiseled in granite. "That won't be for a long time."

We stood in a tense face-off. Finally, I turned and walked to the door. "Well, it's been nice knowing you, Nick. Have a nice life."

My knees shook all the way home and as soon as I got inside my front door I broke down in hysterical sobbing. Have a nice life? Did anyone ever really say that? What had made it come out of my mouth?

Bentley, of course. And there he stood. I knew he'd been waiting for me all evening, probably in that very position, with my bunny slippers in his mouth. I picked him up and held him like a baby and he sighed and rested his head against my chest.

"I can't believe this is happening to me, Bent. Me! Norah the diplomat, out to please the world. And now I have to choose between a man and a dog?"

Just as it occurred to me I might need to have my head examined, Bentley reached up with his tongue and began to gently lick away the tears streaming down my cheeks and collecting along my jawline.

Dog. I am definitely choosing the dog.

Lilly's curiosity outweighed her annoyance with me Wednesday morning as Joe and I sat on the terrace discussing Auntie Lou. It didn't hurt, either, that Connor was in the Java Jockey getting coffee. Nick, who watched me like I was a time bomb set to go off, also joined us even though I tried to give him a daggered look and scare him away. I'm not even sure what a daggered look is. My eyes are probably throwing penknives.

To appear uninterested in Nick's presence, I picked up the newspaper and began to skim the headlines. Nothing I read connected with my brain until my eyes fell on a unique but familiar name in the obituaries—Mazie Henderson. I skimmed the obit to find my fear confirmed. It was indeed Lou's friend who had passed away. An unexpected wash of sadness sluiced over me. It could easily have been Lou's obituary I was reading.

"How long will she be in the hospital?" Joe inquired.

"I don't know, but Dr. Andrews will probably tell us something today," I responded absently.

"Us?" Lilly said.

"Auntie Lou has asked me to be with her. She doesn't have any family, you know, so she really needs someone."

"She sure does," Connor chimed in, even though he barely knows Lou. "Good thing there are a lot of nice nursing homes in the area. Too bad, though. She runs a great antique shop. Shoreside will miss her."

"She's not going anywhere! Not if I can help it," I blurted, surprising everyone, including myself. Mazie's obituary burned in my brain. "You're all talking like she's practically dead."

"Isn't she?" Joe said.

This time I did feel daggers shooting from my eyes as I stared at Joe.

"Not like that, Norah, but how can she work? She lives alone above the store. If she can't lift, do stairs or take care of her personal needs, I don't see how she can…"

"You don't know anything about it," I said stubbornly. "I'm the one who has been at the hospital with her." They all stared at me as if I'd slipped a cog. "Well, I have."

"We don't doubt that, Norah," Joe said gently. "We're just being realistic. Lou's got to be eighty years old, at least. She's been running a business on Pond Street for more than fifty years. If she can't work, the store will either have to close or be sold. If she's not well, no one expects her to go up and down stairs. What else should we think?"

"That she's going to get better?" I suddenly felt very Pollyanna-ish. "Has anyone even considered that?"

They all looked at each other doubtfully, as if none of them knew what to say.

"It's a great thought, Norah, but not practical…" Lilly began.

"None of us has the right to decide for Auntie Lou," Joe admitted. "If she's well enough to come back to the store, I'll be the first one to encourage her."

"You might be giving her false hope," Lilly accused. "That's cruel, if she really can't come back to work."

Cruel? I stared at Lilly. Is that what she thinks I'm capable of now? Cruelty?

I looked up to see them all watching me, waiting for my next outburst. No way would I give them that satisfaction. I stood up to leave. "I'm sorry you all think that way. I don't believe we should give Auntie Lou's eulogy quite yet. I want to believe she'll be back to the store soon and I will do everything in my power to help her make that happen. I would hope that as *friends* of hers you'd all do the same." Then I did a Lilly and swept across the street to my store, more determined than ever to help Lou come home.

"What's shakin', baby?" Winky inquired as I entered.

"My fists, Winky. I'm so mad I could…I could…spit!"

Winky gave an impressed whistle.

"What's up, Norah?" Annie asked, looking alarmed. I'm not a volatile or demonstrably emotional person most of the time. I'd worried her, too.

When I told her about Lou and what her so-called friends had said, she murmured. "That's terrible. I'm so sorry for Lou. She's such a sweetie." Annie paused. "But what if they're right, Norah? What if she can't come back? What then?"

Et tu, Annie?

"Let's cross that bridge when we come to it, shall we?"

"You're right, Norah. Just like you always are."

Yeah, right. That's why everyone is jumping to agree with me on everything I say and do these days.

"Listen, Annie, since you're here this morning, I think I'll run over to the hospital and check on Lou."

"Go ahead, I'll hold down the fort…the Ark, I mean."

I escaped out the door and jogged home to get my car without seeing any of my traitorous friends.

"Lord," I prayed aloud as I waited at a stoplight near the hospital, "help me. I've antagonized or hurt everyone I care about and I still don't quite understand how it all happened. Lilly, Connor, Joe, Annie…and Nick. They all think I'm losing it. Maybe I am. Guide me, will You? Give me the wisdom I don't have on my own. Show me what I am to do in all of this. Oh, and could You help Nick and Bentley become friends?"

When the light turned green and I pulled into the intersection, I noticed the driver to my left staring at me. Oh, great. He must have seen me talking out loud to my Invisible Friend. Now he thinks I'm crazy, too, even though talking to God is the only smart thing I've managed to do lately.

A nurse's aide scurried out of Auntie Lou's room just as I exited the elevator. I caught up with her in the hallway. "Is everything okay with Lou?"

The aide's eyes grew wide. "She's a very strong-willed woman, isn't she?"

I couldn't help laughing. "You could say that. It's what's kept her going all these years."

"Yes, well, it's still keeping her going."

"And that means…" I encouraged.

The aide waved a hand in the direction of the door. "Dr. Andrews is with her. Maybe you'd like to talk to him."

"Right…"

Chase Andrews was leaning against the windowsill, a chart under his arm. He, at least, didn't look ruffled by Auntie Lou.

Lou looked very small in her bed and her eyes were teary. "Lou?"

"Talk to him, Norah. You tell him." She pointed a finger at Dr. Andrews.

"Tell him what?"

"What Lou would like you to tell me," he said with a sigh, "is that Lou's home is handicapped-accessible, that she is able to be at home alone, that her store needs her and that you will make sure she's taken care of."

I stared, wide-eyed, first at Dr. Andrews and then at Auntie Lou.

"But you live on the second floor of the building," I reminded her.

I knew immediately that I had not said the right thing. Lou's shoulders drooped and she looked, if possible, more disconsolate than ever.

The doctor studied her with a single raised eyebrow.

Then Lou's fighting spirit kicked in again. "But I have an elevator!"

That surprised me as much as it did Dr. Andrews.

"Haven't used it in a few years, of course, but it goes from the basement to the second floor. The fellow who owned the building before me needed a freight elevator because he stored things on the second floor. When I had the furnace checked, the technician commented that the elevator was in good shape." Lou bobbed her head as if to punctuate her announcement.

Dr. Andrews turned to me. "Lou suffered another mild stroke. A transient ischemic attack, actually, which is also called a TIA. The symptoms are usually temporary and there don't seem to be any significant complications in Lou's case. She had some moments of confusion, slurred speech, dizziness and weakness in her hands. That is already subsiding although I've ordered physical therapy for her. She's on medication to prevent blood clots which will reduce the chances of future blockages.

"A TIA is often a warning sign for a major stroke to come. In Lou's case, we were fortunate. This gives us time to prevent a subsequent episode. Next time she might not be so lucky."

The medical words were spinning in my head. "So now what?"

"We've already got her on proper medications. Some rest, some physical therapy…"

"…and I can go home!"

"But Auntie Lou…" I began. Then I saw the look in her eyes and recalled the day we'd talked about just such things. She'd talked about her friend Mazie and how Mazie's children were forcing her out of her home. I'd told her I would help her stay at Auntie Lou's Antiques. I'd *promised*.

"Lou should be able to go home in a few days if, that is, there is a home to go to."

A loud snort came from the middle of the bed. "Of course there's a home!

"Barney can fix up the elevator. He's good at anything mechanical. All I really need is food supplies, a telephone and someone to stop in and check on me occasionally. You'll do that, won't you, Norah?"

"I can." My mind raced but my tongue was still in neutral.

"See?" Lou looked triumphantly at the doctor.

"You have a business of your own to run." He studied me with a clinical eye. "Are you sure you can do this? There are several very nice convalescent homes in the area that would be excellent places for Lou to recover."

"You'll have to tie me up and drag me there," Lou threatened. "I'd probably have another stroke at the front door."

She was likely telling the truth. Her color had risen unnaturally even during the conversation.

"Don't get upset, Auntie Lou, we'll work something out." As I said it, two hugely conflicting emotions descended upon me. One was the enormous weight of responsibility I'd just shouldered. The other was a lightness and peacefulness I hadn't expected. *"…learn to do good; seek justice, rescue the oppressed, defend the orphan, plead for the widow."* Isaiah 1:17

"Okay, Lord, if it's Your will then it's mine, but I'm going to need Your assistance with this."

Chapter Twenty-Five

✣

Exhausted, I was thankful to get home to Hoppy, Bentley and Asia who greeted me with a chorus of thumps, yips and squawks. I'd barely had time to scavenge the refrigerator for a snack and share a few carrot sticks with Bentley, who had learned to eat vegetables during one of my dieting frenzies, when the doorbell rang.

"And Nick thinks you're dangerous and might bite him. He doesn't even know you're a vegetarian," I told the dog. "Stay." Not that there was any danger he was going to move. He had half the couch to himself.

I don't know who I expected to be on the other side of the door, but it wasn't Julie Morris.

"Norah, am I bothering you?"

"No, come in." I held the door wide.

She walked into my living room clinging to a small purse with both hands, as though she were protecting it from a street mugger. Every fiber of her body radiated tension. She reminded me of a rubber band stretched to its max and on the verge of snapping.

"Carrot stick?" I offered. "I've got sodas in the kitchen."

"No food, thanks. I'm not very hungry." She perched on the edge of a chair like a butterfly, ready to take flight.

"Chocolate, then." I pushed a bowl her way. "If you need a kiss and can't get them anywhere else, you can always come to my candy dish. I do that quite often myself."

She smiled faintly and took some chocolate. I waited until a piece was melting on her tongue to ask, "How can I help you, Julie? Or is this a social visit?"

Of course I knew it wasn't, but how else was I to start a conversation with a woman desperately swishing the chocolate around in her mouth to comfort herself.

"I don't know anyone on Pond Street very well," Julie began. "I've tried to meet people, having the tea party and all, but these things take time." She looked at me appraisingly. "You've been very friendly to me, and kind."

"I'm flattered that you felt comfortable coming here today." My urge was to take this poor, trembling woman into my arms and tell her everything was going to be all right, but I didn't know what the "everything" might be. As I'd been reminded of so much lately, life offers no guarantees.

"You're a Christian, I think."

"Yes, I am, but how…" The subject had never come up in our brief encounters.

"By the way you are, your being. You seem so genuinely happy and caring. I had a Christian friend once who was like you. But she's so far away…"

Oh, I thought, I was wrong. There is one guarantee in life, God's faithfulness.

"Thank you, Julie. I try to live my life so that my faith shows, but I'm never sure if it's working or not."

"Oh, it's working, all right. It brought me here, didn't it?" Her face was so pinched and pale I was afraid she might faint.

"The police were at our store today. They wanted to talk to us about Bryce. We had such high hopes for this move but apparently his problems have followed us here."

"Problems?" Other than his hair and wardrobe, no doubt.

"Bryce ran with a bad group at our former home. There was a ringleader of sorts, a boy named Anthony. Anyway, Bryce wanted to be part of a group so he did everything Tony told him to do."

She looked up from the floor where she'd been staring. "When Bryce was small, he was very quiet. He loved games and reading. He spent a great deal of time with his grandparents before they passed away and he was so good to them. We never dreamed that a child could change as much as Bryce changed after his grandmother died. He was lonely, I suppose, and then Tony and his teenage thugs came along.

"The first week he started hanging out with Tony, we had the police on our doorstep. They'd been caught letting air out of tires in a car dealership. Fifty of them."

Gotta give the kid credit. He doesn't do things halfway.

"It's been a string of social workers, court dates and counselors ever since. My husband and I believed all along that what Bryce needed most was to get away from Tony. That's why we moved." A sob caught in her throat. "And now this."

"This?"'"

"There's been vandalism on Pond Street and Bryce is their prime suspect."

I noticed Bentley get up from the couch and move toward Julie's chair.

"Do you think he did it?"

"He says he didn't, but what else is there to believe?"

"Does he lie to you?" A funny question to ask, but it popped out of my mouth before I could think about it.

"Remarkably, no. Sometimes he refuses to speak or to answer questions, but he's never actually lied to us when pressed. His grandfather used to tell him liars were 'lower than thieves' and Bryce took it to heart." A choking laugh bubbled up in her throat. "A teenage vandal who doesn't lie. Quite a paradox, my son." She drew a shaky breath.

"He loves animals, Norah. Adores them. You and Bryce have more in common than anyone else I know here. He talks about your parrot all the time. Maybe you could draw him out..." Then she choked back a sob. "Forgive me. It's a ridiculous idea. I'm just so desperate, I'll do or try anything. I had no right to come here and bother you."

He pulled out Winky's feathers! my logical mind screamed, but my heart—the part that usually gets me into trouble—said, *Why not try?*

"What do you want me to say to him?"

"I have no idea. It was a stupid request. I, oh!" Julie

looked down as Bentley put his front paws on her thigh and began to gently lick the top of her hand. It was as if he were saying, "Don't cry, please don't cry."

"What a sweet animal!" Julie stroked his head with her free hand. "So loving."

And so misunderstood, I mused, thinking of Nick's reaction to him. Suddenly, I made up my mind. I saw the beautiful side of Bentley but Nick only saw his surface, his stocky body and jug-shaped head. Was that so much different from what was happening with Bryce? Although Annie had pegged him as a troublemaker right away and we'd all concurred, his mother believed that his heart could still be reached.

Why get involved? Why bother? Obviously the kid is messed up. Then the answer came. *Because he's one of Mine.* And with that, every nurturing, do-gooder, compassionate cell in my body rose up to be counted.

"Oh, why not?" Hardly the gracious answer that should have come out of my mouth, but it was enough for Julie.

"You have no idea how much that means to me. I'd do anything to help my son. I remember the Bryce I knew before Tony."

"Does he see Tony now?"

"Once that we know of. Tony came over on a motorcycle. Bryce said they walked up and down Pond Street and stopped in the shops. We told him it wasn't to happen again and forbade Tony from coming back. Once or twice I think I've seen him in the neighborhood with other boys."

I recalled the day, the day Winky lost his feathers. My chest tightened and my fury was fueled at the idea of having a creature of mine treated that way.

"Julie, is Officer Nick handling this?"

"No, it's the juvenile division who is in charge."

"What if he talked to Bryce?"

"Do you think he would?"

I abruptly wished Nick and I were on better terms. "I could ask him. He was in the narcotics division once. He knows the effects of keeping bad company. Maybe he can talk some sense into Bryce."

If Nick is speaking to me, that is. Keeping a vicious beast like Bentley might have made Nick cross me off his list of acceptable company.

Hope flickered on her features and Bentley, sensing the change, quit licking her hand.

When Julie stood up to go, she flung her arms around me. "Thank you, thank you, thank you. You have no idea what this means to me. You, Officer Nick—" she looked down at the floor where Bentley sat by her feet "—and your remarkable dog. I feel more reassured now than I have in days."

After she'd gone, Bentley and I stared at each other. "Well, doggy, apparently we are the next best thing to comfort food. Can you tell me how we're going to handle this?"

Unfortunately, Bryce and his mother were driven to the back of my mind by Auntie Lou.

I had until Monday, according to Dr. Andrews, to make it possible for Lou to be back in her apartment. He couldn't keep her in the hospital any longer than that. Lou had held my hand tightly and patted it, saying, "My girl, my dear girl," over and over again until I felt breathless and had to escape.

Outside, I tried to gather my wits about me by giving myself a good talking-to. "Okay, Norah, you've gone and done it now. It's one thing to rescue dogs, parrots, cats and hamsters, not to mention goldfish from centerpieces, it's quite another to try and rescue Auntie Lou…"

But I'd *promised*. She deserved a chance to return to the home she loved.

When I got home, I called Annie and asked her to work for me every free minute she could for the next two weeks. Then I called Barney and arranged a time to meet him at the antique store to tinker with the elevator. I sketched out a grocery list of Auntie Lou's favorite foods, ones she could eat without having to turn on the stove like canned fruits, cereal and sardines. I gag at the thought of sardines, but Lou says they make a great sardine and tomato sandwich. For Auntie Lou, a slice of tomato enhances everything it touches. It was simple enough to arrange for the market and the milkman to deliver and hire a cleaning service to come in and go over everything before Lou returned home and then to dust and do bathrooms every couple weeks.

After that, I called my pastor and put Lou on the church shut-ins list to ensure she'd be getting company, casseroles and prayer regularly. Dr. Andrews had given me the name of home health care people and a physical therapist was scheduled to come out after Lou returned to her home.

By evening, I had done everything I could think of to make it possible for Lou to function out of her home. That was the easy part.

The hard part was yet to come—telling Joe, Lilly, Connor and Nick what I'd done.

Chapter Twenty-Six

❧

"You did what?" Joe asked through gritted teeth, his face flushed pink beneath his tan. "Norah, do you realize how much responsibility you've taken on? What are you thinking?"

"You could just look in on her once in a while. If everyone did, she'd be fine. I have everything else set up. All Lou needs is a little company occasionally." At least I hope that is how it will work out.

"You took a lot for granted assuming that we'd all 'pitch in' and do a turn with Auntie Lou."

Joe, until recently, has never been short-tempered with me. In the last week or two, however, he's been irritated with everything that came out of my mouth. I've noticed Lilly going to the Java Jockey more often and staying longer than usual. She's probably shared her suspicions, both real and imagined, with him. If that's the case, he's getting an earful about the incident with Connor.

"I'm sorry. I really can only speak for myself. I shouldn't have dragged you into this."

Joe ran his fingers through his hair. "Norah, you know I'm happy to visit with Lou. It's not that. It's that you should never have encouraged her to come back here. What if she gets sick in the night? What if she falls? She's old, Norah, she could die in there!"

I looked him straight in the eye. "She's not afraid of dying, Joe. She knows where she's going and looking forward to it. She *is* afraid of not having a chance to get well and remain in her own home."

He didn't seem to hear. "Maybe the stroke did something to her mind. Who knows if she's rational enough to make such a decision?"

"She made it before the stroke. She asked me if I'd help her in case something like this happened."

"Maybe she wasn't quite right even then."

How had I missed this thickheadedness of his until now? "If her doctor isn't concerned, why should you be?"

He looked at me and smiled condescendingly. "I guess I shouldn't say anything, Norah. Part of what I like about you is your compassion. I just never thought you'd try to rescue people like you do animals."

That comment stuck with me like a bur. Why wouldn't he think I'd make every attempt to rescue Auntie Lou or anyone else who needed help? I wasn't angry about the remark, but felt instead the heavy burden of disappointment.

Even Lilly, who wasn't speaking to me unless it was absolutely necessary, deemed the news worthy of comment.

"Why'd you help her get home, Norah? You should know better. That's no place for her. She needs to be in a facility for people like her."

Like her? I'm not quite sure what people like Auntie Lou are, considering she's one of a kind.

"It's not your business, Norah," Lilly concluded coolly. "And unlike you, I don't interfere with other's lives."

And don't steal other people's men. I helped Lilly fill in the blank of what she'd left unsaid.

I miss Lilly terribly. She's here, but she's not here, not for me. The only persona she's used with me lately is ice queen, and it hurts. No more shared lunches, movies or quick chats in front of our stores. No more late-night pizzas and certainly no more drop-ins to talk and make banana splits. I'm beginning to realize that, having put all my time and energy into my business, Lilly is the only friend with whom I've really stayed in touch. That leaves Bentley, Hoppy and the birds to hang out with. Such is the pathetic state of my social life.

Connor, the one person I could count on to stop by, has, fortunately, been out of town. Having him on my doorstep just pours gasoline on the fire with Lilly.

"Maybe," I said to Bentley, "I *should* date Connor. He's handsome and sweet, and Lilly hates me anyway."

Bentley didn't even acknowledge the statement. Smart dog. He knows a lie when he hears it. As much as I like Connor, he doesn't make me hear bells.

Even Nick has been lying low since discovering Bentley.

I buried my nose in the dog's fur as I recalled Nick's re-action to Bentley, the horrified look, the backing away....

I went to the refrigerator and got out the ice cream. I had three scoops already in a bowl when I realized that I wasn't even hungry. I thought I'd already hit the bottom of the barrel emo-tionally but not being hungry for ice cream told me that I was no longer at the bottom of the barrel—I was under it.

The hole I'm in is definitely getting deeper.

"That cleaning lady has to go!" Auntie Lou announced the moment I walked into her apartment on Wednesday. She was ensconced in her favorite rocker with a television re-mote, cell phone and Palm Pilot. With that equipment, Lou could rule the world and never leave her chair.

The only world she has been trying to rule, unfortu-nately, is mine.

"We need her, Lou. I don't have time to keep your place clean and dust the shop." I kicked off my sandals so that I wouldn't tread on the newly washed floors.

"Then find someone who doesn't have fingers like sau-sages! She nearly broke three of my vintage china tea cups. The Staffordshire with the old English peonies on it, the blue asters and the Bavarian Vohenstraub with the yellow roses! The entire shelf shook and I shook right along with it."

Auntie Lou is a china expert and the pieces she keeps in her apartment she treats like children. The only thing the cleaning lady could have done to offend her more was to start ripping apart one of Lou's antique quilts to use for dust rags.

"I'll talk to the service. They can send someone else out."

"Everyone's incompetent these days," Lou muttered into her frilly-collared bathrobe. "That physical therapist who comes, what a snippy little thing she is. Next she's going to ask me to put my heels on my head and do a dance on my fingertips. Never dealt with someone so unreasonable."

"Dr. Andrews says you're improving remarkably. She must be doing something right." The smile on my face was beginning to crack.

"That young pup says I can't go back to the shop yet," Lou snorted. "Doesn't he know that would be the best medicine for me? I tell you, Norah, I'm going to go crazy if I have to sit here like a frog glued to a lily pad much longer."

Me, too, Auntie Lou, me, too.

And the mention of a lily pad only reminded me of Lilly. Though she and Joe stop in occasionally to see Lou, neither has offered to give me a break from the daily grind of checking on her.

"Don't be a goose," I told myself. "Everything is fine."

Then I stepped, barefoot, onto a hair ball that Silas had conveniently retched up on the kitchen floor. It was the hair ball that broke the camel's back.

I raced out of Auntie Lou's without another word. I couldn't speak. I couldn't even hold back my tears.

I ran toward home so fast that I didn't notice Nick filling his car at Barney's Gas.

I flung myself onto my porch swing and finally let go of all the frustration that had been building over the past weeks. Everything I did went wrong. I'd alienated my best friend, distanced myself from the men in my life, even chased Nick off for the sake of a dog. I'd still not talked to

Bryce as Julie had requested and Auntie Lou seemed more miserable, rather than less, being at home in her apartment.

Plus, an entire tank of rescued goldfish had come down with fin rot, Winky and Asia Mynah were driving me crazy with their stupid bird conversations, Hoppy seemed listless and I'd switched brands of dog food for Bentley and given him more gas than Barney had at his station.

I'd worked myself up into a good sobbing, hiccuping, belching, red-nosed, red-eyed, puffy-faced cry when I felt a hand on my shoulder.

So I did the logical thing. I screamed. Not one of those little "Eeek, you startled me" screams but a full-on, bloody-murder-type scream that can crack glass and break eardrums. The next reasonable thing I did was fall off the swing.

And that's the last I remembered until I woke up in Nick's arms with a small bagful of ice on my head. The patio stone beneath me was hard and cool and I could feel the rise and fall of his broad chest as my cheek lay against it. I looked up at him and hiccuped.

The face that looked down at me was ruggedly handsome and immensely concerned. His brow was furrowed and, in my addled state, I lifted a finger and tried to scrub out the creases. Then I let my finger drift down his nose, across his cheek and along the line of his jaw. The furrows of concern relaxed but his blue eyes were wide and I noticed little flecks of inky navy in them that I hadn't noticed before.

That realization bumped into the fogginess in my brain and cleared away a little of the mist. Only then did I think that perhaps I shouldn't enjoy being held in his arms quite this much. Especially since he hated Bentley.

Bentley! I started to struggle. How had he gotten into my house to get ice without going by Bentley?

"Hold still, will you? You need to keep this ice in place or you're going to raise a huge bump on your head. When I touched you I had no idea that you'd jump so high you'd fall out of the swing. Nervous little thing, aren't you?"

"Only when I'm sobbing my heart out and someone grabs me. If I don't think I'm being attacked, I usually stay in place." I touched the ice bag on my head. "How'd you get the ice?"

"Your deck door was open. That's very careless, you know. Anybody could have walked into the house."

"It appears 'anyone' did. How'd you get past Bentley?"

Nick frowned. "I forgot about him. I saw you lying there and he was nowhere to be seen."

"Hiding from you, probably. He's scared of people. You were in more danger of being attacked by the rabbit."

"Those two birds screamed at me, if that's any help. One kept yelling, 'Gimme a kiss' and the other one whistled and screeched, 'Nice buns.'"

"That would be Winky," I sighed. "Do you want to help me up? I'd better go in and find my dog. He's probably cowering under the bed right now."

Nick frowned.

"And don't you dare say anything about how dangerous he is. You've seen for yourself what a threat he is to humanity. Want to come inside?"

"I'm sorry, Norah, but no matter what you say, I don't trust that dog."

Unexpectedly tears sprang to my eyes again and leaked down my cheeks.

"Norah?"

"Couldn't you at least *try*? How much could it hurt? Then at least something would be going right."

He brushed the wild curls away from my face. "Something? Does that mean that nothing is going right now?"

"You might say that." I started to struggle again and this time he helped me to my feet. But instead of allowing me to go inside, he guided me back into the swing and sat down beside me.

"Want to talk about it?"

He surprised me so much that my jaw dropped open. "You want to listen?"

"I think I'd better. You were crying awfully hard when you ran past me."

I dug in my pocket for a tissue but came up with only a little lint and a dime. Nick pulled a pristine white handkerchief out of his pocket and handed it over. I mopped up a bit and turned away from my reflection in the glass patio door. Better not to know, I decided, or I'd go looking for a paper bag to put over my head.

"Everything is messed up and everyone is mad at me. I didn't do anything to start any of this and now I'm a pariah on Pond Street."

"The Pariah on Pond Street. Good movie title."

"It's serious, Nick."

Once I started talking, I couldn't seem to stop—not when I fessed up to Connor's advances, not even when I told him that Joe is waiting for me to agree to marry him. I even blathered out everything about my discussion with Julie Morris about Bryce and how she'd asked me to talk to the boy.

"But, what makes me think I can straighten him out? I've mucked up my own life. Even Lou is upset with me!"

"She adores you."

"She doesn't like the people I've hired, she's sick of not being at work and is generally sour as an old pickle."

"That, at least, is good news," Nick commented with a small smile on his face.

"Good news? Then a city-wide breakout of poison ivy would be *great* news."

"It means she's feeling better. People who are very ill don't have the energy to be crabby."

"I hadn't thought about it that way," I admitted, feeling somewhat mollified.

"See?" He lifted my chin with his finger and forced me to look into those unfathomable eyes. "It's all in your perspective."

"My perspective is warped and with good reason."

"Momentarily. You'll snap back." He was so confident I almost believed him.

"I don't know about that, Nick. Lilly is livid, even though she's trying to hold her tongue. Joe's getting fed up…." More tears leaked down my cheeks. "And my fish have fin rot."

"Better them than your friends," he suggested and I felt a bubble of laughter rise within me.

"Julie Morris is depending on me."

"Sounds to me like you've got too many people depending on you rather than on themselves. Let me do a little checking on this Bryce Morris thing. I turned it all over to juvenile so I don't know what they've come up with. Wait a day or so before you try to visit with him."

"Gladly." I sighed. "I wish I could find something to take my mind off this for a few minutes."

"How about this?" And before I realized what he was doing, Nick took my face in his hands and kissed me.

When we broke apart I was blinking rapidly. "Well, that worked. For a minute there, I couldn't remember any of my troubles or even my own name."

"Doctor Nick, that's me," he said softly. "Maybe you need another treatment...."

Chapter Twenty-Seven

❧

When I faced Joe the next morning, I felt guilty, as if I'd been disloyal. Though I've made him no promises, I do love him. I'm just not sure it has matured into the marrying kind of love—yet. Actually I'm not sure of anything other than God knows what's going on and He'll tell me what I need to know. Besides, Nick had sought *me* out. I wasn't wantonly attempting to attract men like Nick and Connor. They just appeared. Is that my fault? Can I be blamed that I fell on my head and allowed Nick to kiss me?

"What's up?" Joe shoved a caramel latte across the counter to me. "You look worn out."

I resisted saying, "You should have seen me yesterday." After Nick had gone, I had floated into my bathroom feeling quite lovely. Then I'd glimpsed myself in the mirror. Red, blotchy, nose raw from blowing, eyes puffy and bloodshot, lips chapped, hair full of static electricity…no, today I looked good. Yesterday I could have scared the green off grass.

And Nick had still kissed me. Wonder of wonders.

"I hate to bother you, but I need a little help with something." I mustered up my courage, knowing how Joe felt about my bringing home Lou in the first place. "I want to use the freight elevator at Auntie Lou's Antiques and I don't want to do it alone the first time. Barney checked it out but I'm not sure what I'd do if I got myself stuck between floors."

"Norah, you know what I said. This is too much for you."

"Come and help me just this one time, won't you?"

Much to my relief, he came around the counter and took my hand. "What am I going to do with you? You're an incorrigible knightess-in-shining-armor, rescuing everything and everyone you come across."

"I've never heard of a 'knightess' before." I snuggled closer to him and he tucked me in the curve of his arm.

"Neither had I until I met you."

Twenty-five sweaty minutes later, Joe and I were sitting on the floor of the freight elevator staring helplessly at one another.

"You're never going to be able to take this elevator up and down alone. It's not easy to work the ropes and pulleys. You need more strength than you have." Joe rolled his eyes. "I can imagine you and Lou stranded between floors."

"I'll bring food for the trip. And a cell phone."

"Seriously, this isn't a one-person job and I can't promise I'll be around all the time to help you."

"I'm not asking you that. Don't worry about it. And thanks for oiling those thingamabobs and whatsits."

"You're going to have to give this up."

"Says who?" The little streak of Irish in my background popped up in the form of good old temper.

"Okay, then. Find out for yourself. I just don't want you to kill yourself in the process. Auntie Lou needs to be in a nursing home, not here."

"Dr. Andrews says it's fine," I said stubbornly.

"Then have him come and work this elevator." Joe got to his feet and held out a hand to me. "Coming?"

"No. I plan to sit here a while and pout."

"Suit yourself. I've got to get back to work." He walked through the open elevator door to the first floor of Auntie Lou's shop. When he turned around, his eyes were anxious and his expression sad. "You've been different the last few weeks. I miss the old Norah." Then he walked away.

"The old Norah?" I felt like pulling my hair out of my head. I was exactly the same Norah I'd always been. It was everyone else who'd gone crazy.

It felt good to sit in the old elevator. The silence was deafening and no one would think to look for me here. As I quieted myself, I began to pray.

Lord, here we are again. Me, looking for answers and You, having them. What am I supposed to do? I thought You wanted me to bring Lou home but now.... A wave of tiredness overtook me and impulsively I curled up on the wooden floor and closed my eyes. I'd rest just a minute. Then I'd figure out how to move Auntie Lou around.

How had I gotten inside the television set?

I peered out from behind the screen. Bryce Morris was there, wielding a joystick and making me leap and run with a barely perceptible move of his hand. I was dodging to the right and to the left, jumping over obstacles and crawling through caves. What on earth…

I awoke with a yelp. I'd fallen asleep and dreamed I was inside a video game being played by Bryce. Sucking my finger, the one I'd just jammed a sliver into, I got to my feet wondering what kind of answer to prayer that was?

The Bed and Biscuit is slowest on weekdays. Other than a dog named Daisy who is here so often that she thinks she owns the place and a kitten determined to shred everything in sight including my skin, the B and B was empty. As I sanitized kennels and washed bedding in the old washer I keep in the back for that purpose, I couldn't get my mind off that dream. What did video games have to do with anything? What even made me think of them?

Or, I mused, as I threw the last of the bedding into the dryer, maybe the video game meant nothing. Maybe it was Bryce I should be thinking about.

And the proverbial lightbulb came on in my head.

Although Nick hadn't gotten back to me yet on Bryce's legal status, that didn't stop me from walking to the Toy Store.

Bryce was alone in the back room playing, what else? a video game.

"Your mom or dad around?"

"Dad will be back in a minute. He went to get a haircut

at Belles & Beaus." The boy looked at me curiously. He's an odd combination of vulnerable and tough, rude and thoughtful. "Do you want something?"

"Actually, I want to talk to you. You've been working at the store a lot lately."

"Kept under my parents' thumbs, you mean?" A flash of anger sparked in his eyes. "I didn't do anything. I didn't mess with the mail or the garbage or any of that stuff, but no one will believe me."

I felt a flicker of sympathy for him. We're in similar situations, Bryce and I. I didn't mess with Connor but nobody believes me, either.

"Auntie Lou has faith in you. I told her what happened and she says she doesn't think you'd do that kind of thing."

"Really? She's a cool old lady."

"That she is. She seems to like you." *Cool old lady* is high praise from a boy wearing more chains than a prison gang.

"She lets me play her pinball machine. I wish her store wasn't closed. Is she going to open it again soon?"

"She'd like to get downstairs for a couple hours every day, but I don't want her hiking up and down the stairs from her apartment to the store. I've got an idea that might work, but I'll need your help."

"Mine?"

"There's an old freight elevator in the building. If Auntie Lou could ride up and down stairs in that, she could at least sit in a rocker and mind the store awhile. If you'd help me, we can make it happen."

He looked disbelieving.

I was skeptical myself. Today his hair was tipped a magenta color that matched a fire-breathing transformer-type creature on his T-shirt.

"I can't work the elevator alone," I continued. "I'm not strong enough. Besides, I can't run back and forth all day making sure she's okay. I thought perhaps I could hire you to put her in the elevator, take her down to the shop and play pinball for a couple hours while she visits with customers. Then you could take her upstairs again. She can't pay you much, but…"

"Play pinball and hang out with Lou?" There was genuine excitement in the boy's voice. "You don't have to pay me to do that!"

And that was how a potential juvenile delinquent, a lady so old she insists that her first church was in the catacombs and I came to be working the freight elevator at Auntie Lou's Antiques.

Lou clapped her hands together as Bryce and I wrestled the elevator to a stop and opened the door. Then she grabbed my hands and held them so tightly that I made a note to tell the physical therapist that Lou had gotten her strength back.

"Norah, you don't know what this means to me."

"I'm sure it feels good to be back here. Look, Silas is happy, too." The big cat shot out of the elevator and headed for his favorite rocker.

"Without you, Norah, I might never have seen my shop again."

"I don't think…"

"Child, you were the one who kept my hopes up. You were the one who promised to help me. God sent you to me.

You're my angel. I'll never forget this." Emotion crackled in her voice. Then she turned to Bryce. "And you're helping her. You're a good boy, aren't you?"

Bryce looked as if that were a new concept for him. He likely hadn't heard that said about himself for some time. I wonder how long it's actually been since anyone truly trusted him. Maybe Lou and I are the naive ones and he'll disappoint us, as well, but I don't think so. Not after that crazy dream and all.

Friday night. Not long ago this would have been girls' night out for Lilly and me. A movie, concert, play or sometimes shopping and a leisurely dinner. It never mattered because the point of the evening was to spend time together. Now Friday night is a long, torturous evening of popcorn, bad television and trimming Bentley's toenails. How had I come to this?

I nearly jumped out of my chair when the doorbell rang and Bentley dived for the underside of the coffee table. Hoping against hope that Lilly had softened, I hurried to the door.

It wasn't Lilly on the other side, but Connor, and he was carrying a dozen long-stemmed red roses.

"You shouldn't have." *You really, really shouldn't have.*

"I wanted to." Connor peered over my shoulder into my living room. "Is this a bad time?"

A terrible time, I wanted to scream, but my good Christian upbringing kicked in and I stepped aside. "It's just me and the pets."

He gave me that glazed look he does when I start to talk about my animals. I noticed it the first time he entered my shop and it's never changed. He doesn't seem to know what to do or say in the presence of all my critters. But he's a sailor. Maybe he prefers fish.

I led the way to my kitchen where I put the roses in water. I buried my nose in one fragrant bloom and breathed deeply.

Connor, who'd taken the stool on the other side of the counter, smiled. "I'm glad you enjoy them."

"I love them, but you can't keep sending me things, Connor. It's too much."

"Nothing's too much for you. I'd like to be able to give you everything."

"Connor, we hardly know each other."

"I know. That's why I'm here tonight. I suggest we remedy that."

My warning antennae set up a ruckus but I kept my mouth shut.

"I'm going to be going to Hawaii in a week or two."

"How nice for you."

"Have you ever been to Hawaii, Norah?"

"No. It's on my to-do-someday list, though. Right up there with skiing in Switzerland."

"Maybe you'd like to come with me."

I stared at him bug-eyed. "With you? To Hawaii? I don't do that sort of thing, Connor."

"Not *with* me exactly, but as my guest. I know you better than that. My family has a hotel on the big island. You could stay there. The penthouse is at your disposal, the food is wonderful and the beaches are beyond belief. No strings attached."

Oh no? There's one huge string in here somewhere.

"We could sightsee and have dinner together when I'm not working and really get to know each other."

There it was, that big string I was looking for.

"It doesn't seem to be happening here, getting to know you, I mean. You're always working or with your friends and now that the lady from the antique store has been ill, I've hardly seen you around."

Good. My invisibility cloak has been working.

"I'm a straightforward, go-after-what-I-want kind of guy, Norah. And I want to get to know you better."

"It's a very flattering offer, Connor, but I can't." I felt Bentley scoot close to my feet, something he does when he needs reassurance—or when I do.

"Don't answer yet. Give the idea a few days to digest." He glanced at his watch. "I'm meeting some people for dinner in a half hour at Ziga's, so I don't have time to stay any longer, but I want you to give the idea some serious consideration."

"I don't accept huge gifts like that. I don't leave my responsibilities like Lou, the store and my pets for long periods of time. I don't travel with men across oceans—not usually even across town—and I don't…"

He held up a hand and put his index finger to my lips. "I understand all that. It's what I find so intriguing about you. You aren't like the other women I know. I know there are women who'd probably say yes without even thinking it through. That's not the kind of woman I'm interested in. Besides, as I've told you before, you're a challenge and I love a challenge."

He shook his head when I tried to speak. "Think about it," he said and he showed himself out the door.

It only took a millisecond to do that, of course. The worst part of this whole thing is that the more I say no, the more interesting I am to Connor. If I'd fallen at his feet the first time we met, we could probably have become friends. Because I don't fall at anyone's feet, except God's, of course, I wasn't all that eager to impress him. That, apparently, has made the chase all the more fun for Connor.

"Maybe I'm not giving him enough credit, Bentley," I said. *Someday I'm going to get a best friend with only two feet.* "Maybe he really is interested in me, but I have a hunch that I'm more attractive to him because he's not accustomed to being ignored by women. I'm probably the exception rather that the rule. He's just like Lilly…."

Bentley whined and rolled to his side.

"That's it, Bent, they're two of a kind. He wants me because I'm not interested in him and Lilly wants him because he's not interested in her. And somehow I got to be the third point on this ridiculous love triangle. Well, I wish they'd leave me out of it."

Funny, I thought as I got ready for bed, all this had likely come about because Connor and Lilly couldn't bear to fail at making a conquest. They were cut of the same cloth. No wonder they'd never get together. It would be far too much competition for one household to take.

Still, that didn't help me figure out how to get out of this mess I found myself in.

Chapter Twenty-Eight

❧

Nick walked into the Ark the following Friday in casual clothing and doing that habitual thing he does, jingling the change in his pocket. Although he tried to be discreet, I saw his eyes scan the kennels for canine inhabitants. The two tiny Yorkie puppies in the window apparently weren't enough to keep him away. Dogs that grow up to weigh less than seven pounds soaking wet are, if not embraced, at least tolerated.

To my surprise, I felt tears forming in my eyes. Quickly, I swiped them away with the sleeve of my sweatshirt. His reaction to Bentley had put up a wall between us that seemed to be getting thicker—for me, at least. Ironic, isn't it? I've always known I wouldn't become involved with a man who didn't share my faith. Never once did I think that it would be a dog that kept me from allowing myself to fall in love with Nick.

In love?

"Is something wrong? You just got really pale?" Nick put a hand out to me. "Do you need to sit down?"

That would be because I just saw Nick and thought "love" at the same moment.

"Norah?"

"No. I'm fine. Thanks." Fine as one can be when one's perspective on the world has just tilted onto its head.

He gazed down at his shoes. When he spoke again, his voice was so soft that I could barely hear him. "We didn't part on very good terms the night I was at your house. I was hoping that we could talk about it."

"Is there something to discuss?" Be still my heart. Just because he's asking doesn't mean we can come to terms. My terms include Bentley.

"Maybe not," he admitted, "but it's worth a shot."

"My house?" I asked, knowing I was being nasty.

Now he paled. "No, mine would be fine. I'm off today. I'm going riding and then I'll buy some seafood and make lobster quesadillas."

"Tempting, but I think my place would be better."

"Norah, I won't…I can't."

"Then there isn't much to discuss, is there?" I felt as though I were dissolving as I spoke.

Nick…me…Bentley. Another ridiculous love triangle.

He turned as if to leave, hesitated and swung back. "You're being difficult about this."

"No more so than you."

"I told you I don't like that dog…."

"And I told you that I love him. Besides, you don't even know him."

"I know the breed."

"Bentley is no breed! He's got more ingredients than a church casserole!"

"His body is pure pit bull."

"And his face?" Bentley's body and head have always looked as though they belonged to two different dogs

"Don't do this, Norah."

"Do what? Invite you to my home? Ask you to like the animals I like? Look at me, Nick? Where do I work?" I gestured around the room filled with birdcages, travel kennels, leashes, collars and food for every creature imaginable. "Have you considered that you might be the one being difficult?"

His jaw tightened, his eyes went blank and I saw something in him that made me realize why he'd been able to work in narcotics for all those years. If I'd been intent on doing something illegal, I'd want him working for, not against me. Then he lowered his head and when he lifted it again, the softness was back. Softness and sadness.

"We'll eat outside."

"I'll set the table."

"I'll bring food."

"I'll make dessert."

"Six o'clock?"

"Seven."

When he left I wasn't sure if we'd set up a date for dinner or a duel at dawn.

Annie walked into the shop at that moment carrying a flat, foil-wrapped box. The grin on her face was wide as a slice of watermelon.

"What have you got there? Something from your new boyfriend?"

"Something from *somebody's* boyfriend." She held the package out in front of her. "Chocolates! I've never seen a box so big. A delivery boy just brought them. Read the card, see who they're from."

"I have a bad feeling about this." I tore open the small envelope.

Sweets for the sweet. Think seriously about Hawaii.

I crumpled the paper in my fist. "Take them, they're yours."

"Mine? I don't think…" Then her eyes grew wise. "Connor again?"

"Who else?"

"I'm sorry, Norah, I figured Joe sent them."

"It's okay. Just get them out of here."

"Can I share them?"

"Whatever. Just don't let me see them." Two months ago I would have given my eyeteeth for a beautiful box like that. I would have delighted in the fun of it. I would have been flattered. Today, I felt only annoyed with Connor's persistence and exasperated with Lilly's obtuseness and mistrust. What should have been harmless fun was now this event of huge *significance,* a phase I thought we'd all grown out of in high school.

I slapped the blank order I'd been vainly attempting to

fill out onto the counter. "I'm going to see how Auntie Lou is doing. I'll be back after a bit." And I made the jump out of the frying pan into what was, hopefully, not the fire.

I heard the whooping and thumping long before I got to the open front door of the store.

"Get in there. Come on, baby, make it happen. Oh no!"

"Auntie Lou?"

She was off her rocker—literally, not figuratively—and standing in front of the pinball machine. Bryce was beside her, patting her on the back.

"You did really well for the first time. I can't believe you've had this thing in here and never played it until now." Bryce's eyes were shining and there was so much of the eager little boy in his face that my heart melted.

"I never knew how much fun it was." Lou patted his shoulder. "You keep playing. I'll talk to Norah."

We moved away from the clanging sound of the machine.

"Looks like you two are getting along." Lou's face was relaxed and happy. Even some of her wrinkles seemed softer.

"He makes me feel young again, that boy. Why, I'm not a day over sixty-five when I'm with him. It was a fine idea you had, asking him to help me."

"He seemed to think so, too."

"Whatever you're paying him, you should give him a raise."

"I agree. Especially since I'm not paying him anything."

Lou's eyebrow arched. "What?"

"He won't take it. He says being here is fun and that he likes it better than being watched by his parents all the time. I'm thinking about putting money into a savings bond so at least he'll have something later."

"I can't figure out why those parents of his fuss at him so much." Lou scowled, a rather ferocious expression on her lined face.

"There's been trouble…."

"He told me. I believe him. I don't think he did anything wrong."

"What about the stuff in your jewelry case?"

"If he'd wanted things from here, he could have been taking something home every day. I wouldn't have noticed."

She has a point but there's still no getting around the vandalism that had occurred. I only hope I haven't brought that vandal into Lou's life.

Then I looked at Bryce. He is a different kid here, playful and childlike. It is as though he and Lou are healing each other somehow. Far be it from me to stop the only positive thing I'd seen happening lately on Pond Street.

I walked back to the store to find Lilly coming at me, eyes blazing. "'I'm not interested in Connor. There's nothing between us.' Isn't that what you told me? Hah!"

"What are you talking about?"

"Why is he sending you a huge box of candy if there's not something between you?"

Annie. I'd sent Annie off with the candy and no instruction not to tell anyone from where it had come.

Now what, Lord? I petitioned silently. That's been my frequent prayer of late. I'm walking in the dark with every step I take and pleading that He'll shine a light on enough of my path so I don't trip and fall on my face.

Lilly stood there glaring at me. I knew with certainty

that our friendship, fragile as glass right now, was either going to be shattered or strengthened by what I said and did next.

As I watched her the scales fell from my eyes. I saw not the stylish, worldly wise woman I knew Lilly to be, but the little girl she'd once been—unsure, eager to please, hungry for affirmation. There, I realized, was my answer, and there was no way to handle this but with the difficult truth.

Lilly opened her mouth to speak but I stopped her. "It's my time to talk and your time to listen."

"I don't need to listen to you. I see your actions."

"What is it you think you see, Lilly? Me asking for flowers and candy and attention? Me making huge plays for Connor's affection? Me trying to push you away so Connor notices me, instead? I don't think so. If you'd truly been looking, you'd have heard me suggest that Connor get to know you better. You'd have seen me turn down dates and even a trip to Hawaii with him. You'd have seen me backing away from a relationship with him as fast as I can."

Lilly gaped at me, but I didn't give her time to speak.

"You, of all people, should understand why Connor is pursuing me. You two are just alike. I'm appealing to Connor *because* I'm not encouraging him, not in spite of it. You do the same thing, Lilly. Don't you see?"

"That's not the point…."

"It *is* the point. You want Connor because he doesn't fall all over you. Come on, Lilly, tell the truth. If he'd come to town and swept you off your feet, would you still be together now?"

"Of course!" She hesitated and her brow furrowed. "I think."

"Neither of you realize it, but this is a game you both play, a game of conquest, not genuine love."

Lilly stared at me, dumbstruck.

"You expect men to be interested in you and when they disappoint you…"

"…I think there must be something wrong with *me* or they'd be interested," she admitted reluctantly.

"So you set out to prove yourself wrong, that there isn't really anything wrong with you. That you can make any man love you."

"Is that what I do?" She sank into a chair as if her legs had given out on her. "Norah, I've been so miserable…I've missed you…the way Connor looks at you…it's been eating me alive." She put her head in her hands. "I've been such a fool."

"We're all foolish sometimes."

She looked up and her eyes streamed with tears. "Oh, Norah, you don't even know the half of it!"

I don't know the half of it?

I rolled Lilly's words around in my mind for the rest of the day but couldn't make sense of them. What else has been going on that I don't know about? Instead of feeling better that I'd finally had it out with Lilly, I felt as if I'd opened another can of worms, nasty ones.

I ran into Joe at the market after work. "Hey, how are you?" I greeted him.

He looked up, his hand midair, reaching for a jar of caramel fudge ice-cream topping. "Norah!"

"Don't look so surprised. I eat, too, you know."

"Of course, I just didn't expect to see you here tonight."

Why not? Joe looked nervous, almost guilty. What is so strange about running into me in the grocery store?

"Looks like we have the same grocery list," I commented, peering into his cart. A bunch of bananas, steaks, ice cream, lettuce, strawberries, dinner rolls, pineapple preserves and whipping cream. "Nice supper tonight?"

"Ah…nothing special. Good to see you, Norah, but I've got to get going. See you tomorrow?"

"Sure, I…" But I was addressing Joe's retreating back.

"Weird," I muttered, reaching for a jar of butterscotch topping. I hadn't had a banana split since the falling out with Lilly, so that's what Nick would get for dessert tonight. I hoped that more than dessert will be sweet if Nick and Bentley meet face-to-face tonight.

Chapter Twenty-Nine

❧

Bentley can read me like a book.

He senses my emotional state almost as quickly as I do myself. Apparently he's reading something in me right now because no matter where I move in the kitchen, he follows and sits on my feet. Tonight I could have worn him instead of slippers.

It must be something in the air. Hoppy won't get out of his litter box even for lettuce and Winky and Asia Mynah are having some sort of whistling contest that forced me to stuff my ears with cotton or go deaf. Still, I was ready before seven and waiting for Nick to come.

I'm not sure why, but I felt the need for candles, so I put an entire forest of them on the patio. In a huge departure for me, I even put on makeup. Not my standard swish of blusher and mascara but foundation and eyeliner. Filled with anticipation and dread, I fortified myself in every way I knew how. My feelings for Nick have undergone a change since the last time he'd been at my home. I find myself terribly afraid that Nick and Bentley can't make peace with each other and am troubled about the idea that Nick may be permanently out of my life. Or maybe I'm acting like Lilly, wanting someone just because I can't have him. Either way, I'm not willing to give up Nick's friendship without a fight.

"You know, Bentley," I said as he sprawled across my legs, "I can't have a serious relationship with Nick if we have to stay outside all the time. This is Minnesota. I imagine the romance would end mid-January at the latest."

The dog made a low whining sound as if to apologize but he made no effort to move. That, I fear, is how it may be—Bentley and I, apologetic but together, and Nick nowhere in sight.

"That was simply amazing." I leaned back in my chair and rubbed my stomach. "You are truly the best cook I've ever met."

"Better than the ones at Ziga's?" Nick asked.

"Top of the heap. And I'm ashamed to give you my fresh-from-the-dairy-case excuse for dessert."

"Banana splits, I hope."

"No homemade fudge topping, no freshly made caramel, nothing." I brightened. "I will cut the bananas myself, however."

"Perfect." Nick rose to follow me into the house but halted so suddenly I heard his shoes skid on the patio floor.

I looked back to see what had stopped him. His gaze was riveted on the floor inside the door. There, peering out the window, were two beggars, hoping for scraps. Bentley and Hoppy looked as pitifully underfed as two fat and pampered pets look, each hoping I'd take pity on them and share my table food.

"Isn't that cute…" I said, then realized that Nick was still frozen to the spot.

Bentley.

"I'll wait out here."

"Nick, this is the most harmless dog on the planet. Trust me."

"I trust you, Norah. I don't trust him. I've had more experience with this than you have."

More than me, dog lover extraordinaire? I don't think so!

The rest of the evening deteriorated rapidly and I, disturbed by Nick's insistence on the dangers of a dog like Bentley, didn't help matters any. I was, in fact, glad to see him leave shortly after dessert.

It isn't working. Nick is not going to change his mind about dogs, nor will I change mine about Bentley. It's ridiculous to imagine that a woman who owns a pet shop could fall in love with a man who hates her pets. What have I been thinking?

Frustrated with myself, I picked up the phone to call Joe. Joe understands me. He likes Bentley and tolerates all the other creatures that have paraded through my home and shop over the past couple years. Perhaps Joe is right and he and I are meant to be together.

But Joe didn't answer his telephone. Instead his answering machine picked up. I didn't leave a message. Puzzling.

In the grocery store he'd sounded as if he was cooking dinner at home. Maybe he'd run back to the Java Jockey. Joe's a homebody. If he purchased food for dinner, surely he'd be home cooking.

The next day, I felt as if I were the sole survivor on an island. Annie told me Joe had taken the day off and that she was covering for him. Lilly's assistant came to work saying that Lilly had gone to market. Nick and Sarge, according to what Nick had told me last night when our evening was still progressing nicely, had an assignment to work a strawberry or apple festival and parade somewhere in the city. Lou had a doctor's appointment and had told me in no uncertain terms that I was to stay at the Ark. She'd arranged for the senior bus to pick her up, take her to the clinic and bring her home again. Even Barney's Gas was being staffed by someone I didn't know while Barney took his vacation fishing in the Boundary Waters of northern Minnesota.

I was so grateful to see Julie Morris walk through the door of my shop I nearly kissed her.

"You look sparkly today."

"Oh, Norah, I *feel* sparkly." She put her hands to her ruddy cheeks and beamed at me. "I've had the best news!"

Great. I could use some good news.

"Officer Haley stopped by the house this morning on his way to an assignment. He told us that he's still looking into the issues with Bryce but that he is very happy to see Bryce taking such an interest in Lou. He said it's good for both of them and a real help to you."

Oh, he did, did he? I hadn't realized he'd noticed.

"And, he told me that you were the one who suggested he talk to Bryce. So guess what?"

I had no idea. Nothing surprised me any more.

"He's taking Bryce to the State Fair."

Okay. Some things do surprise me.

"He is?" I felt a strange twinge of jealousy twanging away at my emotional center. I *love* the State Fair. I want to go to the State Fair. And Nick's taking Bryce?

"The best part is that Bryce is excited about it." Julie grabbed my hands. "I have you to thank for all of this—Officer Nick befriending Bryce, Bryce's job at Auntie Lou's—why, you're God-sent!"

Yes, well, God-sent. At the moment I'm feeling like anything but a messenger from God. I'm hurt, left out, jealous and confused, which also makes me feel small, self-centered and childish. Not pretty.

I was in a weakened emotional state when Connor walked through the door and asked me to join him for dinner.

"I really shouldn't." Lilly would never believe I'd accepted an invitation only because I was feeling forlorn and out of the loop. Forlorn is not one of my normal emotional states but today the description fits.

"My brother is considering the purchase of a restaurant about thirty minutes from here. He wants me to take a look at it. I'd rather not eat alone."

Thirty minutes away? What's the likelihood of crossing paths with Lilly? I weighed the risks and accepted his invitation.

"When can you leave?" Connor looked around the shop. A black-and-white kitten was hanging on the edge of its cage, pawing at him. With a hint of a smile, he let the kitten hook its paw around his finger.

"I can leave anytime. It's almost five anyway. No one will notice that I'm missing."

He looked at me quizzically. "Something wrong, Norah?"

What's wrong? Today it feels like everything.

When I didn't answer immediately, he said, "Let's save that question for later." His gaze turned back to the kitten. "Is it true that cats don't like water?"

"Some do, especially big cats in warm climates. They like to cool off, although I've never met a house cat that likes a bath."

"I never paid much attention one way or the other to animals until I met you. It's the first time I've ever really considered that they have distinct personalities—like this little fellow."

The kitten's purr was audible from where I was standing.

"I've considered getting a pet, but I'm not home a great deal."

"Then I wouldn't sell one to you."

"No?" He looked surprised. "Where's the businesswoman in you?"

"Standing behind the animal lover, I'm afraid. Now if you wanted a dog that you could take sailing with you, I could find you a nice water dog like a Keeshound."

He looked at me in amusement and held out his car keys. "I'll consider it. Shall we go?"

He put the top down on his convertible, I pulled the ponytail clip out of my hair and we cruised the freeways, Connor looking like an escaped movie star and me, well, I looked more like an untrimmed poodle with my curls whipping in the wind.

The restaurant was nice and the location good but it was definitely not Ziga's. Still, we managed to enjoy ourselves on the deck and talk desultorily about nothing until they lit a fire in the outdoor fireplace. Then we ordered dessert and slowly sipped our coffee, allowing the night to drift away.

"Now are you ready to tell me what was wrong back at the shop?" Connor asked gently.

"It's not 'wrong' anymore. I was feeling sorry for myself. But then you came along—" I gestured toward the beautiful setting "—and made everything right."

"Everything?"

Why was he dredging up the emotions I'd been stuffing?

"I don't know what I want, Connor, or what I'm expecting. The parts of my life I thought I had in place have gone topsy-turvy and I've lost my footing."

Joe's become distant, Lilly angry and Nick…what is it with him and dogs, anyway? Sure, some dogs are badly trained and dangerous but couldn't he just give Bentley a chance?

"I've never thought of myself as a control freak, but… Connor, do you believe in God?"

"Sure."

"Do you know Him?"

"Not the same way you do, Norah. We're more passing acquaintances than intimate friends."

"There's something I'm beginning to recognize about myself. My life isn't turning out how I'd planned it would. I feel as though I'm losing control of my world and I'm starting to panic."

"That doesn't seem like you." The waning light softened his features and I saw compassion in his eyes.

"It isn't. I thought I was through panicking about things when—" the aha moment hit me hard "—when I turned everything over to God...."

When *was* the last time God and I had had a really good discussion about what He wanted for me? Granted, I've been calling for His will to be done and petitioning Him right and left—to return Lilly's friendship to me, to make my plan for Auntie Lou work out, for Nick to like Bentley, for Connor to... But when was the last time I asked God what He thought about these things and taken the time to listen to His answer? Had I ever asked Him if Connor, Nick or even Joe was supposed to be a part of my life? Had I assumed that because I wanted Auntie Lou on Pond Street that it was His plan for her? Maybe Lilly and I are done. Is it possible that Lou isn't supposed to live on Pond Street anymore? It suddenly occurred to me that in this relationship I've had with God, I've been doing all the talking.

I groaned and put my head in my hands. What an arrogant, presumptuous fool I've been.

Connor leaned forward. "Are you okay? Can I get you something? Water?"

I looked him straight in the eye and made my decision. "Connor, I'd like to tell you what's been going on in my life. It's only fair because you are a part of it." And I recounted everything that had been happening on Pond Street—including the fact that prayer becomes very one-sided when I do all of the talking and none of the listening.

When I was done, I leaned back in my chair and breathed

a sigh of relief. He deserved to understand what had been going on between Lilly and me. He'd become my friend and deserved my honesty.

As we sat there and the dusk turned to darkness, I tried to explain everything that had been happening since he arrived in Shoreside.

"I see." He spun the straw in his glass between his thumb and forefinger and looked at me appraisingly. "I had no idea what a juggling act you've been attempting to keep everyone happy. What would make *you* happy, Norah?"

I wanted to blurt, "That you fall in love with Lilly, that Auntie Lou get back to her prestroke state and that Joe and I…or Nick and I…" But I didn't. "I want to quit trying to manage this by myself, turn it back over to Him and see what He does."

I want to listen for a change, Lord.

"You're a brave woman."

"Brave? Hardly. Shortsighted? Yes. Mistrustful? Of course." I put my hand over his as it lay on the table. "Whatever happens, I want God to be the one to plan its unfolding, not me. Do you understand?"

Connor laid his free hand on top of mine. "I do understand. I'm not sure *why* I understand because usually I'm not a very spiritual guy."

He looked deep into my eyes. "And now I have something to confess to you."

I tilted my head, waiting for him to speak. When he did, he multiplied my problems tenfold.

"Norah Kent, I love you."

Chapter Thirty

❦

I opened one eye and saw a single eye staring back at me from the other pillow. Then a long pink tongue shot out and licked my nose. Bentley and I lay facing each other, a look of contentment and peace on his features that I envy. All is right in Bentley's world as long as his stomach is full and I'm around.

Me? I'd soothed myself with Ben & Jerry's until I made myself sick.

I rolled over to grab my phone and call Annie, who was opening the store today.

"Norah's Ark. There's nothing like puppy love. May I help you?"

"Hi, Annie. Everything okay down there?"

"Sure. You sound tired."

"I'm on overload. Do you think you can handle it today?"

"No problem. Stay in bed, eat two chocolates and call me in the morning."

"Thanks, I'll do just that. If you need help, don't call me."

"Gotcha," Annie said cheerfully and hung up.

I was pulling the covers over my head, planning to lie there until either my or Bentley's bladder threatened to burst, when the phone rang. I eyed it, wishing I had caller ID. Unfortunately I'm too snoopy to leave a ringing phone alone.

"Norah?"

I bolted upright in bed and Bentley grunted a complaint. "Nick?"

"You sound funny."

I may sound funny, but I feel anything but. "I'm okay. Just a little down in the mouth."

"Would an outing help?"

When I remained silent, he added, "I know you and I have some areas of disagreement, but Bryce Morris isn't one of them. I promised him I'd take him to the State Fair and I was wondering if, maybe, if you wanted to…"

Deep-fried cheese curds. Corn on the cob. Every food imaginable on a stick. Bungee jumping. Kitschy shopping. Horse barns.

"On one condition."

"What's that."

"That no matter how much I eat, you don't say a word."

His laughter unexpectedly lifted my spirits. "We'll pick you up at ten-thirty."

When they arrived, I had my State Fair uniform on—comfortable shoes, a water bottle, sunscreen, hat, a wad of five-dollar bills and a cell phone. I looked like a tourist attempting a two-week tour of every country on the European continent.

Bryce was in a uniform I'd never expected to see on him—baggy khaki shorts, a white cotton shirt and, wonder of wonders, tennis shoes instead of biker boots. Even his hair was tipped in a subdued burgundy color.

Nick, who couldn't look bad if he tried, was in his typical off-duty uniform—jeans and a soft cotton shirt. "Looks like you've done this before," he greeted me as I scrabbled into his car.

Bryce offered me his place in the front seat but I declined. "Stay there. This is your day. Besides, I'm a better backseat driver when I'm actually in the backseat."

We drove to one of the many shuttle stops around the city and caught a bus to the fairgrounds. Bryce was practically bouncing off the wall by the time we got to the ticket stands.

"Haven't you ever been to the fair before?" I asked. "You're acting as if it's your first time."

"It's different today."

"What's different?"

He hesitated before answering. "The past couple years I've come with my friend Tony and his buddies. They don't want to do or see much. They just want to hang out."

"And look cool, right? No rides, no food, just smart comments about people and checking out the girls?"

"Yeah. They could do that at the mall. This is the *fair.*"

"What's first, rides or food?" Nick asked.

"Rides!" Bryce and I chimed together. "You throw up if you eat first," I added.

"I see I'm with professionals," Nick said. "Let's go."

I am not at my best when hanging upside down sixty feet in the air. Spinning. Or having my skin go all flubbery so I look like Gumby at three Gs on the Turbo Force. They've added new rides to the old favorites, all with intimidating names like Mega Drop, Magna, Wipeout and Drop of Doom to go with old standbys like Tornado and Zipper. To prevent any more damage than had already been done to my brain cells I finally had to beg off, leaving Nick and Bryce to ride until Nick, too, decided that he'd had enough whizzing, tumbling and shaking. That left us on the ground while Bryce continued to try everything that moved, including something that looked like a large slingshot which ejected people into space and then let them snap back to earth.

"I'd never live through that," I commented, happy to have both feet on the ground, sharing a bucket of fries with Nick.

"Been there, done that, got it out of my system." Nick dipped a French fry in my ketchup and put it in his mouth.

"You've done and seen a lot, haven't you?"

A look that I'd begun to recognize came into his eyes and made them look like hard, flat bits of obsidian. "Too much."

"Is that why you always shut down when the subject comes up?"

He looked at me steadily. "There are points in my life that I don't want to revisit. Looking back only scratches the surface of wounds that are finally beginning to heal."

Another reason Nick and I weren't right for each other. I

don't believe relationships can thrive when we keep secrets from those we love. That is part of why I've been so miserable over the Connor and Lilly thing. I disliked tiptoeing around Connor to keep Lilly happy. Much too complicated.

And speaking of complicated, Connor's words had run through my head all night. *I love you.*

Last night I'd seen a different side of him. Although he's always charming, last night he'd seemed *real,* approachable, and, well, lovable. I'd been overcome and utterly speechless, which only seemed to endear me to him further.

"Where'd you go?"

I looked up to see Nick waving a pork chop on a stick in front of my nose.

"Away. I just went away for a moment."

"You certainly did. Anywhere you can take me?"

I looked him squarely in the eye. "Maybe, if I felt I could trust you."

"You can trust me."

I shook my head. "You don't trust me with your thoughts, Nick. There are a lot of places you don't allow me to go. It is a two-way street."

He nodded but he didn't volunteer any more about himself.

Bryce's gag reflex kicked up when I wanted to look at all the little shops and stands under the grandstand. "Shopping, Norah? You can do that on Pond Street."

"But where else could I find a sequined red, white and blue T-shirt that, if you touch just the right bit of bling, plays the Star-Spangled Banner? Or this multipurpose cleaning solution that is equally safe for my finest lingerie and my car engine? Or…"

"I'll stick with her, Bryce. You go get some food and meet us at the horse barns in an hour. You've got my cell number if you can't find us."

We watched him walk away. There was a relaxed, jauntiness in his step that I hadn't seen before.

"He's a new kid, isn't he?"

"And he's going to be 'newer' yet, if what I expect comes down from juvenile services and things work out as I believe they will. It appears Tony, that so-called 'friend' of his, may be the one who did all the damage on Pond Street, including stealing the mail and washing checks."

"What was he doing in Shoreside causing trouble?"

"Apparently Bryce was trying to squirm out from under Tony's control when his parents moved him across town. Tony seemed to think that Bryce would be his puppet in Shoreside. Tony has delusions of grandeur and wants to run some sort of gang. He's just a two-bit bully, of course, but one with aspirations."

"Like aspiring to have the penitentiary as his retirement villa?"

"Anyway, Tony and his buddies were doing damage over in Shoreside to get Bryce in trouble, to show him what could happen if he didn't take his directions from Tony. He even lifted a leather wristband Bryce owned and planted it to make Bryce look as if he'd been the one doing the mischief."

"What a little creep."

"You've got that right. Bryce, away from Tony, is turning into a decent kid. Sounds like if they can get enough on Tony, he'll get into the system, off the street and maybe get some help."

"And Julie Morris will get her son back." Just the thought choked me up. Impulsively, between the nail-art booth and the get-your-name-on-a-fake-license-plate display, I threw my arms around Nick and gave him a hug. His strong, muscular body gave no resistance. Instead, he hugged me back.

It wasn't until a lady with a double stroller containing twins and enough paraphernalia and shopping bags to equip an arctic explorer ran into us that we released each other. Red as our cheeks were, you'd have thought we'd both been to the face-painting booth.

"Sorry, I just got so excited."

"Don't be sorry. That was better than any of the rides I've been on so far."

Being the sophisticated and classy woman that I am, I gave him an elbow in the side, grabbed his hand and pulled him toward a booth selling chocolate tacos.

At the end of the evening, while Bryce took a final round of rides—the boy's stomach must be made of cast iron—Nick and I sat on the top of the grandstand in the last row of seating. It didn't do much to dim the sound of the monster trucks, but we were in a private little bubble of our own as the moon hung plump and ripe in the sky over us.

"Norah?"

"Hmm?" I didn't want to talk or move. I was nestled into the curve of his arm, my head on his shoulder.

"I want to say something."

"So say it."

"I know we have our disagreements…"

Bentley. I stiffened.

"But maybe we can work it out."

Get rid of Bentley, you mean?

"You're a very special woman. I want to get to know you better. Much better."

My head was still spinning like a Tilt-A-Whirl when Nick dropped me off at my front door.

There is simply too much going on in my life right now.

Connor loves me. I can say the word and live a glamorous life and be treated like a princess.

Joe has grown distant and appears on the verge of going AWOL.

Lilly avoids me because, as she said cryptically, I don't know "the half of it." Whatever *that* means.

Nick wants to get to know me "much better."

Nick hates Bentley.

I love Bentley.

As long as that standoff exists, there is no possibility of Nick really knowing me at all, because Bentley and his kin are part and parcel of my heart. So there's no point in my even thinking about how I feel about Nick....

No wonder I'm tired.

Auntie Lou is thriving thanks, in part, to Bryce Morris.

"That boy is a tonic for me, Norah. I praise God for him every day," she told me when I came to check on her.

"What do you two talk about anyway?"

"He tells me how it is to be young and I tell him how it is to be old." She looked at me slyly. "It gives us both an advantage, don't you think?"

"His mother says she hasn't seen him this happy since before his own grandparents passed away. She had no idea how much influence they'd had on him or how much he had missed them."

"So I'm still good for something." Lou had begun wearing some of the vintage hats she had in her shop. She looked like the Queen Mum today in a powder-blue straw hat with huge baby-blue cabbage roses. Though I'd never tell her this, she manages to draw the curious into her store just to see what a woman in thick black stockings and a broomstick skirt, hot pink sweatshirt and wide blue hat might have for sale.

"Haven't I always told you that?"

Lou's eyes turned watery and I saw her lips quiver. Quickly she dug in her pocket and drew out a small box which she thrust in my direction.

"Open it."

"What's this?"

"Quit gabbing and open it." She dug again in her pocket and came out with a large men's handkerchief into which she proceeded to blow with a sound reminiscent of a fog-horn on Minnesota's North Shore.

The box had been carefully wrapped. When I peeled back the paper, I revealed a small velvet jeweler's box. The fabric was old and faded and flattened in spots. It had been opened and closed many times over the years. "Lou, you shouldn't have…."

"Never noticed before how busy your mouth can be, dearie. Stop flapping your lips and open it!"

Sensing there was something truly exceptional about this moment, I lifted the box's lid slowly. Inside was a rose gold ring, thinned from long years of wearing, with three stones embedded in the surface, a large radiant-cut diamond flanked by two smaller diamonds. I lifted it out and slid the ring onto the third finger of my right hand. It glided into place like it had been there forever. "It fits!"

"It's yours."

"Oh, I couldn't. This must be very valuable."

"It is valuable. It came from Tiffany & Co. Ordered especially for me."

"It's yours then? Not something you purchased for the store?" I held out my hand and admired the delicate workmanship.

"Biggest purchase Silas made in his entire life," Lou said with a chuckle. "Of course, I took charge of our money after he did that."

"Your husband bought this for you?"

"You're beginning to sound like that stupid parrot of yours, repeating everything I say. Of course he bought it for me! It's my engagement ring."

I stared at the ring nestled on my finger then tried to tug it off. "I'm sorry, I shouldn't be wearing your engagement ring, Lou. I had no idea…."

"It's yours now."

"Oh, no. I couldn't. I wouldn't. Why would you do such a thing?"

Lou looked at me with such loving tenderness that my chest constricted. "Because you are my daughter. Every woman wants to pass her engagement ring on to her daughter."

She reached out and took my hand. "You gave me my life back by fighting for me and bringing me home. I know what happens to old people who don't have family and no one to take care of them. They can't live alone. It's not safe."

"But you said you were perfectly safe…."

"I know, I know." She looked at me impishly from beneath the overpowering hat. "I lied. But you came in swinging anyway and convinced everyone that you and I could do this. And we did!

"The store is doing fine considering that my customers have to figure out how to get here during the hours I'm open. Bringing that boy into my life was a stroke of genius and my cat, well…"

"It's too much, Lou. I can't accept it."

"Then who will I leave it to? The cat? Norah, you are my daughter now. If you don't take it, someday someone will sell it in a shop like this and no one will ever know anything about my husband or me. You have to take it."

I closed my hand tightly and felt the sweet heaviness of the ring's weight on my finger. "It will always remind me of you. And if I have a little girl someday, I'm going to pass it on to her."

Lou's eyes began to sparkle and I knew I'd said the words she wanted to hear. "Thank you, dearie, for so graciously accepting my gift." Then she scowled at me. "Now you'd better quit wasting time and find a father for that *granddaughter* of mine."

Chapter Thirty-One

✤

I like Connor a lot, but not enough to let him be the father of that granddaughter Auntie Lou wants so badly. Nick, other than the fact that he loathes dogs and abhors Bentley, would be an excellent choice for the job. And Joe, patient, loving Joe, the "sure thing" in my life has been highly underappreciated by me of late. Of course nowhere have I heard those bells I want. God knows the desires of our hearts, but…bells?

It is human nature to want what you don't have—thin thighs, for example, or straight hair. People tell me all the time that they'd love to have my mop of curls, while I'd gladly give them away in trade for sleek straight hair.

"Lord, there has to be something in here for me. Show

me what it is." I pawed anxiously through the pages of my Bible, skimming passages and trying to will the Holy Spirit to toss a verse at me.

As I cradled my head in my hands and stared at the page, a verse caught my attention. *"Disregarding another person's faults preserves love; telling about them separates close friends."* Proverbs 17:9.

Nice, but it doesn't seem to apply to my current predicament. Since God always has a purpose I have to assume this is relevant somehow, although I have no clue as to what its significance might be. I'm trying to *listen* for Him now, though, so I'll take this verse for what it's worth.

When Joe called to asked if he could come over, I said yes. If Connor could tell me he loved me, who knew what Joe might come up with?

While I was waiting, I picked up Bentley and staggered to the couch. He's been overeating lately and resembles a furry lump of concrete. "Diet doggy food for you, my friend." He whined pitifully, as if I'd sentenced him to a month of hard labor at a canine penitentiary.

The doorbell rang in minutes. I smoothed down my hair on my way to the door. "Hi, stranger, it's good to…Lilly?"

Joe had not come alone.

Lilly hung behind, urging Joe to enter first. My antennae should have picked that up right away. Not only that, but instead of her usual flamboyant garb, she wore a pair of light tan pants and a fitted blue sweater. Her lobes were decorated in discreet pearl earrings and her hair was pulled into a knot at the base of her neck. I hardly recognized her.

"What's going on, guys?" They both looked somber, as if someone had died.

"Lilly and I have to talk to you, Norah."

"Sure." I gestured them into my living room. Winky and Asia Mynah eyed the pair but neither had a smart remark to make. Winky didn't even whistle.

They started to sit together on the couch, glanced at each other and moved to take the two chairs opposite the sofa. I and Bentley took our places on the sofa, instead.

"You two look like you're on your way to a funeral," I commented, but the joke fell flat.

"We need to talk."

"If it's about Auntie Lou and the past few weeks, forget it. Everything is turning out fine. I shouldn't have expected you to commit to helping with her…"

"It's not about Auntie Lou, Norah. It's about me and Joe."

I turned to look at Lilly. "What do you mean, you and Joe?"

To my amazement, two large tears rolled down Lilly's cheeks.

"Norah, I am so sorry. I was so nasty to you when I thought you were trying to steal Connor away from me."

"It was a misunderstanding, that's all. I would never, *never* go behind your back to compete with you over someone you care deeply about." I thought that would assure Lilly that there were no hard feelings but my words managed to make her cry even harder.

"Really, Lilly, it's okay. I understand that things didn't look good but you can trust me. I'd never…"

"No, but I would!" Lilly wailed. "You have every right to hate me."

This was getting a little surreal for my taste.

Joe cleared his throat. "What Lilly is trying to say, Norah, is that while Lilly thought that you and Connor were…an item…something happened. Something between us. We've been seeing each other."

I looked at Joe and back to Lilly. "You two…"

"I didn't mean for it to turn out like this," Lilly interrupted, "but I was so angry with you and I didn't have anyone else to talk to. Joe listened and tried to help me."

"And I'm ashamed to say," Joe added softly, "that I wasn't so sure you were telling the truth, either. I'm sorry, Norah."

"We both thought that you and Connor…it was hard to believe anything else when the two of you spent the evening together on the *Lady of the Lake*. Then there were the flowers and the candy and you brought Auntie Lou home and we both thought that wasn't a good idea…."

"Are you saying that the two of you went behind my back and started a relationship?" It was ludicrous. "Are you joking?"

"We didn't plan it that way, it just happened!" Lilly's nose was red and puffy. "I blamed you for trying to steal Connor and…"

"And managed to get between Joe and me, instead?"

"It's my fault, too, Norah," Joe said. "I felt like you were pushing me away."

"Appearances can be deceiving," I murmured as I heard my world tumbling down around my ears. "Did anyone ever consider asking *me* what was going on? Or believing I was telling the truth?"

"We know that now. We were both hurting and…"

"And you looked to each other for comfort?" I was dumbfounded. "How many times have I lied to either of you in the time we've known each other?"

"I was jealous," Joe admitted miserably. "And Lilly really needed someone."

"Oh, please! Lilly accused me of being in love with a man she was attracted to, so to get even, she got involved with the man I was seeing?"

This wasn't happening. It couldn't be. I don't live my life like a soap opera and this mess is getting far too sudsy for me.

Disregarding a person's faults brings love. There it was, one of those pesky pop-up Scriptures flashing onto the display screen of my brain just when I'm ready to be good and angry.

"Lord," I petitioned silently, "this is too much to disregard. My dearest friends *betrayed* me." The guilty parties sat across from me, the expressions on their faces alternating between hope and apprehension.

I knew what they wanted me to say. "I forgive you. It's okay. I understand." But if I opened my mouth and said that to them right now I'd be the world's biggest hypocrite. It's not okay. It's the furthest thing in the universe from okay.

Joe! The man who said he wanted to marry me! With my best friend?

How dare he? I'd counted on Joe....

Counted on him.

Counted on him for what? That still small voice that could resound so loudly between my ears prodded me.

To be there, of course, waiting patiently, like Bentley waits for me by the front door holding my slippers. To be there *if and when* I decided I'd marry him. To be there when I need him without much regard to when he needs me. To be there even though I know deep in my heart that he's not the one for me…there are no bells with Joe. I love him but he doesn't make my heart chime with passion. If I'm honest I have to admit that the music between us is missing.

So, that silent yet prodding voice persisted, how dare *I* keep him on hold while I'm looking for someone else?

All this flitted through my mind as we sat in a visual stare-down, each of us bracing for whatever the other would say next. Lilly was poised like a deer on the edge of the forest, watching me to see if I were going to remain calm or raise a rifle to my shoulder and blast her into oblivion.

A profound wave of disappointment washed over me, so deep and strong that I wanted to weep. The disappointment was not that I'd somehow "lost" Joe to her, but that she hadn't trusted me. Had all her talk about becoming a Christian been for my benefit alone? A verbal salve meant to pacify me into believing she bought into my faith? Was it so difficult to believe that anyone could walk the path Christ had laid out for us? A path of honesty, righteousness, compassion and forgiveness…

Ouch!

When God makes a point, He's not always subtle. No matter what else is going on here, between the three of us, love found and love stolen, Christ is in our midst. What would He have me do here and now? In this moment?

Not being Jesus, I knew I wasn't going to handle this gracefully. Maybe I couldn't even be charitable, but I had to try.

"I'm very hurt. And maybe not all that surprised. I have to admit that my first reaction is to tell you both to get out of my life. My second reaction, the one that doesn't come from me but from the One I try to follow, is more benevolent."

My mind galloped through snippets of Scripture like an out-of-control race horse. Proverbs, Matthew, Colossians, Luke... *"Good sense makes a man slow to anger... If you forgive men their trespasses, your heavenly Father also will forgive you... As the Lord has forgiven you, so you must forgive... And if he sins against you seven times in the day, and turns to you seven times, and says, 'I repent,' you must forgive him."*

I wish I could say those verses made me calm, cool and collected, but I can't. What they did do was keep me from putting my foot in my mouth and walking around in there.

"I...I don't know what to say," Lilly said.

"It was never our intention..." Joe began.

"Do you believe us, Norah?" Lilly pleaded.

"Probably more than you believed me when I said there was nothing between Connor and me." *And it certainly explains why Joe wasn't cooking dinner at home the other night.*

Lilly paled.

"Will you forgive us?" Joe asked, misery oozing out of every pore.

"Frankly, at this moment, I don't feel like it." I took a deep breath. "But ultimately I'll have no choice."

They stared at me, baffled.

"It's not because I want to but because He wants me to." I gestured upward for lack of a better place to point. "I know you aren't bad people and it's not wise to throw the baby out with the bathwater."

Lilly began to speak but I stopped her.

"I don't want to talk anymore right now. Honestly, I don't know what I might say."

"We'd better go." Joe stood up. He looked me square in the eyes. "Norah, I think I love and respect you more now than I ever have. You're real. *It's* real, that faith of yours. I'm humbled." And he turned and left.

I stared at the wall for what felt like hours after they'd gone, warring emotions playing out on the front line of my mind. Then I paced around the apartment, Bentley anxiously tailing me, as I spoke my mind—to Joe, to Lilly and to God. When I'd given them all a good talking-to, I sank onto my bed, spent.

No matter how I turn it over in my mind, which I've been doing for days now, the truth is the same. I hadn't loved Joe as he'd deserved to be loved. Since I'd told him I wasn't ready to commit, there should be no reason to be angry when he moved on. That made no sense whatsoever and, if I'm anything, I'm a woman who likes things that make sense.

Worse—or better—yet, there's a crazy, inexplicable part of me that's happy for Lilly. She found what many women dream of. I saw the way she looked at Joe. I could practically hear the bells between them.

I rubbed Bentley's head—he hasn't been more than twelve inches away from me since this entire mess came to light. "God's doing a number on me, Bent. I've been betrayed. I should be angry. I should want to yell and scream and throw something."

Bentley looked up at me, alarmed.

"But I don't feel like it. I feel…quiet, like I know this was the right thing to have happen. It's just plain *weird*."

I suspect it's that "peace that passes understanding" thing. It's divine and there is no way to comprehend it on my own but I am grateful to have it now. It is the only thing that can help me preserve and not destroy my relationship with Lilly and Joe.

I grabbed Bentley by the head and kissed his nose. His little tail thumped wildly and I know he tapped in Morse code, "Welcome back, Norah. Welcome back."

Chapter Thirty-Two

Forgiving is one thing, forgetting is quite another.

I feel raw when I think about Lilly and Joe, even though I know logically that my relationship with Joe would never have progressed any further than it had already. Lilly is so ashamed of having done what she, ironically, accused me of doing, that she's constantly trying to ingratiate herself with me. She doesn't need to, not for my sake, but for her own. That's the way it is with God and us, too. He's already forgiven us but we just can't seem to accept it and are always trying to make ourselves "good enough" for Him. It is as hard to receive forgiveness as it is to give it.

Fortunately Annie asked for more hours this week because she's decided to take classes at the University this winter to become a veterinarian. I'm so excited for her that I'd pay her way if I could. In lieu of that, I'm staying away from work so she can earn a few extra bucks.

I was bottom-up, digging in my garden, when I heard a man clear his throat directly behind me. I turned around and nearly gave Nick an appendectomy with my garden trowel.

"You shouldn't surprise a woman with a weapon," I warned.

"Good thing I have fast reflexes or you could have eviscerated me with that thing." Nick had his hand in his pocket, jingling loose change, hardly the pose of a frightened man.

"I doubt it. It's not doing anything to these weeds except maybe giving them a bad scare. The little roots just go into hiding until my equipment is in the garden shed and then they start growing again." I scrabbled to my feet and dusted off the knees to my jeans.

"Need help?"

I thought about Nick's green thumb and was tempted. "I'd like to say yes, but the manners I was raised with tell me I should ask you if you'd like some iced tea, instead. Besides, I could use a break."

"Anything I can do to be of service is fine with me." He dropped into a chair and watched me peel off my garden gloves.

"I'll be right back. I even baked chocolate chip cookies today." I looked down at my shoes. "Not like yours, of course. These are from a roll of cookie dough in the refrigerated section. Does that count?"

"It does in my book." Nick looked so at ease and right sitting on my porch that he could have been a permanent fixture in my life. Then I turned to go into the house and saw Bentley waiting patiently on the other side of the patio door with his adoring eyes fixed on me. I don't ever want to have to choose between Nick and my other permanent fixture, Bentley.

The telephone rang as I walked through the patio door. It was my mother, ready for a chat. After five minutes I got a word in edgewise and promised to call her after Nick had gone. It wasn't until I'd poured the tea and put the glasses on a tray with the cookies that I realized that I hadn't shut the patio door behind me. My four-footed detainees had been sprung from the joint and were enjoying freedom on the patio with Nick.

More accurately, two out of three were enjoying freedom. Hoppy had found the lettuce I'd planted for him in my flower bed and was gorging himself like a professional glutton.

Bentley, who didn't like to be outside except on my patio, was, to my surprise, showing curiosity toward the tall, handsome stranger backed up against my fence. Bentley, who is afraid of everyone and everything, was sniffing Nick's shoes.

I was interested in Nick, too, especially the ashen color of his face and the way he gripped the wrought-iron railing that encircled the terrace. He was as frozen looking as my lawn ornament of an erect toad holding a fiberglass umbrella.

"Bentley, leave Nick alone," I ordered. Actually, it was more of a suggestion. Bentley doesn't do well with raised voices. Still, it was enough. He slunk off, tail between his legs, as though I'd screamed at him at the top of my lungs.

"You can move now," I told Nick. "He won't be back unless he's invited."

I saw the tension seep out of his expression and his shoulders relax. Nick had felt truly in jeopardy from a dog that's scared of his own image in a mirror.

"You'd better tell me about it," I murmured as I handed him a glass, "because otherwise I don't get it. Not you, a policeman and a horseman."

Nick glared at me as if I'd loosed the Hound of the Baskervilles on him.

"What? Did your mother get scared by a Doberman when she was pregnant with you? Or was it a hundred and one Dalmatians?" My joke fell flat.

"I almost died because of a dog like that." His words were soft and fierce.

"Like *that*?"

I turned to stare at my dog. Bentley was sitting in the baby pool I keep outside for him on hot days. He was holding a rubber bone in his mouth and looking about as bright as a burned-out lightbulb.

"A pit bull mix."

"Staffordshire terrier and beagle with a few other lineages thrown in," I corrected automatically, my mind trying to get around what he'd just said. "You almost died?"

Nick had gone too far to go back now. "Drug raid. We'd been watching the house for days. There were some nasty operators in there so we had plenty of backup, but none of us had any idea that they kept attack dogs inside the house."

He lifted his arm. In the sunlight, the ribbons of scars on his arms stood out in stark relief.

"Dogs did that to you? I thought maybe you'd had a car accident and gone through a window."

"Not dogs, just one dog. I was on my way to the second floor of the house when he came flying out at me from the top of the stairs. His razor-sharp teeth—" Nick shuddered and had to gather himself together to continue "—looked like they'd been honed with files. He grabbed me at the shoulder and as I tried to shake him loose he hung on. He slid down my arm without easing up, his teeth taking my flesh with him."

I stared at him in horror as I imagined, from the shape of the grooved scars, how it had happened.

"I fell backward down the stairs and he came with me. When I landed on the ground, he went for my neck.

"I'd almost bled to death by the time I got to the hospital. They gave me several pints of blood and lost count of the stitches somewhere after five hundred. The bites got infected and for a while, the doctors weren't sure they could save my arm. I was in the hospital for two weeks and in physical therapy for months." He paused and drew a deep breath. "All because of a dog like yours."

Bentley stared at both of us with an innocent "Who? Me?" expression on his face.

"And now I wish you'd put him inside, Norah, because he's making me very nervous."

I jumped to my feet and grabbed Bentley out of the pool. I wrapped him in a towel lying on the deck chair and hurried him inside. As I went through the door, I heard Nick say, "Be careful, Norah. Never trust…"

I returned to the patio with a sickly knot lying lumpishly in the pit of my stomach. A vast chasm had grown between us in the time I was gone.

"Nick, I am so sorry. I've been so blind. I had no idea…."

"I should have told you before, but I didn't want…" He paused to stare at me. "I didn't want you to know I was afraid."

"Afraid? Why wouldn't you be afraid? In a situation like that you would have to be crazy not to have been afraid. And now you feel this way about all dogs?"

"I know it's irrational but I can't seem to shake it. Especially not around dogs that look like…" His gaze rested on Bentley on the other side of the window and I knew that sweet and stupid face I love so much provoked only horror in Nick.

"Oh, boy. Big obstacle to overcome," I murmured with exquisite understatement.

"You could say that. Walking through the door of your shop makes my heart pound like a trip hammer. What if there's a dog loose in there? What if you've got Bentley with you at work? It's not rational, but fear doesn't have to be rational. Coming so close to death made me reevaluate my own life. It's when I turned to God. That's the gift that came out of being on death's doorstep. I'm not ungrateful for that. Much as I want to I don't know how to shake this phobia. I'm sorry, Norah, but I cannot tolerate one of the things you love most—dogs."

I thought about the Bed and Biscuit and about Bentley and Hoppy who were staring curiously at me, their human.

"Are you sure?" I ventured. "Never?"

"I can't imagine it. I'm sorry."

Well, that's that. My only consolation is that I've never heard bells when I'm with Nick, either.

* * *

Winky has become fixated on body parts and romance.

"Great legs, sweetheart. Vavavoom!"

"Better than yours."

"Nice buns! You make my heart sing."

"You make my head ache." No wonder. I'm carrying on a conversation with a bird. Between him and Asia Mynah, I could have been chatting all day long.

"Come 'ere and gimme a kiss, baby!" Winky has perfected smooching sounds to go with his catcalls and whistles.

"Not on your life, bird beak."

I poured myself another cup of coffee hoping the caffeine would kick in soon. I'd slept very little last night and when I did, I dreamed that Nick was being assailed by a dog that got larger and fiercer in every dream. If that had happened to me just hearing about the attack, I can only imagine what Nick's nightmares must be like.

I have a fear of heights that has no rational explanation, but every time I come too close to a twentieth-floor hotel window, my stomach feels like it has been on a roller coaster ride; my breath grows short and my heartbeat escalates. It's nothing I elicit or intentionally think about. It just happens—like what happens to Nick when he sees Bentley.

I'd resent someone pooh-poohing my experience or telling me I'm being silly. It was only five years ago that I learned to sit in the IMAX theater with its steeply graduated seats and watch the movie's wild camera angles. I still cover my eyes when my heart can't take it.

"Great buns! Groovy."

"Actually, it's a muffin, Winky," I said, wishing his previous owner had taught him to say, "You look lovely today."

Then Winky nearly split my eardrum with a wolf whistle. Even though I was sure he'd caused permanent damage to my hearing, I had to smile. Winky seldom uses his wolf whistles on me.

Then I glanced up and saw Lilly standing on the far side of my patio door.

I put down my muffin muttering, "Oh, sure, you save those for her. Well, my friend, you'd just better remember which side your birdseed is buttered on."

Lilly looked unsure, so I waved her into the room.

"Is it okay that I came?"

"Of course. Coffee? Muffin? Juice?"

"No thanks. I just wanted to stop by and tell you something."

I took a deep breath. If this is about her and Joe, I don't want to hear it.

Lilly hurried on. "I miss you, Norah. I miss you so much I can hardly stand it."

"I haven't been anywhere, Lilly. You're the one who disappeared."

"I know. That's what makes it so much worse. I cut you out of my life. I did the very thing I accused you of doing. I called myself your friend and then acted as though you were my worst enemy." She bit her lip as she looked at me. "I'm so ashamed."

"It's done now. Past. There's no way to unwind it, so we have to move on." As I said it I realized that I really did believe that and had shockingly few regrets about it. If this had been a test to really discover how I felt about Joe, then I had my answer.

"I said something else to you for which I'm ashamed."

Wolf whistles and confessions before breakfast. What next?

"I accused you of being a lousy Christian and told you that if you were what a Christian looked like, then I didn't want to be one."

"Or else I wouldn't have 'stolen' your man? I remember."

"I've come to take back what I said." Lilly raised her chin. "You have been more gracious and forgiving than I dreamed you—or anyone—could be. I recalled what you told me about Christ living in you." She looked at me as if I were an oddity in a carnival sideshow. "He really does live in you, doesn't He?"

"He sure does. I'm not the best condo He has, but He's here." I pointed to my chest with my index finger. "All moved in and ready to stay with me forever."

"I see that now. It's not just about going to church and being 'good,' is it?"

"You've got that right."

"The change takes place inside you first and *then* you are able to act the way you did when I betrayed you?"

"Only by God's grace. On my own, I would have scratched your eyes out."

"Norah, I don't know where this thing will go with Joe and me but we want to see it out. What I *do* know is that I want what you have, that kind of faith. I want to be more like you."

I shook my head and pointed upward. "More like *Him*, you mean. Do you want to talk about it?"

It's pretty cool how God works. He doesn't waste an opportunity to further His kingdom, no matter how miserable, awkward or uncomfortable the circumstance might be.

Feeling pretty good on Wednesday morning despite Winky's admonitions to go play in the street and Asia Mynah's suggestions that I'm overworked and underpaid, I decided to take Bentley for a walk.

"You're getting a little tubby, my boy," I told him. His tail was wagging slowly as if he knew that this was not going to be a short walk around the park. Bentley has an approach-avoidance attitude toward outdoor activity. He loves it and he's terrified.

"I know too many people with phobias, Bent. I can't have a dog with them, too. You've got to get over this fear of fresh air."

I hadn't even coaxed him to the front door when someone started pounding on it.

When I opened it, Bryce Morris bolted in with a whoop which set off Winky and Asia. When the din subsided and I got him to sit down, I could finally ask him what was going on.

He beamed at me, his grin so wide I could see his molars. "Auntie Lou gave me the pinball machine! Can you believe it?"

Frankly, no, I can't. It's an expensive item and since being in the hospital, Lou's income has dropped. I don't believe she can afford to give away something as large and pricey as that pinball machine.

"Wow," I finally stammered. "How did that come about?"

"I just came into the store and she said I could have it."
He paused. "Oh, yeah, and she said I was supposed to come
and get you because she needed to talk to you."

Not even thinking of the fire hydrants Bentley would
have to pass on the way to Auntie Lou's Antiques, I dragged
him out the door behind me.

Chapter Thirty-Three

❦

Bryce and I were almost to Auntie Lou's when I realized that Bentley had not dropped to the ground or refused to move. His little legs churned along willingly and he passed two fire hydrants without flinching, an inexplicable phenomenon in Bentley's world.

Bryce was busy telling me how cool it was that Lou had given him something as awesome as her pinball machine. I, on the other hand, was growing more alarmed by the moment. Was there something she wasn't telling me? Normally people don't start giving things away until they think they aren't going to be around to use them much longer.

Lou had an appointment with Dr. Andrews the other day. Had he found something? An aneurysm? A blockage of some sort?

I heard my heart pounding in my ears by the time we got to the store. Auntie Lou was in one of her rockers wearing— do my eyes deceive me?—a purple dress and a red hat, just like the mob of older ladies that sometimes come by the bus-load to shop on Pond Street and do a dinner cruise. She was wearing black stockings and black slippers and, I could tell by the expression on her face that she thought she was very foxy.

"There you are! I was afraid that Bryce wouldn't find you before I left." She had her teeth in and, wonder of wonders, lipstick on her lips.

"Left?"

"Julie is giving me a ride to her church. There's a group going out to lunch and then to a play. I'm going to go along."

I hadn't even noticed Bryce's mother until Lou gestured toward her with her cane. Julie was standing there, gazing at Lou, looking as proud as a mother hen.

"Doesn't she look wonderful? Lilly brought her the outfit."

"Amazing." I had no idea Lilly allowed clothing like that into her shop.

"I take a couple days off and look what happens!" I couldn't help smiling. Lou looked so happy—and so charmingly ridiculous—that it warmed my heart. "And Bryce told me about the gift you've given him…."

"He's been such a help to me it was the least I could do," Lou said. "Besides, he's leaving it right where it is so he can visit me whenever he comes to play."

"Is that right, Bryce?" I turned to the boy who'd suddenly turned shy.

"Sure. Why would I want the old pinball machine without Auntie Lou?"

Why, indeed? Since Bryce and Auntie Lou had teamed up, he'd gone through a complete transformation. His clothes were not always black, his hair was often without its neon-colored tips and there was often a smile on his face. Auntie Lou and Nick had managed a turnaround in this kid that was miraculous.

"Who's going to mind the store while you're off gallivant-ing around?" I teased. "Silas?"

"That's my other bit of news." Auntie Lou straightened proudly. "I've taken on a partner."

One more surprise and I'm going to fall over.

"Julie Morris is now half owner of Auntie Lou's An-tiques."

I turned to stare at Julie who wore a wide, delighted smile.

My mouth was opening and closing but no sound came out. For a woman who's never at a loss for words, it's a pretty eerie experience.

"Julie told me that her husband has expanded into Inter-net sales and since he is always at the store during business hours, there's no need for her to spend so much time there. She said she wished she could think of another business to open on Pond Street." Lou made a grand gesture with her hands. "And I said 'Why not antiques?'"

"It's going to be perfect," Julie added. "Lou will make all the buying and selling decisions. She'll work the store the hours she sets and I'll take the rest of them. I can do the things that she'd like to cut back on—dusting, cleaning and bookwork. If she doesn't feel well one day, I'll open the store for her. If she feels wonderful and wants to work, she can hang out in the store as much and often as she likes."

"It will ease my worry about what will happen to the store," Lou concluded, "and I'll have both income and what the Morrises are paying me for half ownership. If I do need more help and can't be upstairs any longer, I'll be able to call my own shots and decide where I want to go." She looked at me and smiled serenely. "And it will take some of the pressure off you, Norah. I know how you've been concerned about me."

"I…ah…oh, Lou, I'm so happy for you! It's perfect."

It was a huge load lifted from my not-so-broad shoulders. Auntie Lou would have others in her life. We can share her. She certainly has enough personality to go around.

At that moment, we all heard a hiss so loud it sounded like a leak in a blimp. I spun around to see Bentley quivering like an aspen leaf but holding his ground as Silas tried to intimidate him into retreat. The pair were nose-to-nose. Silas's fur was standing on end and his tail looked like a bottle brush. His teeth were bared and he looked very fierce. Even I would have been intimidated by him at that moment. Amazingly, though, quivering, gelatin-kneed Bentley was not backing down. He was making a sound in his throat that was half growl, half plea for mercy.

As we watched the scene play out, Silas grew bored with his theatrics, gave one last hiss, turned his scrawny rump toward Bentley and stalked off. With a leap, he jumped into his rocking chair, made three circles around the cushion, sat down, closed his eyes and fell asleep.

Bentley, when he was sure the cat was serious about abandoning the game, sank trembling to the floor like a KO'd boxer.

"You did it, Bent. You stood up to that cat. Good boy. Brave boy." I felt a little like a mother whose sweet but clumsy child had just managed to hit a home run or send a free throw swishing through a basketball hoop. Whatever had possessed the dog to choose today to become brave, I have no idea. I'm just glad it happened at all.

"Bryce," I asked, "will you run Bentley home? I think I'll stop by the store and see how Annie's doing."

Again, to my surprise, Bentley trotted off without a backward look at me. What was going on with him? Has he been watching therapy sessions on the medical channel?

Before I went home, I stopped at the market to pick up something for dinner. As I made my way to the checkout counter with my low-calorie frozen dinner and a pint of Ben & Jerry's, I ran into Nick, who had jumbo shrimp, colorful red peppers, a steak, onions and fresh mushrooms in his basket.

"Looks like you've got a balanced meal planned," he commented. "Protein, vegetables, dairy—plenty of dairy."

"There's something really annoying about a man who knows more about cooking than I do," I shot back.

He whistled under his breath. "Touchy?"

"I just learned something that surprised me. I should be used to bombshells by now, considering all the times that I've been targeted lately."

Without a word, Nick plucked the frozen dinner and the ice cream out of my basket and handed them to a shelf stocker who was passing by. "She's changed her mind. Could you put these back?"

"What am I supposed to eat? Bread and water?"

"How about shrimp cocktails and shish kebabs?"

"You're making that for yourself?"

"If I don't, who will?" He smiled at me. "And I'd like to have you join me, if you would."

How could I resist? Especially in a case where the cook is as delicious as the food he cooks?

"That's nice of you."

"I heard about Joe and Lilly," he said softly. "Are you okay?"

"I am. Really. Fine, actually. I feel slam-dunked but definitely not out of the game."

"You're a remarkable woman."

"Not so remarkable. Joe deserves someone who's not constantly putting him off. He's the kind of guy who wants to settle down. If there's any chance Lilly is the one for him, then I wish him all the best."

"See what I mean about remarkable?" Nick took me by the arm and steered me into the street. "Let's go home. I'll start dinner and you can tell me what else happened today."

His house, warm and inviting, cocooned me within its walls. With Nick calmly filling skewers with meat and vegetables as I sat at the counter and watched, a sense of tranquility descended over me. There was jazz music playing in the background. With a glass of iced tea in my hand and a moment without any responsibility whatsoever, I finally began to relax.

"What else happened?" Nick asked. He stabbed a wedge of yellow pepper on the tip of his knife and held it out to me.

I popped it into my mouth and chewed thoughtfully. "Auntie Lou sold half her business to Julie Morris. And she gave Bryce the pinball machine in her store."

Nick looked up. "How do you feel about that?"

"I feel fine, Dr. Freud, thanks for asking."

"About doing this without your knowing, I mean. That's a big decision and you've been Lou's main confidante for some time now."

"It's a relief, frankly. I've been wondering what was going to happen to her and the store when she couldn't be there any longer. It appears she's taken care of that all by herself. Julie's willing to let Auntie Lou be as active in the store as she likes. She wants to learn the business and she'll be able to take it over someday."

I reached across the counter and grabbed another pepper, red this time. "And I think the fact that this happened is, in great part, due to you."

"Me? I doubt it."

"You helped them with Bryce. Now that he's out of trouble and away from his old friends, he's turning into a great kid. It wouldn't surprise me if someday he went into geriatric medicine or something. He's wonderful with older people."

"You give me too much credit. I was just doing my job."

"You take everyone you deal with to the State Fair?"

"No, sometimes I take them to an equally thrilling county facility," he joked. Nick picked up the plateful of skewers and carried them to the grill. When he returned, he put out his hand and beckoned me into his living room.

"Sounds like things are changing in your life, Norah."

"Too fast. Joe, Lou, Lilly...nobody except Bentley and the other animals seem to need me anymore. I'm beginning to feel a little...irrelevant." Instead of being pivotal in my friends' lives, I'd suddenly become superfluous. Lilly had

Joe. Lou had Julie and Bryce. Only Bentley and Hoppy have me. Ever since Connor told me he loved me, my mind has been doing cartwheels about that bit of information and it was clear that despite his charm, his money and his good looks, he isn't the guy for me. No bells. Not even a tinkle.

Nick studied me in such a manner that I might as well have been standing in a police lineup. He scrutinized my face with such intensity that I could practically feel his gaze searing my skin. "Who do you want to be important to, Norah?"

I hadn't thought of it like that. I've focused on what is slipping away, not what I now could bring in to my life.

"There's always God. His love for me doesn't change. My family, my pets, those are all givens. Who else? I don't really know."

"So the pets rank right up there with God and family?" His voice was curiously flat.

"Every person has a purpose on the planet, Nick. It's evident that mine involves animals. Taking care of them, protecting them, showing others how much joy they can bring. Animals are a huge part of the Biblical story—Christ was born in a barn—His birth witnessed not by kings and politicians, but by God's creatures. We call Him the 'Lamb of God.' Scripture is filled with references to nature. A dove was the first to let Noah know the earth was no longer covered with the waters of the flood. The Holy Spirit descended like a dove. Daniel in the lions' den, sacrificial lambs…"

"And in Proverbs," Nick reminded me, "it says that 'Like a dog that returns to his vomit is a fool who reverts to his folly.'"

"You would know that one, wouldn't you?"

He didn't say anything but went to the deck and returned with the food. We ate in silence and when we were done, he held out his hand to me and led me to his couch. The music swelled around us and I sank down beside him. It felt perfectly right and natural to lean against him with my head on his shoulder.

I dozed off and when I awoke, Nick was gently curling a strand of my wild black hair around his finger.

"Sorry I'm not much company. I didn't realize how exhausted I was until I finally relaxed." I sat up and turned my body so I could look at him. A lock of dark hair fell onto his forehead and his eyes held such kindness that it nearly took my breath away. "You're different from anyone else I've ever known, Nick. You're a…a…safe place to fall."

"Safe? That's the kind of description a man really likes to hear from a beautiful woman." He touched my cheek with his finger and I felt a shiver of pleasure throughout my body.

"You know what I mean. When I come here, it's like coming to a place I most want to be. Being with you is like… coming home…for me."

He looked at me oddly and was quiet a very long time before he spoke. "And you're like that for me, Norah, except…"

The hairs on the back of my neck stood up—another Scriptural thing. *The hair of my flesh bristled….*

"Except?'"

"I can't feel the same way about animals as you, Norah. I might have at one time, but it's no longer in me."

"Sarge…"

"Is the exception. What you care about most is what I prefer to avoid."

"And you believe that's never going to change for you?"

"It hasn't so far. I don't anticipate it will now."

"Then this is pointless, isn't it?" I looked longingly at his arms, wishing they were around me again.

"I don't like it this way, Norah, but I don't know what to do. I'll never share your passion for animals. You'll never understand the hurdles I've had to jump just to stay in the same room with a dog, even in a kennel."

"Miracles happen, sometimes, don't they?"

"They usually have to do with things like walking on water and healing the sick, not helping people getting over phobias about dogs."

"But it could happen," I persisted.

"I don't know that it's something I could even pray for, Norah."

"So whatever we have is over before it begins?"

"Unless you can figure out what to do about it."

He said it with the finality of a slamming door. I knew what he meant. *Unless you are willing to give up Bentley.*

When I returned home, I sat on the sofa scratching Bentley's ears.

Even though Nick couldn't pray for an answer to this and likely thought it too trivial to bring before God, I will. He wants to be in relationship and fellowship with us, His children. Certainly He'll be interested in what I have to say about a man and a dog.

Chapter Thirty-Four

❧

After the evening at Nick's house, Bentley and I holed up in my bedroom for two days drowning my frustrations in prayer and food. The prayer part was smart. The food? Not such a good idea.

"Bentley," I said, "what am I going to do? You don't want to be the one to stand between Nick and me, do you?"

I'm pretty sure he shook his head in the negative, but without corroboration, no one would believe it anyway.

He's made so much progress lately—sailing by those hydrants and all—that I feel as though we're on the edge of a breakthrough. Or maybe it's a breakdown, considering I'm thinking all this about a dog.

Besides, it's not just about Bentley. It's any puppy I

bring into the store. My passion is Nick's aversion. That sums it up pretty well and leaves Nick as accessible to me as Joe is now.

I've seen him and Lilly together every day and they are both smiling more than I've seen them do in many weeks. We've been walking a tightrope without a net. At least now Lilly and Joe have something to hang on to—each other.

Before I could start to feel sorry for myself, a gigantic burp echoed through the room, followed by a series of intestinal noises one might hear in one's own stomach during a bad bout with the flu. Then the gassy, growling sounds became a dreadful smoker's cough accompanied by hacking and spitting. The concert ended with a wild, maniacal cackling laughter that would have been great in a horror movie.

Winky.

I moved to his perch and stroked his feathers. "You're bored, aren't you, big boy? After all the fun you had in the shop, my house is a drag. Now that we know that Bryce didn't pull your feathers, I suppose you could go back to the shop—if you'd only shape up."

Winky responded with a guttural mumble and a phrase or two that shouldn't be said in good company.

When he'd arrived on the doorstep of Norah's Ark, I almost hadn't accepted him because of his colorful language. But it wasn't his fault. His previous owners had tried their best to ruin the appeal of this smart, beautiful bird and I couldn't let them win. But now, since he'd been out of the shop and alone except for Asia and Bentley for most of the day, he was dredging up more and more of his unappealing behavior. He'd also begun to repeat my side of every phone conversation and tormenting the dog by telling Bentley to "lie down" every time the dog moved. I hadn't realized it was happening until one day I heard Winky give the order and Bentley drop flat on his way to his dog dish. It certainly explained why Bentley had started waiting for me to get home to eat his food and drink his water.

I stroked his feathers and tickled his armpit—or is it wing pit? "What am I going to do with you? And quit making those smooching noises. You aren't going to romance me out of thinking about this."

Ironically, the one sound Winky can't duplicate is the sound of bells.

"It doesn't matter. When I meet the right man, I'll hear bells, I just know it." But I said it without conviction.

Then, at that moment, a bell did start to chime—my doorbell.

It was Connor.

I invited him in and Winky greeted Connor with an enthusiasm I hadn't seen in a while.

"Hello, big boy. Awwwk. Aren't you handsome? Awwwk. You make my heart sing." And then he shyly tucked his beak in his armpit as if he'd said too much.

"Looks like you have a fan."

"Rather perfect, isn't it? Traditionally, pirates had parrots as pets. He must be able to smell the saltwater in my veins."

"Why do you think parrots and pirates have always been paired together like that?"

"I'm sure the pirates discovered parrots on islands in the Caribbean."

"And the parrots would have been relatively tame considering that they hadn't experienced man as dangerous."

"Imagine if you'd found a bird who could mimic your voice," Connor pointed out. "It would be irresistible to tame it and keep it as a pet."

I studied the two of them. Connor stroked Winky's head and Winky leaned into it much like Bentley moves closer when I'm petting him. It was quite charming.

"What brings you over?" I finally asked.

"I heard about Lilly and Joe."

"Yes, well, so it goes."

"Are you okay? I know you were fond of him."

"I'm okay. Ironic, isn't it? I thought you and Lilly would make a perfect couple. Obviously I don't know what I'm talking about."

"And I thought you and I would be that ideal pair." His gaze skimmed my face. "With time, I still believe it would have happened."

"'With time?' I don't understand."

"I'm leaving Shoreside. I have another business opportunity in Hawaii. One of the reasons I returned to Shoreside was because I thought that prospect had dried up. Now, it appears, we have the chance to develop a commercial business ferrying people between the islands. It will, of course, require that I run the operation for some time to come. I'm leaving the end of this week."

Just like that? The bonanza of eligible men in Shoreside had peaked and bottomed out in what seemed like a nanosecond.

"I'm sorry, Connor." I truly was. If it hadn't been for the

trouble with Lilly, Connor and I would have become, if not an item, at least good friends.

He gave me that devastating smile of his. "I still think that you and I could have been a great couple, Norah. Unfortunately, long-distance relationships don't work like face-to-face ones." He rested the palm of his hand on my cheek. "But never say never."

Just then Winky spoke up. "Winky wants a cracker."

Connor turned to study the bird. "You know, I've heard you say in the past that you'd like to sell Winky. Is that still true?"

"Why, yes, I suppose so. He needs a place that has lots of action, though. When he's entertained his language is much improved. He hasn't been happy here with us. Frankly, I think he considers Asia Mynah a dimwit."

"How would he like to be first mate on a ferry that travels between the Hawaiian islands? He'd be treated like a king and there would be plenty of activity." Connor studied the bird. "In fact, I might just name one of the ferries *The Winky*. I can see people wanting to ride that particular ferry just because of him. He'd be good for business and I'd be good to him." Connor was now talking more to himself than to me. "We're going to develop a new logo. Maybe there's a way to work him in…he'd be great for television and print commercials…."

Winky, a television star with his own line of ferries? A tourist attraction? A parrot with his own personal buccaneer? And that buccaneer would be Connor!

Connor turned to me with a light sparkling in his eyes. "If you would consider selling him to me, Norah, I'd make him the most famous parrot in the Pacific Ocean. I'd even hire a bird specialist to take care of him, if necessary. And I'll pay whatever you want."

His expression softened. "And, even though I'm in Hawaii and you are here, I'll feel like a little bit of you is there with me when I have Winky."

Awwwwwww.

The decision, even though I will miss Winky desperately, was easy to make.

"He's yours."

"Are you sure?"

"I'd hang on to every animal that comes through my shop if I could. And I've been known to refuse to sell a pet to someone I don't think has the patience or disposition to treat an animal well. But I know how movie stars are treated. How could I say no to letting my ham actor Winky go on the stage?"

"I'll send you updates on him and, once we're up and running, newspaper clippings. Who knows? Maybe he'll be on Leno one day?"

"As his mother, it would make me very proud."

When Connor and I parted, he left knowing that he would always have a little piece of my heart.

Three down, none to go.

That pretty much sums up the eligible male population on Pond Street. To my surprise, I find it exceedingly troubling.

I, independent, self-sufficient Norah Kent, am lonesome.

Chapter Thirty-Five

❧

BENTLEY: PLAY NORAH, PLAY!

NORAH: I don't know what's gotten into that dog lately. He's pestering me all the time to play with him. Ease up, Bentley. I don't feel like playing.

BENTLEY: SCRATCH ME, SCRATCH ME.

NORAH: Maybe I should get him some flea powder. He's begging to be scratched all the time and it's driving me crazy. My energy is really low these days.

BENTLEY: TOSS THE BALL!

NORAH: He keeps following me around with a soggy old tennis ball in his mouth. What's gotten into him?

BENTLEY: What's gotten into her?

NORAH: I don't know what I'm going to do about you, Bentley.

BENTLEY: I know *exactly* what I'm going to do about you, Norah.

I put a pillow over my head but even that didn't smother Bentley's caterwauling by the front door. How a dog can howl and hold a Deputy Dawg leash in his mouth at the same time is beyond me. Maybe he, instead of Winky, should be on television. Finally, I rolled off my bed and stomped through the house.

"Okay, already! I'll take you for a walk. Since when did you start liking walks anyway?"

Ever since Joe and Connor stopped coming to the house, Bentley has been a dog on a mission. What mission, I have no idea, but he's been a royal pest, wanting to go outside, pulling me up and down Pond Street past fire hydrants and everything. He doesn't pay much attention to Lilly or Auntie Lou, but he is fascinated with Silas. Every time we walk past Auntie Lou's Antiques, Bentley wants to go inside and stick his cold nose into Silas's sleeping face. It's almost as if he's using it as a test, just to see how far he can go before he chickens out and turns tail and runs from the cat.

Ironically, the tables have turned where Lou and I are concerned and she's worrying about *me* now.

"You haven't been yourself lately, Norah. Are you feeling okay?"

"Fine, but thanks for asking." *Fine, but lonesome.*

"You'd tell me if something were wrong? You wouldn't try to handle it on your own?"

"I know you are here for me, Lou." *Besides, there's nothing for anyone to handle. Joe and Lilly are happy, Connor is off having fun with Winky, and Nick hates dogs and that's that.*

The other one Bentley has become fascinated with is Sarge. He doesn't dare get too near the big horse, but every time we see Sarge, Bentley takes one step closer to him than he did the time before. At this rate, Bentley and Sarge will be best buddies by the year 2010.

Today, however, Sarge was nowhere in sight and Nick was giving out traffic tickets as if he was in a no-parking zone filled with cars. The violators were a little young to be written up however. None of them had a driver's license although several did have training wheels on their vehicles.

Nick was surrounded by a gaggle of kids on bikes watching him write up a ticket for a little girl in pink overalls, frilly white blouse and scuffed tennis shoes. The child was wide-eyed beneath her pink-and-white bike helmet.

With a flourish, Nick whipped the ticket from his book and handed it to her. She looked up at him in amazement, put her feet to the pedals and nearly ran over his foot in her getaway. A moment later another child *did* run over Nick's foot jockeying himself into position for the next ticket.

Bentley and I watched the proceedings until the crowd subsided. When Auntie Lou came out of her store to sit in the sun, I gave her Bentley's leash and sauntered over to find out what was going on.

"They're a little young for traffic tickets, don't you think?"

He looked up and grinned. "Not this kind." He pulled one off the official-looking pad and handed it to me.

To whom it may concern: _____(name)
Was pulled over on _____ (date)
No wrongdoing was observed. However, because

_____(name) was in possession of and wearing a bicycle helmet while riding, they are cited for good behavior. This ticket may be exchanged at the drug store or ice-cream truck for one free treat of choice. Receiving this ticket does not preclude you from receiving another if caught again using a bike helmet while riding.

Officer Nick and the Shoreside Police Department

"Cute. Whose idea was that?"

"Yours, actually."

"Really? I must be losing my memory. I can't recall coming up with it."

"I've heard so many times about your adoption ceremony for pets purchased at Norah's Ark, that I thought I'd try something similar to encourage children to wear their bike helmets. Shoreside is busy in the summer months. A child without a helmet could be in real danger."

"So you came up with reverse ticketing. Great idea."

Nick looked at his watch. "I'm off duty as of ten minutes ago. I could write us tickets for sodas, too, you know."

"Graft and corruption in the police department!" I chided. "But I'll come if you promise to pay your way."

"Deal. Just a minute. I have to…"

He stopped abruptly and his eyes widened. Before I knew what was happening, Bentley broke away from Auntie Lou, ran past a *fire hydrant and across the street* to Nick.

Bentley simply does not do these things. Fire hydrants and streets? Uh-uh, no way. And yet here he was, flinging himself against Nick's well-polished shoes.

Fortunately Nick didn't go for a billy club when Bentley made his move. Instead he froze in place. Then Bentley fell at Nick's feet and rolled over. Panting and wearing a stupid doggie grin, Bent rolled onto his back, exposed his vulnerable belly and begged to be scratched.

"What's he doing, Norah?" Nick asked through gritted teeth. He'd lost some of his color, but he, too, was acting against type by not moving away from Bentley.

"It's his submissive pose. Animals don't offer you their exposed, defenseless undersides unless they trust you. He's asking you to rub his tummy."

"But I don't trust *him*." Nick was doing a remarkable job of remaining calm.

"I think he's trying to make the first move. I've never seen him do anything like this before now." Bentley's behavior bordered on the miraculous.

"Get him away from me." Nick's face was now growing pink.

"Sure, if you want me to. But couldn't you just give him one little scratch?"

"Norah…"

At that moment a little girl named Chrissy, the daughter of one of the hair stylists at Belles & Beaus dashed between us, dropped to her knees and started rubbing Bentley's tummy.

"Hi, Bentley," the little girl said. "You're such a good doggy. When are you going to come and visit me?" Chrissy often comes to Norah's Ark to look at the animals and spends a good deal of time on the floor with Bentley.

Nick reached out as if to protect the child but drew his hand away when he realized that there was no protection needed.

"Have you scratched him, Officer Nick?" Chrissy inquired sweetly. "He's so soft. Feel."

Chrissy pulled on Nick's hand and reluctantly Nick knelt beside the little girl. She tugged his hand to Bentley's round belly. "See?"

In all the years I've worked with animals, I've never seen anything quite like it. It was as if Bentley knew that there was someone even more frightened and timid than he. As Nick, under Chrissy's firm direction, touched Bentley's fur, Bentley licked Nick's wrist.

"He likes you!" Chrissy crowed. "Isn't he sweet?"

"Yeah, sweet." But Nick didn't pull back. Instead he moved his hand to tentatively scratch Bentley's neck. Bentley squirmed with pleasure.

Chrissy jumped to her feet and ran off when her mother called from the front steps of Belles & Beaus, leaving the three of us in an odd little tableau on the sidewalk.

"Do you want us to leave?" I asked, even though Nick hadn't quit scratching the dog and Bentley was transfixed.

Nick unfolded his legs, still keeping an eye on the prone animal at his feet. "I…I don't know."

"Come on, Bent. Come." I tugged at the leash but he wouldn't move. "Now!" Bentley looked as apt to move as a piece of the sidewalk.

"Come on, boy," Nick ventured.

And Bentley leaped to his feet, wagging his tail and drooling on Nick's shoes.

"Want to walk with us?" I offered.

I could tell that Nick was as baffled as me at Bentley's behavior.

"Just a few steps."

I started out but Bentley held back, waiting to see if Nick was coming. When he dragged his furry little feet, I impulsively handed the hot-pink leash over to Nick.

I have got to get this dog a more manly leash!

As soon as Nick took it, Bentley started trotting happily in front of us, past the fire hydrant and even past a motorcycle parked in the street.

Nick and I were quiet, mostly because neither of us could think of a thing to say about the strange turn of events. Bentley had become practically *macho!*

We walked onto my patio and sat down. Bentley sat down beside Nick and started licking his shoe.

"Okay, Bentley, why are you kissing up to him and not to me? Are you trying to win *him* over all of a sudden? What about me?"

"What about you, Norah?" Nick said softly, still staring at my dog with a bewildered expression on his face. "What happens if he does 'win me over'?"

"Then we…you and I…we can…" I trailed off in a flood of embarrassment and pleasure.

"Can what?" To my astonishment, Nick dropped his hand down and stroked the top of Bentley's head.

"Can, you know…be friends again."

"Just friends?"

"Good friends. The kind of friends we would have been already if Bentley hadn't been standing in the way."

"Tell me what kind of friends that would be." His blue eyes were on me now and I felt helpless as a bug on a pin.

"Close friends?" Now I was asking the questions!

"How close?"

"Really close, I guess." *As close as two people can get without hearing bells.*

At that moment a small gust of wind shuffled the leaves on the trees in my yard and set my wind chimes in motion.

Wind chimes?

Comprehension dawned like a blinding sunrise.

Bells have been ringing in a chorus all around me. I simply haven't been paying attention. Could they be the bells I've been waiting to hear?

The change in Nick's pocket that he's constantly jingling, the ice-cream truck, the doorbell each time he walked into my shop, the wind chimes around his house, the sound of the ice-cream truck coming down the street, Auntie Lou's sleigh bell on Sarge's headstall…bells, chimes, a whole carillon! All pealing, ringing and clanging around me every time I saw Nick—and I'd missed it all.

Never, when I was with Joe or Connor, had I noticed the ice-cream truck's melody. Not once had my heart quickened when the doorbell rang and one of them was standing in the doorway to my shop. Never once had I noticed either of them jingling the coins in their pockets. And Sarge—he was decked out in sleigh bells! What could be more obvious than that?

Chapter Thirty-Six

It's been three months now since Bentley took on the responsibility of getting Nick and me together. He's grown bolder every month. Last week he even used a fire hydrant for the purpose for which it was created—other than providing water to put out fires, of course.

Nick has changed, too. He and Bentley sit on my couch together eating crackers and watching television. Sometimes they fall asleep together, Bentley's head and paws on Nick's lap. In fact, Nick's even started talking fondly about dogs from his youth, before the accident soured him.

I've been collecting wind chimes and hanging them in every free spot around my yard and I never get tired of listening to them.

Lilly and Joe are still dating and the jury is still out. We have, however, been able to get together as couples—Lilly and Joe, Nick and me—and laugh and have fun.

Auntie Lou and the Morrises are just like family now, although she tells me that even though she loves Bryce like a grandson, she's still waiting for me to provide her with a beautiful new granddaughter. She also tells me to get busy about it.

I hear from Connor regularly. He is so entranced with Winky that his e-mails sound like those of a young father proud of his firstborn. "Winky does this… Winky does that… Winky says… You should have seen Winky… The people love Winky…." The logo for the ferry line is amazing—brilliant parrot colors in a fluid circle with Winky's face peering out of the middle. Connor also sends digital photos. In one, Connor had a bright kerchief tied around his head, an eye patch and Winky sitting on his shoulder. I'm afraid he's gone as bonkers over Winky as I am over Bentley.

Fortunately for me, Nick has decided that it is possible to love me and my dog.

God does honor and answer prayers—in His own time and in His own way. Fortunately His way is always smarter and better and more wonderful than mine. Without Him, Joe, Lilly and I would be at loggerheads, Connor and I would probably not be friends and…I wouldn't be marrying Nick next month at our little church here in Shoreside. We can hardly wait.

Oh, I did make one concession. Bentley is not going on

the honeymoon. He, Hoppy and Asia Mynah will stay at the Bed and Biscuit with Annie and I think they'll like it.

And I've picked out Nick's wedding present, I can hardly wait to give it to him.

Epilogue

❧

"That's an awfully big box for a wedding gift." Nick pulled me toward him and planted a kiss on my lips. "Why did I have to wait until we got back from the honeymoon to open it?"

"You'll see."

Bentley, Hoppy and Asia Mynah sat in a row in the living room waiting for the unveiling. Bentley has a particular interest in this because he got to make the final choice in the selection of options we had.

"I'm not sure what to think, Norah. You've been awfully secretive about this."

"I wanted it to be special. Like your wedding gift was to me."

And special it was—a beautiful dun gelding to join Cocoa

at the stable. And with him came full tack including a light-weight Western saddle that I can put on the horse without knocking myself unconscious. We named the gelding together. His name is Miracle because that's what this marriage feels like for Nick and me. I don't know how God manages these things but He knew Nick and I needed to be together and He let nothing stand in the way. It took a while, of course, and it wasn't without trauma, but the results are definitely worth the wait.

"Well, are you going to open it?"

"For some reason I feel nervous," Nick admitted. "Life is one surprise after another with you."

"I'll give you a hint. It is something you'd expect from me. And, like Miracle, it's an 'us' present. We'll care for it together."

"Care for it? You mean it's going to be work?"

I bit my tongue and stayed quiet.

"Okay, here goes."

He lifted the big box up to reveal a kennel. Inside was a small brown wrinkled lump snoring slightly.

"What on earth?" Nick bent down and fished the lump out of the kennel and held it close to him.

"What is it?"

"A Shar-pei puppy, of course. A dog you can train yourself."

"His skin is too big for his body."

"That's what makes him cute. Besides, I thought you needed a fresh start with a dog of your own."

"What about Bentley?"

"He picked him out of the litter. They get along beautifully. Finally Bentley has someone more innocent than he to teach."

Nick cuddled the dog close to him and leaned over and

kissed me. "He's perfect. I know that with all your quirks you and Bentley will give me gray hair someday soon. Now I'm guaranteed wrinkles, too."

"I am so proud of you, Nick. You've made me feel like a princess. Overcoming your dislike of dogs is like slaying dragons for me." I wanted to be light but my throat constricted. I love him so much and I know how much he loves me.

"Does he have a name yet? Wrinkles? Crinkle? Crease?"

"Actually, I did have something in mind, but only with your permission, of course."

"What is it?"

"Beau-tox."

When he laughed out loud, little Beau-tox snuffled and buried himself deeper into Nick's shirt.

Nick gathered me in with his free arm. "Norah, if I'm going to be set adrift at sea on an ark, there's no one I'd rather travel with than you." Then he kissed me in that way he has, the way he wipes every sane thought out of my head and leaves me seeing stars.

Auntie Lou, you'll get that granddaughter of yours yet!

QUESTIONS FOR DISCUSSION

1. Do you relate to Norah's affection for animals? Is there a favorite animal or pet in your life? Please describe.

2. Though Lilly is a close friend of Norah's, it turns out that Lilly is also jealous of Norah's friendship with Joe. Have you ever been jealous of someone's friendship or relationship? Would you address it? How?

3. Norah says, "I want the elderly to be given the chance to make their own decisions as long as they can...so I'd better start now to make sure that's in place when I get on the far side of the far side of over the hill." What steps will Norah make to ensure that happens? What about you?

4. Should Auntie Lou have been put in a nursing home? Do you have someone in your family who is aging and needs help? How will you handle it?

5. Three wonderful men—Joe, Connor and Nick—pursue Norah in the book. Is this a problem or a blessing? What would you do if you were in her shoes?

6. Norah doesn't tell her best friend, Lilly, that Connor has asked her out to dinner, knowing full well Lilly has a huge crush on him. Was this wrong of her? Would you have told Lilly right away, or held off to spare her feelings?

7. Auntie Lou allows troubled teen Bryce to hang out in her store and play the old pinball machine. Was it naive of her to trust him when no one else did? Why or why not?

8. Norah discovers that Nick doesn't like or trust Bentley. Is there a way to come to terms with loving someone who disagrees with you on something very important, as Nick does with Norah where Bentley is concerned?

9. The reason Norah gives for not wanting to marry Joe is that she doesn't hear "bells" when she's with him. Does this seem logical or silly to you? Do you or someone you know create reasons to date or not date someone?

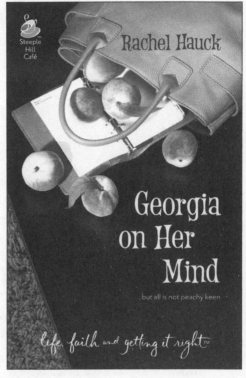

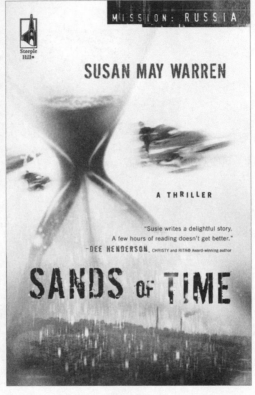

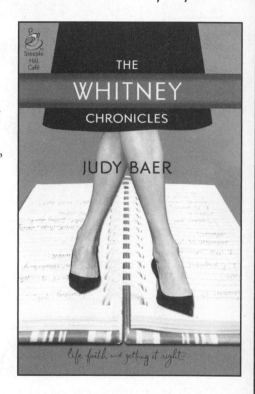

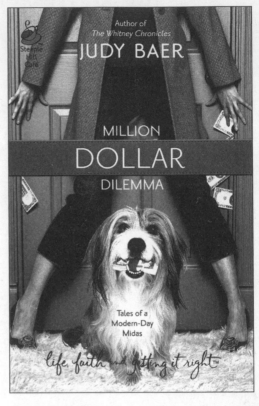